ANNA

Linda Sawley

LINRIC PUBLISHING
ENGLAND

Published in 2010 by Linric Publishing
18 Victoria Lodge
READ, Lancs.
BB12 7SZ

British Cataloguing in Publication data
Sawley, Linda
Anna
I. Title
Classification: Historical Fiction

ISBN 978-0-9557258-2⁴

Cover design by David Eaves

Digially printed by Sherwood Print Services
Unit 5, Sherbrook Business Centre
Sherbrook Road, Daybrook
Nottingham, NG5 6AT

Dedicated to the late Madeleine Pelner Cosman whose book (Women at Work in Medieval Europe) inspired my character. And to Ian Mortimer who made the 14th Century come alive for me, with his book 'The Time Traveller's Guide to Medieval England'.

A donation from the sale of this book will be given to two charities - Derian House Children's Hospice and Ribble Valley/White Rose Ladies Luncheon Club, raising money for cancer research for children in the north of England.

Praise for Linda Sawley's books

Everyone Else's Children
'I just wanted you to know how much I enjoyed reading your book. It was compulsive reading. There were parts that had me laughing out loud like a mad woman! And others that brought a lump to my throat. It was truly an enjoyable read. Looking forward to the next one!!!'
—*Melanie*

A Ring in Time
'Absolutely brilliant! When I got to page 49, I read it straight through at one go.'
—*Marian*

The Key
'Blissfully romantic, a tragic and uplifting adventure of a girl in a man's world'
—*Santa Montefiore - novelist*

Changes
'Changes is an addictive read. I have just finished the story which has taken me through the highs and lows of life, love, emotion and business. Although set in a time when society was organised differently, and being a woman in a predominantly man's world was a difficult, if not oppressive situation, there are similarities with modern day life of being mother, partner, wage earner and women. This was an easy flowing story and I look forward to passing copies to my family members in their Christmas stockings.'
—*Sandra*

The Survivor
'Once I started reading this book, I couldn't put it down.'
—*Richard Bell - Competition Editor for Writers News*

ANNA

Chapter 1

Anna de Rexar ran as fast as her twelve-year-old legs would let her, her dark hair flying behind her. She was late. Very late, and she would be in serious trouble when she got home. Anna skirted the edge of the wood and followed the rutted path that led to her home, holding up her kirtle as she ran. Her heart was pounding but she daren't slow down, despite the pain she was feeling.

The setting sun was sinking below the height of the trees so she knew that it was long past the time for the evening meal. As she approached the front of the house, Anna looked out for tell-tale signs that she was in trouble but there was little activity outside the house. It lulled her into a false sense of security, as her mother or one of the servants was usually outside, scouring the countryside for the errant daughter of the house.

Anna slowed down as she entered the courtyard and hastily tidied her clothes before quietly entering the main hall. She would sneak up the side stairs that led directly into her bedchamber and pretend she'd been home earlier.

'Where have you been?' an angry voice demanded. Anna's heart sunk. She hadn't seen her mother standing by the table. Anna looked at her in awe. Her mother was amazing when she was cross. She seemed to stretch up and become taller, her cheeks reddened and her arms folded across her slim body. Yes, she really liked looking at her mother when she was angry.

'Are you listening to me? I've asked you two questions and you haven't even acknowledged me or responded to either of them. Come back girl, you're in your dream world again. You really are the limit. Where have you been?'

'I'm sorry mother; I was playing with Donald and Christine down in the village. We didn't realise how late it had got.'

'It's about time you three grew up. I was married when I was not much older than you. Besides, it's time Donald was starting work. His father is far too soft with him. Most children start work at seven years old and he's nigh on fourteen years. It's about time he learned to take responsibility and helped with the business.' Anna remained silent, knowing it was better to let her mother rant on for a while; she'd calm down soon enough. Instead Anna concentrated on her mother's new garment, thinking how much the colour suited her. She let her mind go blank again: wandering off into a distant space.

'Are you listening to me, girl?' her mother's voice exploded into Anna's consciousness, dragging her back from her musing.

'Yes, of course I am.'

'What did I say then?'

'Er, let me see, you said that . .' Anna prevaricated, hoping for a clue from her mother.

'See, you weren't listening at all. Just dreaming as usual. Well, there was a surprise for you tonight but you don't deserve it now, so . . .'

'Oh mother, please, what was the surprise?' Anna interrupted. 'Oh please tell me. Has father brought some new material home from the dyers? Am I to get a new kirtle? Or a cloak? Oh do tell.'

'You don't deserve a new garment because of your behaviour, but it wasn't anything like that anyway. But you won't find out tonight because you're going straight to your bedchamber with no food. I'll teach you to have me worrying about you.'

'Oh but please, do tell me.'

'No, it's too late. Straight to your bedchamber.'

'But I'm hungry. I haven't eaten for ages, not since I left the sisters.'

'Perhaps that will teach you to behave. Now go.' Her mother walked briskly away from her and out of the main hall. Anna knew better than to argue further. She slowly trailed up the flight of circular stone steps to her bedchamber and threw herself on the bed.

Anna was angry. She hated being denied surprises. She hated missing her meals too; she loved her food, but she wasn't really worried about that. Young Flossie would bring her a tray up later and sneak it to her room, as she'd often done before when she'd been sent to bed without a meal.

What on earth could it be? she pondered. Perhaps it was the Jongleurs visiting. Oh, she hoped it was. It'd been ages since they'd been, so they were due for a visit. They always made her laugh and she loved to learn their new songs and tunes, and watch them juggle and dance.

Anna ran over to the door and listened carefully. There was no sound of music – just the normal sounds of early evening, when the house was quietening down for the night. Sighing, Anna walked slowly back to the bed and sat on the edge of it. There was a gentle tap on the door. It would be Flossie. Anna jumped up and ran to the door.

'Flossie,' shouted Anna, opening the door and peering down the stairwell, 'what's the surprise?' but there was no one in sight. Flossie would have put the food down and hurried away quickly before she was caught. It would be more than her life was worth to be seen defying the mistress of the house. Anna looked at the tray. There was a bowl of hare stew and a hunk of bread. Huh, thought Anna, not much for an evening meal. But then at least she was getting something, thanks to Flossie. She must remember to be especially nice to her tomorrow. Anna wolfed the food down quickly and got into bed. She might as well go to sleep early. Taking her kirtle off, pulling her night kirtle on and jumping in to bed, she pulled the blanket over herself and cuddled down to sleep. Then she jumped out again, remembering that she hadn't said her prayers. She knelt by her bed and quickly recited some Hail Mary's and then made the sign of the cross and jumped back into bed.

Next morning, Anna was up early and hurried downstairs to the main hall.

'Morning Peggy,' Anna shouted gaily, 'how are you today? Is breakfast ready? Where's Flossie? Is my mother up yet?'

'Well, Miss Anna, which question would you like me to answer first?' chuckled Peggy. She was a tall stout lady with grey hair, and had worked for the de Rexar family for thirty years, having started as a cooking helper like Flossie.

'Your mother hasn't come down yet. She was late going to bed. Too much talking,' she laughed.

'Why was she talking?' pestered Anna. 'What was the matter? Was there trouble? Mother doesn't tend to stay up talking.'

'Now then, Miss Anna, you're at it again, asking all these questions before I get chance to answer the first one. She was up late talking 'cos your Aunty Judith is . .'

'Aunty Judith? Here? When did she come? Why did nobody tell me?'

'You're at it again. You'll be the death of me, girl. Your Aunty Judith came yesterday morning. If you'd been at home where you should be, learning how to run this place with your mother, you'd have . . .'

'Aunty Judith? Here? And nobody told me. Oh, I'll never forgive my mother, never,' Anna screamed.

'Never forgive me for what?' asked a quiet voice. Anna stopped screaming instantly and hung her head in silence, knowing she would be in even more serious trouble than she had been last night. 'Well? I'm waiting. What can you never forgive me for?'

'I . . er . . I was wishing I'd known that Aunty Judith was here,' Anna whispered.

'You should have been home then, girl. Now will you learn to behave? I'm sure Christine doesn't behave like this with her family. Now get your breakfast and get yourself to the sisters.'

'But I want to see Aunty Judith, can't I stay here for today? I'll be very good and help you in the house, like you want me to. Oh please maman,' wheedled Anna, using the softer form of address to her mother to add to her entreaties.

'No, you will go to the sisters now.' With that, her mother turned and walked off, leaving no chance for any further discussion. Anna stood with her head drooping, trying to fight back the tears. She didn't want to go to the sisters today. She'd much rather stay at home and listen to the women chattering and especially see her Aunty Judith, but she knew when she had gone too far with her mother.

Sighing, Anna walked to the large fireplace that took up one side of the hall. Peggy and Flossie had been quietly getting on with the breakfast whilst all the arguing was going on. Peggy put a bowl of porridge down on the table and called Anna to come and eat.

'Here, get this down you, girl. Sometimes you push your mother too far. Flossie, get some food together for Miss Anna, and then she can get going. If she's still here when her mother comes back in, we'll all be in trouble.' Flossie hurried round to the large table with a parcel for Anna. It was a soft piece of cloth containing a large chunk of freshly made bread and a piece of cheese.

'That'll keep you going, Miss Anna,' said Flossie quietly, with a little conspiratorial smile. Anna smiled her thanks, whilst finishing the porridge quickly. Jumping up, she grabbed her cloth parcel, threw a fine woollen cape round herself and ran out of the house. She stopped suddenly and ran back into the house.

'Thanks for my supper last night, Flossie, I was very grateful,' said Anna.

'That's all right Miss Anna. I just told Peggy I was still hungry. It's a good job that your mother is generous with the servants and not penny-pinching like they are next door. Your Miss Christine's maid wouldn't have been able to get extra food for her. Her grandfather is really mean. I've heard their servants talk. Hadn't you better be going, before your mother finds you still here? I think you're in enough trouble already today,' giggled Flossie.

'You're right. See you tonight,' shouted Anna as she ran through the yard.

Normally Anna loved going to the sisters. She adored learning and didn't find it hard to do, but seeing her Aunty Judith was far more important. It just wasn't fair. Her mother was so mean. As she went along the path from her house, she saw her friend Christine de Ribbleside coming out of her house and her mood lifted. Christine was fair, with a widow's peak at the front of her hair, a curvy figure, a ruddy complexion and a round smiling face. Anna loved Christine dearly.

Christine's home was a large manor house like Anna's. The two houses had been built in a similar style to each other over a hundred years ago. Christine's grandfather, Jack, was the Lord of the Manor in the village of Ribbleside and a previous Lord had had twin sons. Anna's house had been built for the younger son, so that he could have a separate household but still be near to the main family house. The only difference was the amount of land. The Lord of the Manor had nine hundred acres; Anna's parents had three fields! Anna and Christine waved at each other.

'I'm in trouble again, Christine. I got sent to bed with no supper last night. Mother was very cross. I thought she was going to hit me,' Anna moaned, as they walked down the path together. 'Did you get into trouble for being late as well?'

'No,' replied Christine quietly, 'nobody seemed to bother that I was in late. Do you think your mother would hit you?'

'Not really,' replied Anna, 'but she looked ferocious. And would you believe it, my Aunty Judith is here and she didn't tell me last night and still sent me to bed and she wouldn't let me see her this morning either but sent me to the silly sisters straightaway. It's not fair,' complained Anna bitterly.

'At least she cares about you,' replied Christine. Anna noted the downcast look on her friend's face and the sad tone of voice.

'Oh Christine, are you all right? Are things not good at your house?'

'No, my grandmother is very ill. You know she's with child again? Well, she doesn't seem to be getting along very well this time.'

'Isn't she a bit old for having children now? She must be well past her fortieth year.'

'Yes,' replied Christine mournfully, 'I think my Grandfather still wants another boy.'

'Should have looked after the ones he had then, shouldn't he?' said Anna sharply.

'Oh Anna, that is cruel. It wasn't his fault that the little ones died with the plague, and anyway my Uncle Max is still alive.'

'Yes, but they've fallen out haven't they? How long is it since you saw him?'

'Many years now, not since I was a little girl. But I'm glad he left because him and grandfather were always arguing. I used to be so frightened. He says he's never coming back whilst Grandfather is still alive.'

'Hey, come on you two slow worms,' shouted a young boy called Matthew. 'Lessons will be over before you get there.' The two girls visibly brightened when they also saw Donald running towards them. He had joined the path from his home, which was also the local forge. It was situated on the outskirts of the village so that shooting flames from the fire didn't burn the huts down in the main village.

They soon arrived at the small bridge that forded the River Ribble from where the village got its name. The entire village was on this side of the bridge and the only building across the river was the convent. It belonged to the Little Grey Sisters of Mary, so named because of their grey habits.

Two large carp ponds were at the back of the convent, and the villagers often bought carp from the sisters to supplement their diet. The convent's magnificent gatehouse overawed new travellers as they crossed the bridge but these children had become accustomed to it. The children crossed under the gatehouse and went in to the laypersons house where their lessons would take place.

Settling down on their seats, the children listened and could hear the final Dominus of the mass that the nuns were singing. Soon they would be singing the Amen and then lessons would begin. The children spoke quietly. They knew instinctively to behave reverently in this hallowed place.

Eventually, Sister Bernadette arrived in the room and stood in front of the children.

'Good morning Children,' she said quietly. The children all jumped up and bowed to Sister Bernadette and replied 'Good morning, Sister.'

'Today, before we start our lessons, we will say the Hail Mary, in honour of the mother of our precious Lord. Why do we also call the Blessed Virgin Mary the rose? Margaret, do you know?'

'Yes, Sister,' replied Margaret. 'It's because the Blessed Virgin is pure and beautiful like the rose.'

'That is correct, Margaret. Well remembered. Sometimes it is difficult for you children to understand the mysteries of religion but you will learn, as you get older. Now let us all pray.'

The children recited their prayers in unison. When they had finished, Christine raised her hand. The children were not frightened of this gentle nun who always spoke in a whisper. She was tiny and bird like in appearance, her grey woollen robes and her white cowl atop her robes accentuating that impression.

'Please Sister Bernadette, could you say a prayer for my grandmother? She's not well.'

'Certainly my child and I will ask the sisters to pray for her as well at the next prayers. And ask at the kitchen for some soup for her, before you go home. Now let's get on with our lessons.' The children shuffled around to get comfortable on their small benches but listened carefully to what Sister Bernadette was teaching them. They knew how lucky they were to receive any teaching, especially the girls. Most lessons were given in the richer homes and only to the boys, but the sisters were of a teaching order and didn't differentiate between boys and girls, or rich or poor, saying they all needed to learn their lessons so that they could worship God. They were probably hoping that some of the girls would become nuns and the boys monks, or serve as laypersons in the convents and monasteries. As well as teaching, the sisters also nursed the sick and had a small hospital in the convent.

After a while, the nun stopped her teaching and the children all drew out their small meals, of bread and cheese mainly. Chattering was constant during this small rest and then the teaching began again. One of the laypersons, Mistress Joan, came to show them how to write their letters and illuminate the capital letter. She was the opposite of Sister Bernadette. She was tall and thin and spoke with a sharp squeaky voice. As a layperson, she didn't wear the robes like the sisters, but wore a simple kirtle, similar to the girls in the class. Christine and Anna were quite good at writing their letters but Donald always struggled with this part of the lessons. He wasn't a neat writer, being a more practically minded person.

At the end of the day's lesson, the children were given a meal of fish stew in the kitchen, before they all ran out of the building. Because the three of them lived at the far end of the village, Anna, Christine and Donald always walked home together. That is, sometimes they walked home. Mostly they wandered off into the woods and fields, watching the animals, climbing trees, and looking at things growing.

Sometimes they watched the men and boys at archery practice on the field. Jack de Ribbleside may have ignored some of his duties as Lord of the Manor, but mandatory archery practice was not one of them, and he provided the field, butts, and bows and arrows for the men in the village.

It was usually Anna who instigated the adventures after lessons were finished, and today was no exception.

'Let's follow the Ribble down to Clitheroe,' she suggested.

'Not today, Anna. I want to get home to see how my grandmother is,' replied Christine.

'Oh of course, I'm sorry Christine, I'd forgotten.'

'Besides, I need to take this soup home that the sisters gave to me.'

'I can't stay out either, I need to go straight home,' said Donald. 'I'm having to give my dad some help at the forge this afternoon. He's got a big order on.'

'Oh, see if I care,' retorted Anna and walked on ahead of the other two. Suddenly she stopped and waited for Christine to catch her up.

'I'm sorry Christine, that was mean of me. Of course I care. Can I come in and see your grandmother? Look, I'll pick some of the flowers in the field and we can take them to her.' Christine brightened considerably.

'Thank you Anna, that would be nice.' The two girls picked some wild primroses, then linked arms and walked home, saying goodbye to Donald as they reached his lane.

Soon, they reached Christine's house and went through the door into the main hall. Everybody seemed to be bustling about and ignored the girls. Christine caught the eye of one of the servant girls and quietly asked what was the matter.

'Your grandmother is starting with the baby, Miss Christine.'

'But her time isn't due yet, is it? I thought they said it would be nearer midsummer?'

'Yes, but it's starting anyway,' replied Ethel, the young servant.

'I've brought some flowers for her,' said Anna.

'I don't think it will be good if you stay here, Miss Anna, begging your pardon, but they all seem a bit flummoxed at the moment,' said Ethel.

Anna put the flowers down on the table and after hugging Christine, quietly slipped out of the house. She walked slowly along the path, thinking about Christine, then suddenly remembered her Aunty Judith. Running the rest of the journey home, Anna ran into the house and looked for her mother and aunty. They were nowhere to be seen.

'Flossie, where are my mother and aunty?' she shouted.

'Your mother has gone down to the village to visit the family who've had a new baby and your aunty has gone home,' Flossie replied.

'Gone home?' shouted Anna aghast, 'she only came yesterday, why has she gone home again so quickly? And she hasn't even seen me. Oh how could she? How could my mother make me go to the sisters this morning?' Anna stamped her foot.

'I don't know Miss Anna, they don't tell me,' muttered Flossie. At this point Anna's mother returned from her errands.

'Goodness, Anna, you have excelled yourself. I've never known you to be home so early. Perhaps going to bed with no supper worked after all.'

'Why didn't you keep Aunty Judith until I got home? Why did you let her go home when I hadn't seen her?' railed Anna.

'Aunty Judith hasn't gone home. She was on a special journey for some new herbs, and was only staying the one night, as she has to get to Yorkshire. She's hoping to get to the next convent or monastery for a nights sleep tonight. She'll probably come back for a night on her way through.'

'Oh I do hope so. By the way mother, Christine's grandmother has started with the baby and it isn't ready yet.'

'How do you know? I'd better go round there and see if I could help.'

'Well, I went round with Christine but they sent me away, so they might not let you go in either.'

'Yes, but I'm a woman, Anna. I might be able to help. I'll go right away.' Anna watched her mother pick her basket up and put some food and old linen in, before setting off to the Manor House. Left alone again, Anna went outside to the stable at the back of the house. She loved going in to the stable and talking to the animals, especially when she had nothing else to do.

'Hello cow,' she said stroking its back. 'Have you given us some nice milk today? I hope so. Your milk is always so creamy and good. Not like the cows at Donald's house. I'm sure they are not happy cows. Their milk isn't as nice as yours.' The cow murmured as if in reply. Anna had learnt from a young age not to give the animals a real name. It was too painful if they had to be slaughtered for eating. So she always called them just cow or pig or goose. It made it less personal somehow. She wandered aimlessly round the rest of the animals, talking to them all.

Glancing across to Pendle Hill, Anna noticed that it looked moody and grim; a light mist floating over the top of it, obscuring the topmost portion of the hill. It has so many moods does Pendle Hill, thought Anna, and today, it reflects my own mood. She sighed disconsolately.

Wandering back into the house, Anna sat by the fire. She wasn't cold but it was her favourite place in the house. When the fire was lit, which is was most times of the day, she would look into the flames and see shapes before her eyes and make stories about those shapes. There was a gentle snoring coming from the side of the fire. Peggy had fallen asleep; her hat all askew. Anna giggled quietly. She knew better than to wake Peggy up. She could be grumpy if she was woken suddenly. The noise of a horse arriving alerted both Anna and Peggy that someone was coming. Anna ran to the door to see who had arrived.

'Father,' yelled Anna, cheering up instantly, 'how good to see you.' Before Richard de Rexar was properly down off his horse, a small whirlwind had collided into him.

'Careful Anna, you nearly knocked me over,' he remonstrated.

'I've missed you so much and you have been away so long,' replied Anna, hugging him and smiling her biggest smile.

'No Anna, only my usual weekly visit to the woollen markets. Have you been a good girl?'

Anna's face fell at this and she let go of her father.

'Ah, I see how things have been whilst I've been away. What have you done to upset your poor mother this time?'

'Oh, just the usual, getting home late from the sisters. And shouting at her.' Anna's head drooped lower.

'Shouting at your mother? That is not good, little Anna. What made you shout at her?'

Anna refused to answer at first, but after repeated looks of enquiry from her father, she muttered 'Aunty Judith came and I didn't get to see her. So I was cross.'

'Really Anna, you are such a crosspatch at times. What am I going to do with you? How will I marry you off to a nice rich man if you are a crosspatch?'

'I will try harder, father, and please don't talk about marrying me off to anyone. I just want to stay here and look after you and mother when you are old.'

'That's not the way of things Anna, as you well know. Besides,' he said laughing again, 'I want some nice grandchildren to play with when I'm old. Most men my age have already got some by now. Most of my friends have.'

'Well you'll just have to wait, 'cos I'm too young for marriage,' replied Anna, turning her head as the door opened. 'Oh look, here's mother. Mother, father's home.'

Anna watched as her parents embraced gently, but she could see the strength of passion in their eyes for each other. Perhaps marriage wouldn't be too bad, Anna thought to herself, if she found a lovely husband like her father.

She went off into a daydream, imagining her wedding day, with her beautiful new clothes, and riding away with her new rich handsome husband, in his specially decorated wedding cart, to his amazing big house. There he and his large number of servants would wait on her hand and foot, and he would look at her like her parents were looking at each other now, and then he would take her upstairs and they would begin their married life together, which would be blissful.

Anna frowned a little about the going upstairs together. She wasn't quite sure what happened between a man and a woman, but she knew it must be nice, because her parents always went upstairs together when her father had been away from home. And told her not to follow them. And her mother always came down later looking very happy, so it must be very nice, being married.

'Anna,' a voice cried, making Anna jump. It was her mother. 'See Richard, this is what I have to put up with all the time. She just goes into a trance and I can't get any sense out of her. Tell her to behave will you?'

'Did you say something, mother?' asked Anna.

'Did I say something? Did I say something?' her mother exploded. 'I was telling your father that Aunty Judith has been here but you missed her.'

'Yes, I did. Mother wouldn't let me stay away from the sisters to see her.'

17

'And rightly so. You are very lucky to receive teaching from the nuns. And I believe Judith is coming back again soon?'

'Yes, Richard,' replied his wife, Jane. 'She's going to the herb gardens in Yorkshire. Hopefully she will return when you are at home.'

'I hope so; it's a long time since I've seen my little sister. I'm always away when she comes.'

'Well stop at home father, then you won't miss her.'

'Is that a good idea, Anna? We won't have any money to spend on fine clothes for you if I don't go to the wool markets and the weavers.'

'Oh,' said Anna reflectively.

'I thought that would change your mind, little miss,' laughed her father. 'Now wife, is there any food ready in this house for a poor working man?'

'Of course, I'm forgetting my duties. Come Anna, we will serve your father his meal.' Richard de Rexar sat down at the large oak table in the middle of the main hall. He quickly demolished a large dish of roasted carp and vegetables, with nearly half a loaf of bread, all swilled down with a tankard of ale.

'That feels better. Now, tell me of your doings little one,' he said to Anna as he pulled her on to his knee. 'What have you been up to since I was last here?'

'Lots of work with the sisters, and some playing out with Christine and Donald. Oh, and do you remember that little pigeon that had a broken wing? It's flown away now – all better.'

'That's good, Anna. You seem to have a way of healing with animals. Perhaps you get that from my sister Judith.'

'I do hope so. I would so like to be like Aunty Judith when I am fully grown.'

'Looking at you, you seem to be almost fully grown now. I'll swear you've got bigger since last week.'

'I'm not surprised,' chipped in Anna's mother, 'she eats like a horse. Come now Anna, I'm sure it is time for you to go to your bedchamber.'

'Oh mother, it's father's first night home; surely I can stay up a little longer? It's only just going dark.'

'No, we'll be going to bed soon, so off you go and then Peggy and Flossie can get the pots cleared away before they settle down for the night. Hurry now.'

Reluctantly, Anna kissed both her parents good night and taking her candle, went up to her bedchamber. Just as she thought, her parents wanted to be alone together. Never mind, it would be her turn one day. She went to bed, dreaming about her handsome rich husband.

Chapter 2

Despite using every excuse not to go because her father was at home, Anna was sent straight to the sisters next morning. Christine didn't appear on the way to the convent, nor did Donald but Anna thought nothing about it as she often got all the way to the convent without either of them catching her up.

On arrival, Anna talked to the little ones. She loved helping the younger children, who sometimes struggled with their work, and she liked some just because they were funny, especially young Matthew Fox. The whole family were called Fox on account of their hair, which was the colour of a fox's fur. Learning all came so easy now to Anna, but she could still remember when it had seemed a mystery. Sister Bernadette had a sad expression on her face when she entered.

'Good morning children. Sit down. I have some news about two of our pupils today. Donald will no longer be joining us. His father has decided that it is time that he started to learn his job in the forge and so he is finished with lessons. Also, Christine will not be here today, or for a few days probably, as her grandmother died in the night, and the little baby with her.'

Anna let out a gasp. Poor Christine, and poor grandmother, and poor little baby. Oh, how sad her friend would be. Christine had really loved her grandmother. She would go after lessons and visit her. Anna was feeling very sad, too. Her two closest friends not with her at lessons. All on the same day. She would visit Donald on her way home as well as Christine. Oh, she couldn't bear so much at one go and slowly the tears that she had been trying to hold back, trickled down her face.

'Sister Bernadette, Anna's crying,' lisped little Mattie, the Miller's daughter.

Sister Bernadette turned round quickly and looked at Anna. 'What is the matter, child?'

Anna sniffed back her tears and wiped her face and nose on her sleeve. 'I'm just so sad about Christine's grandmother. And I'll miss Donald at lessons as well.'

'We'll all miss Donald but you will be able to see him at the forge some days. As for Christine, it is sad news but these things happen. We must all pray to the Blessed Virgin for the soul of our dear departed sister, Edwina de Ribbleside and her child. Come children, we will start our morning prayers with just that prayer.'

Sister Bernadette and the children started to intone their prayers, all except Anna, whose tears continued to roll down her cheeks. At the end of prayer time, Sister Bernadette looked at Anna and told her to come to the front of the class.

'Would you prefer to have a little time to yourself today, Anna?' she asked gently. Anna merely nodded. 'Then go home child and come back tomorrow. I don't think you will learn very much today, with all this sadness.'

Anna smiled her thanks and ran out of the classroom. Rushing through the grounds, she ran out of the convent and sat by the side of the River Ribble and watched the river flowing gently and inexorably out towards the sea, many miles away. Her thoughts were with Christine and her family but also with Donald. It felt as if today marked a big change in their lives: as if life would never be the same again. Getting up from the riverbank, Anna slowly walked towards home but didn't feel ready for going there yet. She took the side lane towards the forge, feeling the heat coming from the fire inside as she got nearer.

Standing at the doorway to the forge, Anna waited. The children knew that they weren't allowed to enter the forge, in case of accidents from flying pieces of cinder or metal, so Anna stood and waited. Eventually, Donald's father saw her.

'Hello Miss Anna, looking for Donald?' he asked cheerily.

'Yes. Is he not helping you today? Sister Bernadette said he was.'

'That's right, he is, but I've sent him an errand this morning. Why are you not at your lessons?'

'I wasn't feeling well, not after hearing about Christine's grandmother.'

'Yes, a sad business. Died in childbirth, I hear?'

'Yes,' replied Anna.

'Well, give them my condolences when you see the family, won't you. And Donald will probably be around later today if you want to see him.'

'Thanks Mr Tom O'the Forge. Goodbye.'

Mr Tom O'the Forge nodded and turned back to his work. Anna plodded slowly home and entered the house. Her father was sat by the fire and Anna went to sit next to him.

'You're back early, child.'

'I know. I got upset when I heard about Christine's grandmother, and also Donald has finished coming to lessons now.'

'Oh dear, your two best friends not there with you? I'm surprised Sister Bernadette let you home though. She's usually quite stern.'

'I think she saw that I was upset today. I've been to see Donald on the way home but he was out on an errand. Where is mother?'

'She's gone round to the Manor House to see if she can help. I think she is going to bring Christine back for her evening meal.'

'Oh that would be good,' replied Anna, visibly brightening. 'I'll look forward to that. Shall I ask Peggy to make her favourite meal?'

'Yes, you do that. And perhaps you can help Peggy in the preparation. That would really please your mother.'

'Oh, all right,' said Anna, less enthusiastically, not looking forward to helping Peggy. Housework and cooking were such a bore, Anna found. All that hard work, and then in less than a trice, it was all eaten, and it would soon be time to start it all again. Not to mention the cleaning of the plates and pans beforehand. With a big sigh, Anna went off into the dairy to find Peggy, but she wasn't there. Anna eventually found her in the brew house.

'Peggy, my father said that you might need some help. Mother is bringing Christine home for her evening meal. What shall I do? Shall I make some bread?' It was about the only chore in the kitchen that Anna enjoyed.

'Nay lass, don't you think I'd have done the bread by now? What sort of person do you think I am? What woman wouldn't have made her bread by this time of day? No Miss Anna, you can help with grinding the barley for the ale, that's what you can do.' Anna's heart sank. It was the one job that she really hated. It was so boring a job was grinding, nobody remembered you and it took forever. Once you were grinding, you could be there for hours. Anna sighed loudly.

'Is there no other job to be done, Peggy? It's so boring is grinding.'

'Aye it is, Miss Anna, very boring, but it has to be done. And no, there isn't any other job to be done, so I suggest you get on with it.' With that, Peggy stomped off back into the house. Anna picked up the grinding stone and worked hard at crushing the barley, letting her mind drift over the events of the day: so many new things that had happened in one day.

It was there that her mother found her.

'Anna, what are you doing? You've nearly ground the barley and the stone. Oh what am I going to do with you? When will I be able to leave you to get on with a job without supervision? What were you thinking about? No, don't tell me, you were in one of your trances. Now leave that alone and come in the house.'

'How was Christine?' asked Anna sadly.

Her mother stopped in her tracks and turned back to look at Anna.

'She was upset, as you can imagine, dear. Can you remember when your grandmother died?'

'Only just, I do remember being sad, but I didn't really understand what death was in those days. Christine will really miss her. Is she coming round for the evening meal?'

'No, her grandfather wouldn't let her.'

'Why not? Oh he's a mean man, I hate him!' growled Anna.

'Anna, how could you! That is an awful thing to say when the poor man is bereaved. I've a good mind to send you to bed again.'

'Oh mother, you want me to act like a grown woman and yet you send me to bed. Don't you think I'm too old for that?'

'Not with the way you act. You can't even do simple jobs. I think it is time that you left your lessons and learnt to be a woman of the house. After all, you will be getting married in the next year or two. I was married when I was not much older than you are now.'

'Yes, but that's ages off, mother. I will learn, I promise you, but don't make me leave my lessons yet. I enjoy it so much with

Donald and Christine and the little ones. Ohh,' Anna stopped in mid-sentence.

'What's the matter, Anna?' asked her mother.

'I'd forgotten, Donald has left lessons today. He's working at the forge with his father from now on.'

'You see, my dearest girl,' replied Anna's mother more softly, 'all three of you are growing up now Anna. You really must try to be more adult. Come, have a hug,' she said, extending her arms to Anna. The two women hugged each other and then went slowly into the house, for once at peace with each other.

For the rest of the evening, the family enjoyed each other's company and talked about Judith's impending return, and about Richard's travels. As the evening darkened, Richard lit candles for all the family to take to their bedchambers, leaving some lit in the main hall for the servants to settle down to sleep with. He was a generous employer and could easily afford candles for the family. It helped that there was a candle maker in the village from whom he got his supplies. It also helped that the candle maker was Peggy's brother, so he was able to get them cheaper.

Most of the villagers made do with burning rushes or cheap tallow candles but they weren't good enough for the de Rexar family. Richard had done well for himself. As a much younger brother in a family, it was often hard to get a living, if you didn't want the army or the church, but he had been fortunate in his life. He had married his wife Jane, whose father was a rich wool merchant from York. Jane's father had died young and the business was given to Richard to continue working at. They also inherited the house, which they now lived in. It was a house that Jane's father had taken as payment of a debt many years before, but they had always had tenants in previously. When Jane and Richard went to look round everything that they had inherited, they fell in love with the house and its setting in the remote village, nestling under Pendle Hill, and decided to settle there in Ribbleside.

The next day, despite her protestations that she wanted to stay with her father, Anna was sent to her lessons. She eventually went but decided she would not go tomorrow, whatever her mother and father said. She would think up some scheme so that she could stay at home with her father for a day or two.

'Anna de Rexar, did you leave your brain at home today?' Sister Bernadette's voice pierced the reverie where Anna was planning a foolproof story for staying at home.

'Er no Sister, sorry Sister, I was just thinking,' stuttered Anna lamely.

'Well, that's good. I'm glad you were thinking. Perhaps you can tell us all what you were thinking?'

'Er, well, I was thinking that when I'm grown up, I'd like to be a physician.'

The class all laughed.

'It's usually men what is physicians,' laughed Jack o'John's. 'You'll just be a wife like the rest of you girls. You don't do jobs like us men.'

'We can if we want,' replied Anna hotly, 'my aunty Judith is a physician and she's a lady, so there! And Sister Bernadette is a lady too and she works,' replied Anna triumphantly.

'That is true, Anna, some women do work,' said Sister Bernadette, 'but we sisters don't see it as work. We see it as a divine calling and vocation. Perhaps you could become a sister with us Anna, and help in the infirmary, if you are interested in healing work.' Anna gulped. She had no intention of ever going to be a nun but how could she get out of this situation without offending the sister?

'Maybe, Sister Bernadette, that is something to think about,' replied Anna demurely, whilst her thoughts were thinking the exact opposite. Just at that moment, Mother Margaret Mary, the head of the convent entered. The children all jumped to their feet and bowed to her.

'Good morning Mother Margaret Mary,' they all chorused.

'Good morning children. Do sit down again. I've come to see how you are all doing with your lessons. And also to tell you about a special visitor who is coming to the convent. Mother Gabrielle is coming to visit us. She is from our sister house in Skipwith in Yorkshire. She too will want to know how you are learning your lessons. How are they doing, Sister Bernadette?'

'Very well Mother. Would you like to test them?'

'Yes, now who shall I ask? Young Matthew, what year is it?'

'The year of our Lord 1335, Mother,' piped up Matthew.

'And Mathilda, what season is it?'

'It's Spring, Mother,' answered Mathilda dutifully.

'Ah yes, but what is the next season that we are almost in?'

'Summer, Mother,' replied Mathilda.

'Correct. Now, let's look to the older ones. Anna, what is the French word for house?'

'Maison, ma mère ,' replied Anna.

'Très bien, ma fille,' Mother Margaret Mary replied. She then proceeded to ask the children questions about religion and was pleased with all their replies.

'Well done children, you are all learning well. But there doesn't seem to be a full class here today, Sister Bernadette?'

'We have lost one child this week. Donald has gone to work with his father.'

'In the forge?'

'Yes, Mother.'

'Good, that is honest and worthy work and he will be a help to his father and the village. But who else is missing today?'

'Young Becky is helping her mother with the new baby today. It was born yesterday morning. Martha hurt her leg on the way home yesterday so is staying at home today. Oh and Christine's grandmother died, so she isn't here.'

'Yes, that was sad news. The baby too, I hear?'

'I'm afraid so. But we do have some good news. Anna is seriously thinking about joining us in the infirmary. She wants to do healing work.' Anna coughed to cover up her shock at what Sister Bernadette had said. What could she say now? But there was no need, as Mother Margaret Mary just beamed at her and said she would talk to her later. But for now, she said, she had to go and prepare for Mother Gabrielle's visit.

Anna let out a sigh of relief and smiled politely at Mother Margaret Mary as she went out of the classroom. The lessons dragged on for the rest of the day and eventually Anna was able to go home. Once home, she was delighted to hear that her father was still at home. She ran up to the solar, where Peggy said her parents were. As she entered the room, she heard her father speaking.

'Yes, it's a good idea. I think it'll do Anna good. She is getting a bit difficult at the moment.' Humph, thought Anna, difficult indeed. What were they saying about her? She opened the door quickly before they could say anything else about her and rushed into the room.

Her mother and father were sat on their own chairs but there was someone else in the room, sat in the fireside, so that Anna couldn't see who it was. As she got further into the room, Anna screamed.

'Aunty Judith, when did you get here?' She rushed over to the fireside and flung herself into her aunt's arms. Judith stood up to greet her. Both tall and slim and dark of hair, and the same delicate features, they looked more like mother and daughter than aunt and niece.

'Stop strangling me and let me speak, you minx. I got here this afternoon. Have you enjoyed your lessons with the sisters today?' Anna pulled a face.

'Not really,' she muttered.

'That's not like you,' said Judith, 'what happened today?'

'Sister Bernadette got it into her head that I wanted to be a nun,' replied Anna glumly. The whole family roared with laughter.

'I couldn't imagine anyone less likely to be a nun than you, dear Anna,' said Judith. 'You would never do as you were told, or you would be dreaming all day and forget to pray!'

Anna grinned at this correct assessment of her. 'You are right; I'd make a terrible nun. But I've no intention of being one. Besides, I've just remembered, what were you planning to do with me as I came in the room? You said it would do me good? I hope you are not going to stop my lessons.'

'Not at all,' replied her mother. 'We just think it's time you learnt a bit more about the world and how other people live.' Anna's mind was working feverishly. What could they be planning for her?

'Yes?' she asked tentatively.

'We've decided that you can go and stay with your Aunty Judith for a little while,' said her father. Anna let out a sigh of relief. Far from being the punishment that she was expecting, this was a real treat. She had often asked to go and stay with her aunt but was always told that she was too young.

'Truly? To stay with Aunty Judith? How long for?' Anna asked with a silly grin on her face.

'For a month or two,' replied her father. 'You'll need to come home before the winter starts anyway.'

'A whole two months? Why that's wonderful. And I promise you all that I will be very good.'

'You'd better be,' threatened her father, but with a twinkle in his eye, 'or Judith will send you back straightaway!'

'Oh but, I'll need to see Christine first. Are we setting off now?'

'No, it's Christine's grandmother's funeral tomorrow, so you can go the day after that,' explained her father. 'Besides, we'll need a day or two to rest Judith's horses and get your things ready. Perhaps you can see Christine now?'

Anna needed no further prompting. She dashed out of the house and ran across the path to Christine's house. The door was shut but Anna was used to going in and out of the house at all times, so she barged into the house as usual. Christine was sitting by the fireside, looking glum. Her face lit up when she saw Anna.

'Anna, I'm so glad to see you. Where have you been?'

'My mother said that I shouldn't come, with your grandmother and everything but she has let me now because I have something to tell you. I'm going to stay with my Aunty Judith in Brun Lea, over the other side of Pendle Hill. A full days journey away.'

'Oh,' said Christine quietly.

'Aren't you thrilled for me?' demanded Anna.

'Yes, I suppose so, but you'll be leaving me, just when I need you. I'll be so lonely without you. Especially now my grandmother has gone. Everyone I love seems to die. First my parents, and my brothers and sisters and my grandmother and now you're going,' Christine burst into tears.

Anna ran to her side and hugged her.

'I'm not dead! I'm only going away for a very short time. I'll be back before you know it and I'll have lots to tell you. And I'll bring you a present back. There, that's something to look forward to. What would you like me to bring? A set of ribbons for your hair? A bangle or necklace? What shall it be?'

Christine smiled sadly. 'You don't have to bring me a present back. Just come back yourself. That will be enough. Never mind, I'll have Donald to keep me company.'

'Oh no,' replied Anna, 'Donald has left the sisters. He's started work ing the forge with his father.'

'Well at least I can still see him sometimes, not like you.'

'It won't be for long, I promise you and then we can just take up where we were before. It won't spoil our friendship.'

'That's true,' replied Christine. ' I suppose we'll have a lot to talk about when you get back. When do you go?'

'Day after tomorrow.'

'I'll call round and see you before you go, if grandfather permits it.'

'Why wouldn't he permit it? He doesn't usually speak to you much.'

'I know, but he's being strict at the moment. Keeps going on about our position in the village and how we must set an example.'

'Well, try to come anyway. If not, I'll call round and see you, shall I? Or will he not approve of me either?'

'Who knows? He's certainly strange at the moment.'

'My mother says that grief takes people in different ways,' nodded Anna sagely, sounding older than her years.

'Grief? I don't think he's bothered. All he's bothered about was that the baby was a boy and it died with her,' said Christine sadly.

'Well I'll try and come. I'd better go back now. Bye Christine.'

'Bye Anna. Thanks for telling me about your trip.'

Anna left the house and went home and told her mum how concerned she was about Christine but her mother just said that it was to be expected. Anna went early to her bedchamber that night. Even the excitement of having Aunty Judith in the house was lessened by her concern for her friend, and she said a little prayer for her before she went to sleep.

On the following day, Anna's father went to the funeral, whilst Anna's mother went to help prepare the funeral food at the Manor House. Anna didn't get chance to see Christine but managed to sneak into the house very early on the following day. The two girls hugged each other, and then Anna returned to her own house, before Christine's grandfather saw her.

Despite her elation about going with her Aunty Judith, Anna set off with a heavy heart, knowing that her friend was so sad. When she got back to her own house, the cart was being loaded up with food and other supplies, including a new piece of woollen cloth that Richard had brought for his sister. Aunty Judith's henchman, Rupert, was fastening the horse to the brackets on the cart. Anna watched him from the doorway.

Rupert was a tall strong young man, who could lift anything. He was not very bright and couldn't read his letters or add up, as many children couldn't, but he was fiercely loyal to Aunty Judith, after her husband rescued him from being tormented in the market at Brun Lea. He had worked for Judith ever since and always travelled with her wherever she went, to protect her.

Eventually the horse and cart were ready. Anna and Judith climbed on to the cart and Rupert patted the horse gently on his neck, as a sign to set off. Jane and Richard waved their only daughter off, with some misgivings. They would miss her but still felt that it would be a good influence in her young life.

Anna gave a last look at Pendle Hill as she left. It was bright and sunny today, and again reflected her mood. She wouldn't miss the hill whilst she was in Brun Lea, as her aunt said that it could be seen from her house, but for now, she was going over the top of Pendle Hill; a journey she had not made before. A journey into the unknown.

Chapter 3

The journey would take all day, so they couldn't dally and Rupert set off at a brisk pace. They travelled thorough Pendleton hamlet and then started climbing up the side of Pendle Hill, towards the natural dip in the top of the hill which was always referred to as the Nick of Pendle. Near the top, they met a packman sat by the side of the track.

'Hallo there, Tom the pedlar,' shouted Rupert brightly.

'Good day to you, Rupert, and to you Mistress Physician. And to the young lady, too,' replied the pedlar, taking off his hat in salute to them. He was an elderly man with a ruddy complexion, from his hours spent outside in all weathers.

Anna and Judith returned his greeting.

'We were just going to rest and have some food, whilst the horse rests. Do you mind if we sit here with you?' asked Judith.

'Not at all, I'd be glad of the company,' replied Tom. 'And who is the young lady?'

'It's my niece, Anna. My brother Richards's girl. She's coming to stay with me for a while.'

'Greetings to you, Miss Anna. Can I tempt you to a trinket from my pack?'

'Not today, unless you can deliver it back to Ribbleside for me,' Anna replied.

'I'm not due back there until next month, I'm afraid.'

'That will be fine; it will get there before me. Have you got some ribbons?'

'Of course, what sort of packman would I be if I didn't have ribbons? What colour would you be wanting?'

'Red,' Anna replied, 'it's for a friend who needs cheering up.'

'What about these ones?' asked Tom, holding up the fripperies.

'Perfect. Can you deliver them to the Manor House at Ribbleside please? For Miss Christine?'

'Certainly. Now what about yourself?'

'Not today, thank you. Christine was the most important person I wanted something for. Another day perhaps?' she said handing her coins to him. Tom chuckled to himself.

'She's a chip off the old block, isn't she? Just like you Mistress Physician. Always caring about others before herself.'

'She certainly is,' replied Judith beaming.

Anna felt embarrassed. Some of the time she was a bit selfish but she did really care about others, that part was true.

They settled down to eating their cheese and bread and then set off again to the top of the hill and over the Nick of Pendle. Giving the horse a light breather as he got to the top, they then set off down the other side, going steadily downhill towards the hamlet of Hey Houses.

'Here's where I leave you,' said Tom. 'I'll see you again shortly, no doubt. I'll be in Brun Lea by Wednesday or Thursday at the latest. Cheerio!' He gave them a hearty wave and turned into the village square, whilst they started the climb up the next part of the hill.

Conversation flagged as they climbed up the hill out of Hey Houses and then they rested again and ate some more bread and cheese.

'Come on,' chivvied Judith, 'not long to go now. Through Higham, and then we'll soon be into Brun Lea. We should be home by dark.'

'Good,' said Anna, 'I'm tired and ready for a sit down by a nice warm fire.'

Judith laughed. 'You'll have to make it yourself then. I let all my servants have time at home with their families whilst I was away. They don't know when I'll be back.' Anna laughed too, at the thought of trying to light a fire all by herself.

They trudged along the tracks and as the sky started to darken, they eventually reached Brun Lea. They walked past the church and up the road heading towards Colne for a short time to Judith's house. It was a stone built building, built over three floors and had been in Judith's husband's family for many years. The ground floor was given over to the animals, then the main living quarters of the house were on the second floor and the bedchambers and solar were on the top floor.

32

Rupert settled the horse in the ground floor stable and then came upstairs to find Judith laughing at Anna trying to light the fire.

'Shall I go and tell the others that you're back, Mistress?' asked Rupert.

'No, leave them. They might as well have another night at home. News travels fast; they'll know I'm back by morning. All we will be doing tonight is going to bed after we've had some food. Perhaps you can help Anna with the fire or else we won't be having anything warm to eat tonight. Better still, teach her how to do it properly for the future,' shouted Judith over her shoulder, as she took her travelling bag up to the bedchamber.

Within the hour, the fire was roaring in the chimney and the stew that Peggy had given Judith was bubbling merrily over the fire. After a hearty repast, the travellers made for an early night. True to Judith's theory, the servants all turned up next morning, chastising Judith for not sending messages.

'I knew you'd all get to know I was back fairly quickly. Nothing happens much in Brun Lea without everyone knowing about it!'

'But we could have had the fire lit and a meal ready for you, Mistress,' chided Mary, Judith's cook. Both Anna and Judith laughed.

'What have I said?' demanded Mary. 'Don't you believe me?' Mary put her hands on her hips in high dudgeon.

'If you had seen Anna trying to light the fire last night, you would know what we were laughing about. This girl has a lot to learn about running a home. Perhaps you can teach her, Mary?'

'Of course, Mistress, I'd be happy to oblige,' replied Mary, calming down and looking happier.

The servants weren't the only people who had heard that Judith was home. A small stream of people visited the house for medicine and advice and Judith was busy for most of the day. She had a small outhouse built behind the house where she saw the patients who could travel to visit her. There was also an herb garden, so that Judith could grow some of the herbs she would need for treatments and making tisanes. In the afternoon, Judith and Rupert set out to visit some outlying houses and farms. Anna was left in the house to help in the kitchen, which didn't please her at all. During the evening meal, Anna asked Judith if she could watch her consultations and go on the visits but Judith declined.

'It's important that my patients can speak to me in private. You are only a young girl and it . .'

'But I want to be a physician like you,' Anna interrupted. 'How will I learn if I don't come with you?'

'Anna, you're too young to think about becoming a physician. You will be married and have a family to bring up soon. There is plenty of time for being a physician later in your life. Concentrate on being a woman first.'

'Talking of being a woman, Aunty Judith, I have my monthly curse just started and have a tummy ache. At home, Mother lets me have a bath to ease the discomfort. It works really well. Is it possible that I could have a bath?'

'Of course dear. Fancy, you having your monthly curses already. You are growing up to be a woman now. I'll brew you a tisane to help with the pain, too. You go and get your things ready. Have you got some cloths with you?'

'Yes, Mother packed me some.'

'Good. I'll get Fanny and Aggie to fill the bath for you in your bedchamber.'

Anna was amazed at how quickly the servants got the wooden bath ready and she sunk into the water with pleasure. Before the water had even started to cool, Judith brought her a cup with steaming liquid in it. It smelt lovely.

'What's in it, Aunty Judith? What have you made it from? It smells of mint.'

'Never you mind for now. Just enjoy it. I'll teach you about tisanes later, if you really want to know about my work.'

Anna got into her night attire then climbed into her bed, falling asleep straightaway.

Next morning, when Anna arrived downstairs, there was nobody about. She helped herself to a bowl of porridge from the pan on the fire and ate it quickly. As she was scraping round the bowl, Mary entered the kitchen.

'Oh, I see you're up at last, Miss Anna,' she remarked.

'Why, am I late?'

'Your aunty has seen all her patients and gone on her rounds. She's got to go up to Briercliffe hamlet today and then Marsden hamlet. They're both a long ride for her. She'll be away most of the day.'

'What a shame, I could have gone with her for company.'

'She's got Rupert for company. Besides, you should have got up early if you'd wanted to go,' replied Mary brusquely.

'Perhaps I will tomorrow, do you want me to do anything for you today?'

'No thanks. Everything is done; I suggest you look round the village. It's market day today,' said Mary.

Anna nodded. She felt that Mary didn't want her around so decided to take up her suggestion. She got her cloak and a basket and asked Mary if she wanted anything from the market. Mary replied in the negative, so Anna took some money from her little hoard that her father had given her and set off.

As she walked into the market place she was amazed at the array of stalls that were available – far more than she was used to in Ribbleside. But then, Brun Lea was a far bigger village. And really, it wasn't a proper market at Ribbleside, just villagers putting their wares outside their huts on tables, for anyone who was passing. At Brun Lea there were some of the same stalls, such as wicker baskets; bread and candles, but there were also stalls selling more exotic goods and every kind of game. Anna could see spices from far off countries, and she inhaled their pungent smell.

There were swans, larks, partridges and pheasants hanging from the wooden frame of the stalls. Ready-made garments were hanging from another stall, with kirtles, hoods and under garments all available. Most of the garments were serviceable ones but there were also some brighter and fancier garments too. Shoes of every type and colour were arrayed on another stall; the cordwainer's talent being in evidence. Stallholders cried out to the people; advertising their wares.

The smell of warm food assailed her nostrils, making her hungry, especially the mutton pies. Anna decided she would buy a large mutton pie for Judith, as a little thank you for bringing her to Brun Lea. After paying for her pie, chosen to be large enough for all the family and servants, Anna laid it carefully in her basket and carried on her journey around the market. As an afterthought, she also bought a rich cheese. She was sure that Aunty Judith would be pleased with her purchases and hurried on home with her precious cargo. It might even please Mary, too.

After going upstairs to the living floor, Anna took her purchases and put them on to the kitchen table, under Mary's watchful eye, waiting for nods of approval. They did not appear. Indeed, Mary looked frozen faced at Anna and left the room. Anna was puzzled. Her mother loved it when her father brought home some delicacy from one of the markets he had passed through on his travels. But before she sorted this puzzle out, Judith came through the door.

'Aunty Judith, how glad I am to see you. Look, I've been on the market. Isn't it a big one? Much bigger than the one at Ribbleside. Where have you been today? Why didn't you wait for me? Can I come with you next time?'

'Anna, calm down. That's so many questions you've asked me. Let me ask you one back. Where's Mary?'

'Don't know, she went out when I came back from the market. I bought some things from the market for us but she didn't seem at all grateful,' moaned Anna.

'What things?' asked Judith quietly.

'A lovely big pie and some nice cheese. Look here they are,' Anna said as she pointed at her purchases.

'Oh Anna, Mary makes the best pies in Brun Lea and she makes her own cheese. And have you been to market like that with a bare head? No wonder your mother despairs of you. Now, I'm off to find Mary. You'd better put those foodstuffs in the food cupboard for now. I'll sort them out later.' Judith hurried out of the room, leaving

Anna dismayed and not a little puzzled. What was wrong with her presents? And why should she not have a bare head? And why was her aunty shouting at her? She'd never shouted at her before. Life was certainly different in Brun Lea, Anna decided. She went up to her bedchamber and rested on the bed. She supposed there would be no evening meal until later. Time would tell, she decided.

Anna had not long to wait. An irate aunty entered her bedchamber after a sharp knock.

'What possessed you to insult Mary in that way? She has been with me for many years and my husband's family before that,' she demanded.

'I thought I would save her from making an evening meal,' stammered Anna, 'I had no intention of offending her. I meant to help her.'

'Well you did offend her. She's threatening to leave my service. Now come downstairs and make your peace with her. At once!'

Anna jumped off the bed speedily and followed her aunty down to the next floor. Mary was stood by the doorway.

'What have you to say to Mary, Anna?'

'I'm very sorry Mary. I didn't intend to offend you. I wanted to give you some help in the kitchen by buying the food. Please forgive me, I have a lot to learn,' muttered Anna in a low voice. Mary looked unconvinced

'There Mary, it was all a misunderstanding. Anna wasn't trying to teach you your job. She was only trying to help you. Now come on Mary, you know I can't manage without you,' wheedled Judith.

Mary shrugged her shoulders.

'Well if it was a mistake, then perhaps I'll stay. But if there's any more of this, I'm going to my sisters and that's final,' she said, retying her pinafore and going over to the fire. Judith let out a sigh of relief.

'And you Miss,' she said turning towards Anna, 'I'll speak to you upstairs in the solar.' Anna stood rooted to the spot for a while until another glare from her aunty made her set off upstairs to the solar. It was all very puzzling. She had never seen her aunty like this before.

As soon as the door was shut, Judith started lecturing Anna all about offending long-standing servants and knowing her place in this family. Anna let her carry on for a while, trying not to burst into tears. Eventually Judith stopped berating Anna.

'Well? What have you to say for yourself?'

'I'm sorry Aunty Judith, for offending Mary, I will try to learn from you all, but why shouldn't I go into the market with my head bare?'

'Anna,' replied Judith in an exasperated voice, 'you are not in Ribbleside now. Brun Lea is a far more important village and no decent woman is seen without her head covered. Understood?' Anna nodded, but couldn't stop herself making another comment.

'But I'm only a girl, Aunty Judith. There were other girls who had nothing on their heads in the market.'

'You came here to learn a little about what it means to be a woman, so it's time you started learning. So in future, you will always have your head covered in public whilst you are living with me. Right? Now I'm tired and I want something to eat and an early night. I've had a busy day.'

'Oh, how was your day, Aunty Judith?' chirped Anna, trying to make amends.

'If you want to know, I had a small patient who died and the parents are distraught. The last thing I wanted was trouble in my own house. The day had been bad enough. Now are you so serious about making healing a career?' With that, Judith flounced out of the room and went into the kitchen. Anna slunk into her own bedchamber, deciding she wasn't hungry after all. And she knew that there was no Flossie here to sneak a meal up the back stairs to her. Anna went to bed and pondered all these things in her heart and decided tearfully that growing up was not much fun.

Next morning, Anna was up early and was determined to make amends to both her aunty and Mary. She tried to make the fire and only succeeded in upsetting Mary again, for scattering ash all over the floor. In her efforts to please her aunty at breakfast time, she knocked over a flagon of milk and further irritated her. Eventually, Anna dissolved into tears.

'I'm so sorry, I do want to learn, but everything I try to do seems to go wrong and makes things worse. Please help me, Aunty Judith,' Anna cried.

'There, Anna, dry your eyes. Spend some time just watching Mary and the others working today, and then tonight, when I've finished my chores, I'll talk to you. How does that sound?'

Anna nodded at Judith and wiped her eyes.

'Now I'm off to do my visits. See if you can stay out of trouble for a day, will you?'

'Yes, Aunty Judith,' replied a chastened Anna. As good as her word, Anna carefully watched all that Mary did and asked questions. In the afternoon, Mary set her to preparing the vegetables with Susy, the cooking helper. Nodding her approval of this new industrious girl, Mary said that she'd make a woman of her yet. Anna beamed at this rare piece of praise from Mary. She was so keen to show Mary her new capabilities that she offered to grind the barley for her, although strongly hoping that Mary would say no.

'Why, thank you dear. That would be most kind of you. Grinding fair hurts my joints nowadays,' grinned Mary. Anna's heart sank but she gritted her teeth and went into the brewing room and started grinding. If this is what it took to get in favour with Mary and her aunty Judith, thought Anna, then so be it. But her heart ached at the thought of this becoming her regular chore.

After the evening meal, which consisted of the mutton pie, Anna noted, Judith said that they would talk in the solar.

'Come Anna, I'll groom your hair, and we can talk,' said Judith kindly. Anna sat on the floor in front of her aunt and Judith checked her hair for the constant fight against lice that was prevalent amongst even the cleanest families.

'Now I'll show you how to fasten your hair up so that it is more womanly. You can also choose some of my head coverings for yourself. Or you can buy some in the market. You'll find that most decent women will keep their head covered when out of the house and I want you to do that too.'

'I will Aunty Judith, whatever you say. Now, will you tell me the story about how you met your husband, my uncle Edward?'

'You've heard it before, Anna.'

'I know, but I love to hear it,' replied Anna.

'Well, as you know, we lived near York . . .'

'Was I born yet?' interrupted Anna.

'No,' laughed Judith, 'your mother and father were married, but they hadn't moved to Ribbleside yet. They still lived in Jane's family home in York with her parents. I had gone to stay with them for a while as your mother was expecting a baby.'

'Was that one of the 'lost' babies,' interrupted Anna again.

'Yes, your mother lost several babies, as you know, before she managed to get to full term with one.'

'My mother always said she missed the lost babies, even though she never really saw them,' said Anna quietly.

'You always do,' replied Judith even more quietly, but Anna didn't understand the implication of her reply, so ignored it.

'So what happened next?' Anna asked.

'I got taken with a fever and was very ill. They sent for their physician but he was away and so his apprentice came to see if he could help.'

'And what did you think of this apprentice, when you first saw him? Did you like him? Was he handsome?'

'Heavens girl, let me tell the story. I hadn't a clue what he looked like, as I was well nigh unconscious. But as soon as I was better, I decided that I liked this man.'

'Describe him to me, Aunty. I do wish I'd met him.'

'Well, he was medium height and build with very dark curly hair and a magnificent curly beard. He was very handsome, except for a deformity of his nose. He had broken it when a boy and it was never quite straight. And he loved to laugh and he made me laugh too.'

'So how did you get to know him?'

'Well, he started coming to visit my brother, your father, as a friend, after I was better. But then he started coming when your father was away and I realised that he was really coming to see me.'

'How did that make you feel? Were you excited?'

'Very. I knew that I could live with this man and love him.'

'How did you know? What did it feel like?'

'Oh Anna, what a lot of questions. You are certainly growing up. You will know when you fall in love. You can't stop thinking about them, or talking about them for that matter. You want to know their opinion on everything and want to touch them and hold them, and spend lots of time with them.'

Anna sat quietly for a moment, thinking about this prospect of falling in love and getting married and what it would be like.

'You've gone very quiet, my lamb?' said Judith.

'Just thinking, that's all,' Anna replied.

Judith laughed. 'I can see that we are going to have to look round the market in Brun Lea to see if we can find a suitable match for you. What do you think about that?'

'Oh,' said Anna blushing, 'I don't think so. I'm too young yet. Besides, I think I would like to marry Donald. He is quite a nice boy. I like to talk to him and spend time with him and I like to hear his opinions about things, so perhaps I already love him a little.'

'Donald? The boy from the forge?'

'Yes. We spend a lot of time together.'

'I don't think that your parents would want you to marry Donald,' said Judith tentatively.

'Why not? They know him and they like his parents?'

'But Anna, he is not the same as us. He is from peasant stock. His father is a worker.'

'But my father works. What do you mean? Are you saying that he's not good enough for me?'

'Not necessarily, but your father may have a richer person in mind for you. He may have already talked to some of his friends about a prospective husband for you.'

'But I don't want to be married off to someone my father chooses. I want to fall in love like you did.'

'It doesn't happen very often though, Anna. Most girls marry their father's choice. Now let's get on with the story,' chattered Judith brightly. 'Edward was coming to the end of his apprenticeship and had been promised help in setting up a business in Brun Lea, where his family came from, so he asked Richard if he could ask for my hand in marriage, with my father already having died.'

Anna was enthralled by the story again and sighed appreciatively: her own worries about an arranged marriage forgotten for the moment.

'And did you say 'yes' straightway?' sighed Anna.

'Of course. I wouldn't have risked offending him, or losing him. He was moving the following week.'

'So did you have a quick wedding, then? So that you could go with him to Brun Lea?' asked Anna.

'Yes, we were married that week and I moved with him to Brun Lea. We were married for ten years,' she added sadly.

'So what happened to him? I was never very sure. I just knew that you were a widow.'

Judith swallowed. 'It was quite sudden. We had a small boy ourselves by then, called Gregory. He was three years old. There was a nasty fever going around town and of course, Edward was out all hours, trying to help people. Eventually, he got the fever and died very quickly.'

'That must have been awful for you, Aunty Judith, so what happened to Gregory?'

'He got the fever and died the following week.'

The two women were both silent, thinking their own different thoughts. Eventually Anna broke the silence.

'And is that when you decided to become a physician?' she asked quietly.

'Not straightaway, but yes. I couldn't stand being alone at home all the time, with nothing to do. I didn't need money, so I was more fortunate than many women in my position, but I needed something to do. One of Edward's friends in Lancaster offered to let me live in his house and teach me all that I needed to register as a physician. It was my salvation. I had a reason to get up in a morning again.'

42

The silence resumed; both women deep in thought.

'That's what I want to do, Aunty Judith. Will you teach me?'

'No, not now. You are too young and besides, there will be a man out there somewhere to come and woo you,' sparkled Judith, trying to lift the solemn atmosphere.

'I'll start looking at next market day,' quipped Anna. And she did. The very next market day, Mary was amazed at how early Anna was up and ready for shopping. She even offered to grind the barley again. On arrival at the market cross, Anna wandered round the stalls very slowly. To any observer, she would just be another housewife, checking out the contents of the stall. In part, that was true, but Anna was carefully looking at all the young men on or at the stalls, or who were visiting the alehouse across the road.

I wonder, she thought as she looked at a fine young man, with rich clothing, and vivid red hair and beard. He seems very striking. Could he be a possibility? But then a woman came away from a stall and took hold of his arm possessively. Perhaps not, giggled Anna to herself. But this first abortive attempt didn't stop her looking at all the other young men around. Tall ones, fat ones, thin ones, laughing ones, rich and poor ones, they all came under her scrutiny. By the time she had done her shopping she was quite exhausted, and told her aunty so when they had supper together, that evening.

'So have you found your ideal husband yet?'

'No, not really, but I've had a lot of fun looking,' she replied laughing.

As the weeks passed by, Anna learnt a lot more from both her aunty and her staff. She learnt about being a woman from her aunty; about caring for her animals from Rupert; about household duties from Mary and Susy; and how to manage money and buy from the market. Anna was very pleased with herself. During these few summer weeks, she felt that she had grown up immensely and realised that perhaps she was ready to leave the sisters soon. She was ready for the next phase of her life. After all, she was now thirteen years of age. Truly a woman.

Chapter 4

It was the morning of her return to Ribbleside. Anna was excited and yet sad. She had thoroughly enjoyed her time with her aunt but was itching to return home. She wanted to see how her parents were, and how Christine was, and Donald. And her animals. She guilty reflected that she had hardly thought about them for the last few weeks, but now she was going home, she couldn't wait to see them all.

Judith had offered to let Rupert take her back to Ribbleside but Anna was worried that her aunty would be lost without him as he accompanied her on all her travels.

It was Anna's idea that she travel back with Tom the pedlar. He would make sure she was safe, and it would be part of his journey to go to Ribbleside anyway. Tom wasn't sure at first either, but Anna soon persuaded him. It meant that Anna could also buy gifts for all the staff and her aunty from the pedlar, before they went.

They set off together, with Anna in high spirits on a little pony that Tom owned. She enjoyed stopping at all the villages and joined in the banter when people were choosing their wares. Because of the stops at villages, they had to stay at his sister's house overnight, but this added to the pleasure of the journey for Anna. She was well received by Tom's sister. Hers was a plain but warm hut on the outskirts of a village on the lee of Pendle Hill and Anna enjoyed the company of the small children.

On the next day, Pendle Hill could not be seen at all. The driving wet rain of Lancashire obscured the view of the magnificent hill. Tom's sister laughed when she saw the weather.

'Knew it was too good to be true. We've had fine weather for three days on the run. That's pretty rare near here. Y'know what they say round here, Miss Anna? If you can't see Pendle Hill, it's raining; and if you can see Pendle Hill, it'll be raining later.' They all laughed. 'Have you got a thick blanket to cover yourself with?' Anna assured her that she had and dragged the blanket round her. It was a miserable journey, as eventually, the rain trickled in through the blanket, thick as it was. Anna was becoming increasingly uncomfortable and wished that Tom had a modern covered coach to transport her. Not that she wasn't grateful. She couldn't have set off home on her own; not with all the rogues and vagabonds that were around in the countryside.

Anna was soon within sight of her beloved village. Her excitement grew as she got nearer the house. She would be glad to get out of the rain. Ignoring Tom, she jumped off her pony and ran across to the house. Peggy was the first person she saw.

'Peggy, how good to see you,' she said, enveloping Peggy in a wet hug. 'Where is my mother?'

'Well Miss Anna, nice to see you, even if you are sopping wet. Now get those wet clothes off you at once, before you get a chill.'

Anna took the two outer wet garments off and placed them on a chair near the fire. Peggy continued, 'your mother is in her solar. Do you need to get your belongings off the pedlar? Do we need to pay Tom for transporting you here?'

Anna jumped round. 'Oh sorry Tom, please forgive me. I'd quite forgotten you in the excitement of being home again. Do come in and have some refreshment and get dry. Come over here, sit yourself right by the fire and get warm. Flossie, could you see to him, please?' Anna commanded. Peggy and Flossie stared at Anna and then at each other. Was this the little girl that had gone away two months ago? She was certainly grown up now. Before either of them could answer, a quiet voice spoke out.

'Anna, how good to see you, and to see that you are caring for Tom,' said Jane de Rexar.

'Oh Mother, it's so good to see you. I have so much to tell you,' replied Anna, hoping that her mother hadn't heard Peggy having to remind her about caring for Tom. Jane hugged Anna and then Anna pulled away.

'Oh, I have presents for you all. Bought at Brun Lea market. It's so much bigger than ours at Ribbleside; even bigger than Clitheroe. Here mother, this is the latest design in headwear for ladies. Isn't it lovely?' said Anna as she placed a hat on her mother's hair. 'And

45

Flossie, I've bought you some ribbons for your hair and I'll show you how I've learnt to do my own hair now. And Peggy, I've bought you a lovely wicker basket for when you go to market. I hope you like it. And where is father? Is he here? And I've got a present for Christine as well. Can I go round there?'

'Anna, you haven't improved in your talking. Questions, questions, questions, without giving anyone time to give you an answer,' replied her mother laughing. 'Your father will be home tonight and Christine is gone to Clitheroe so you will have to wait to see her. Now let me look at you. You do look grown up with your hair all braided, I must admit. But first things first. We must remember our manners. Have you got enough to eat Tom? Will you require a bed for the night?'

'I thank you kindly Mistress, but I'll be on my way as soon as I've eaten, if that's all right with you?' replied Tom. 'I'm wanting to get to the next village before nightfall if I can.'

'That's fine. And at least let me exchange your wet clothes for dry ones. You can bring them back next time you are passing. Do we owe you any money for your trouble?'

'No, Mistress Physician gave me some extra for my trouble. But I must say, it was no trouble. She's a delight to have aside of you,' remarked Tom.

'No trouble?' said Jane, 'then truly, my sister in law has worked a miracle. She gives us nothing but trouble usually.'

'Oh mother, I'm trying really hard now,' complained Anna.

'You've always been trying, dearest, trying our patience,' quipped Jane, and then laughed as she saw Anna's crestfallen face. Anna said goodbye to Tom, thanking him for accompanying her to her home and then went upstairs to get some dry clothes on and to put her things away in her bedchamber. It felt nice to be back in her own bedchamber. She had enjoyed being at Aunty Judith's, but it was nice to be in your own home and your own room again. Hearing a horse approaching down the lane, Anna looked out and saw her father. Running downstairs, she threw herself at him, hugging him tightly.

'Father, I've missed you so.'

'And I've missed you, my dear. My, how you've grown. You look a proper lady now. I like your hairstyle; very grown up.' He turned to his wife, who had just come in the door, having heard the commotion. They hugged tenderly and Anna felt that they had quite forgotten her. She stood and watched them. Adult love was becoming very interesting to her.

'I've got you a present, father. Look,' she said, proffering her gift. Reluctantly, he moved his gaze from Jane and looked at the gift Anna was holding. It was a leather satchel for when he was out on his travels.

'My, that's a smart satchel, Anna. That will be very useful. The tooling is very fine. Where did you get this?'

'At the market at Brun Lea. Oh father, it's a massive place, not like here. There must be about two hundred houses and the market has many stalls. Life is so much faster there.' Richard laughed at Anna.

'So you like the faster pace of life, do you? Perhaps we should move to York, or even Canterbury.'

'Oh well, I do like here as well,' backtracked Anna. 'It's just been nice for a change. And I have so enjoyed living with Aunty Judith. I'm sure now that I want to be a physician when I'm older, but Aunty Judith tells me I need to get married first and be a physician later.'

'So have you anyone in mind to marry, Anna?' teased her father. 'Did you meet anyone at Brun Lea?'

'No,' said Anna, trying not to blush, 'nobody special.'

'Are you sure?' asked Richard laughing.

'Quite sure, father, but I did enjoy looking.'

At this, the whole family laughed out loud.

'Well, young lady, perhaps we'd better advertise that we have a daughter of marriageable age now and see what we can come up with. We could put a notice outside the house to that effect.'

'No, you wouldn't,' gasped Anna, completely mortified at the thought of a notice advertising her.

'Well, why not? Now let me see, it could say

To the highest bidder:
A young lady who never stops talking,
hates cooking and housework and has a temper,
yet is kind to animals.
Apply within.
No reasonable offer refused.

'Yes, that should do the trick. I'll get someone to prepare it now. I wonder what response we will get?' continued Richard. By now, Anna was pummelling her father with anger, but he started tickling her and eventually they both fell back on to the settle laughing.

After the riotous return to her home, Anna soon settled in to her life, but quietly took up more of the duties of a woman within the home. Her mother praised her for even small tasks that she did, to encourage this new mature behaviour. It was never discussed, but Anna was no longer sent to the sisters for learning. It was as if the visit to her aunt's marked the change from childhood to womanhood.

Anna loved being treated as an adult, even though she did miss the little ones at the convent. But she saw them out at play when they were not at the convent and kept in touch with the minutiae of their little lives. Christine and Anna also went to visit Donald at his forge, but more and more, he seemed to be too busy to talk to them, and eventually they stopped going.

Since her grandmother's death, Christine had not attended the sisters either and was expected to start learning about housework like Anna. They spent their free time talking about everything under the sun and walking around the village. If it was raining, they tended to stay in Anna's house, as Christine was unhappy in her home. Things had not improved since her grandmother had died, and her grandfather had become even more difficult to live with.

In early September, Richard had stayed at home for a week and he and his wife had spent a lot of time talking together on their own. Unusually, they seemed to be having a disagreement about something, but never mentioned it to anyone. Eventually one evening, they asked to speak with Anna in the solar. Anna skipped into the solar, happy with her life and beamed at both her parents.

'Did you want me? Is it to discuss something nice? Are we going to York? Or to see Aunty Judith? You both look very serious. What is it?'

'Sit down, Anna,' said Richard, 'we want to talk to you about your future.'

'Oh good, am I going to work with Aunty Judith and become a physician?'

'Anna, be quiet,' said Richard sternly, 'not another word until I've finished. This isn't easy for me. You are now thirteen years old and it is time that we thought about getting you married. We have had an offer for your hand, which we have accepted, after a lot of thought. It is someone who can give you status and riches and an even more comfortable life than you have now.'

'Is it anyone I know?' burst in Anna, unable to hold her tongue any longer.

'Yes,' replied Richard simply, 'you do know him. It's Jack de Ribbleside.'

Anna laughed. 'Goodness, he's got the same name as Christine's grandfather. I hope he's a lot better than him.'

'It is Christine's grandfather,' said Richard quietly. Anna continued laughing, until she realised what her father had said.

'You want me to marry Christine's grandfather?' she asked in horror, 'but he's an old, old man. He must be forty or fifty years old at least. You can't be serious, father. Anyone but him. He's not even nice. He's horrible. I can't marry him. No, I'll not even consider it.'

'I have said you will, Anna. You have no say in it really. I am your father and I will do what is best for the family and this offer is a good thing for our family.'

'How can it be a good thing for the family? It's awful. It's the worst thing for the family.'

'Nevertheless, Anna, you will marry him. I have given my word as a gentleman.'

'Well take it back then,' said Anna angrily, 'I won't do it. I can't marry him.'

'But you will, Anna,' said Richard determinedly.

'I'd rather go as a nun first. That's what I'll do.'

Her mother spoke for the first time. 'Don't be silly Anna. You wouldn't make a nun. This marriage is fortuitous for us and you will be in a position of power in the village.'

'I don't want a position of power. I don't want to marry yet. I'm too young. Let me have a little longer being at home with you. Please?' she implored her parents, the tears streaming down her face.

'I'm sorry but you have no alternative,' said her father grimly. 'The honour of the family is at stake. I cannot tell you the full reason, but trust me Anna, I wouldn't insist on this marriage if there was any other way out. You will marry him, so go to your bedchamber and reflect on this. I won't talk to you again until you are in a more reasonable frame of mind. Go.'

Anna froze. She couldn't believe that this was her father speaking to her like this. He had always been so caring and loving and full of fun. And her mother. She was no better. She wasn't even taking Anna's side like she usually did, but agreeing with her father. She made one last attempt.

'Mother, I'm too young to marry,' Anna wheedled.

'No child. You are not. Do as your father says and go to your bedchamber. At least you can see Christine all the time when you live there,' her mother cajoled, 'and you won't be far away from us. You can call round and see us at anytime. If you married somebody from away, we would hardly ever see you again. This way, we can see you often.'

But Anna was rooted to the spot, not taking in what Jane was saying. Her thoughts were with Christine. What would Christine make of this? Would she be pleased? Anna thought not. How would she have liked it if Christine had married her grandfather? It didn't even bear thinking about. Not only was she to be married to an ancient man who was horrible, but also her best friend would hate her. Anna knew that she would get nowhere tonight with her parents, so she slunk up to her bedchamber, without even taking a backward glance.

On reaching her bedchamber, she threw herself on the bed and howled uncontrollably, banging her fists on the pillow. It wasn't fair. Her whole life would be ruined. She couldn't bear it. Perhaps she should go and be a nun. At least she wouldn't have to marry that hateful man. Yes, that was the solution. She would be a nun. Her sobs subsided eventually but no one came to see if she was all right. Neither did any food appear outside her bedchamber from the faithful Flossie. Well, she didn't care if she never ate again. She didn't even care if she died, because that way she couldn't marry him. Eventually she sobbed herself to sleep, but spent a fitful night, as she kept waking up and remembering the fateful news that she had received the evening before.

Next morning, with puffy face and tired eyes, Anna went downstairs to find a subdued household. Nobody looked her in the eye and they barely passed the time of day with her. She went out to the animals and told cow how unhappy she was and cow mooed sympathetically. Anna sat up in the hayloft and spent time in thinking. She went round and round the problem again, without finding a solution.

Her father had been so adamant that she had to marry and that was strange in itself. He was so rarely adamant about anything and her mother could usually talk him round to anything. Her father had hinted at family honour, but she knew from the steely look to his eye, that he wouldn't give her any more details, so it was useless to ask. Anna sighed. Life was so unfair. Eventually her rumbling stomach made her go inside and even though she had decided last night to starve herself to death, the reality of hunger overruled her young body.

Helping herself to gruel, Anna sat at the table and listlessly spooned the food in to her mouth. Her mother found her there when she was finishing her food.

'Good morning Anna, I'm glad to see you are eating something. You must be feeling better this morning,' her mother asked softly.

'How can I feel better?' Anna grumbled, 'I'll never feel better again. Not if I have to marry him.'

'Oh Anna,' said Jane, 'don't start again. You heard what your father said. And he repeated it again this morning before he left.'

'Father's left? Without speaking to me?' cried Anna incredulously, 'but I wanted to talk to him today.'

'There was nothing further to say. Besides, he has business to attend to. Money doesn't make itself, as we know only too well. Don't make it harder for your father. If there was any other way, he would have taken it.'

'But what . .' started Anna, but she was shushed by her mother.

'I can't answer any more questions Anna. You'll just have to accept that we know what's best for you.'

'But he's so old, mother and I'm so young,' Anna wailed.

'Don't worry dear; when older men marry a young woman, they often wait until the girl is older before taking her to the marriage bed. And at least they are experienced and can guide the young girl.'

Anna gulped. The marriage bed. She had forgotten about that. She would have to sleep in the same bed as Christine's grandfather. Oh no, she couldn't think of anything worse. But then she did. The marriage bed thing, that which happened between men and women. That was worse. But her mother had said that he would wait until she was older, of that she could be thankful. She hoped that he would wait a long time for her to grow up.

'I think I'll go back and sit in my bedchamber and think,' said Anna quietly. Jane nodded and let Anna go upstairs, thinking that it would give Anna time to come to terms with her impending marriage.

Anna alternated between lying on the bed and looking out of the open window. Her thoughts went round and round; still trying to come up with a solution. After a long time of thinking she realised that she had four options. Firstly, she could run away and never come back. Yes, that was a good solution. That's what I'll do, Anna thought. But when she started planning her escape, she realised that it wasn't so easy. Perhaps she could go to York to her father's cousins, she thought in excitement, but then she knew that they would just send her back. And anyway, how would she get there? She had no money of her own; she had no one to travel with; and the roads weren't safe for women travelling around on their own. No, perhaps running away wasn't an option after all.

Her second idea was to kill herself. Anna thought about this carefully but knew that it was a sin against the Holy Church and she could never do it. Besides, she had too much living to do yet. She was too young to die. No, perhaps that wasn't an option either.

That just left either marrying the Lord of the Manor or joining the church. Marrying the Lord of the Manor, or following the rose-like Blessed Virgin. Wife or nun. Being married to the man or married to Christ.

Anna thought long and hard about joining the sisters. She tried to imagine herself in the rough grey habit, her hair shorn, her life dictated by bells and prayers, of leaving her family and friends, of losing her own will and having to submit to another's will, of never having choice again. But the alternative, she thought, marrying that man. No, I can't marry him; I'll join the sisters.

A feeling of peace descended over Anna. That was it. Perhaps the conversation with Mother Margaret Mary had been a sign that she should think about a vocation of caring with the sisters. Whether it was or not, she would become a nun. She went to look out of the open window again, strengthening her resolve to enter the cloister. She looked at the river running nearby, the lambs frolicking in the fields, the cows munching the grass. A peaceful idyll. Being in the convent would be peaceful, she convinced herself. Never again to have to make decisions, they would all be made for her. Anna nodded to herself. Yes, peace. No decisions. Making the sign of the cross, she went back and lay quietly on her bed, deciding how she would tell her mother and father.

The sounds of children running past the house trickled into her mind. They sounded happy and carefree, as she had been only yesterday. How her life had changed in one day. She went over to the window and watched the children at play. Yes, she thought, they are free and I would not be if I were in the cloister. Her new decision started to waver. I would never be free to roam round the hills or the village; never free to live my life, as I want to do; never free to have children myself, she thought. No children. That was a blow. She had always imagined in her dreams that she and her rich handsome husband would have lots of beautiful children, who would look after her in her old age. Did she want to renounce having children of her own forever? But she could always teach like Sister Bernadette, she reasoned with herself. But that wasn't the same as having her own children, she realised.

And some part of the days she would have to be silent. Could she ever achieve that? She found it so hard not to talk or make a comment about something. Could she be silent? She doubted it! Anna tossed and turned again, her former peace destroyed: becoming a sister seemed to have lost its attraction.

But that only left the other unbearable option. Marriage to Christine's grandfather. Could she do it? It seemed the only option that her father would gladly accept. Still, at least he was very old so he probably wouldn't live long. Oh God and Holy Mary forgive me, thought Anna, as she made the sign of the cross. What an awful thing to think. Wishing a man dead who hadn't done anything wrong to her. That was so evil of me, she thought. God would probably strike her down dead for thinking such a thing. She jumped off the bed and knelt down on the floor, praying out loud.

'I'm sorry God, I really am. I didn't mean that. Please forgive me. I will marry him, just to show that I'm sorry, but please don't strike me down dead. Holy Mary intercede for me,' she begged. Lifting her head, she opened her eyes and then gingerly stood up. Nothing happened. She stood staring at the bed where she had said such an evil thing, hating herself. She moved slowly, as if each step was causing her pain and walked over to the window, pressing her face against the rough opaque pane of glass.

Married. She couldn't believe it. Her life seemed to have taken a wrong turning away from the plans that she had made for herself. But those were child's plans, she reasoned with herself. She was a woman now. Deciding she must go and tell her mother, Anna slowly turned away from the window and moved towards the spiral staircase, to go downstairs. She would speak with her mother before she lost her nerve.

Chapter 5

The kitchen was quietly busy when Anna entered the room, looking round for her mother.

'Where's my mother, Peggy?' Anna asked.

'Feeding the chickens,' replied Peggy, without looking round.

'Thanks. I'll go and find her.' Anna wandered outside and looked in the fields surrounding the house.

'Oh there you are, mother. I was looking for you. I wanted to tell you that I have decided that I will marry Christine's grandfather. I know it is father's will,' said Anna listlessly.

'I'm so pleased Anna, what brought about this change of mind?'

Anna couldn't tell her the truth, but mumbled something about thinking things over and seeing what was for the best. Dear God, thought Anna, I'm now adding telling lies to my list of sins. For the best? What was she saying? But as she looked up, she saw that her mother was smiling. Jane held her arms out to Anna and hugged her close.

'You won't regret it, Anna. It will all work out. Now, we must choose your trousseau. What would you like to wear?'

'I'm not bothered. You choose for me, mother,' replied Anna and walked back into the house. Jane watched her daughter walking back with a dispirited look about her and sighed. Even though it was best for the family, it was a hard thing to expect Anna to do, giving up her dreams of the rich and handsome husband, who was also young. Jane pulled herself together and followed Anna back into the house.

Anna decided that she would go and see Christine, but didn't tell her mother. Walking to Christine's house gave her a strange feeling. Soon she would be living there. It would be nice to have Christine always around, but she hoped that Christine wouldn't find it difficult. Anna walked through the door and looked anew at the décor. It was a gloomy house compared with Anna's own home; the furnishings stark and dismal. Perhaps she could brighten it up, she thought to herself. That would give her something to do. She and

Christine could go out travelling and buy new furnishings, or even make new tapestries to hang on the walls. Brightening a little, Anna shouted for Christine, who came running down the stairs.

'Anna, thank goodness you've come. I need to talk to you. Come on outside.' Christine grabbed Anna's hand and ran out of the door and along the path away from the houses and village. When they eventually stopped they both sat down on the grass and Christine started to speak.

'I'm so unhappy, Anna, I've just heard that my grandfather is to get married again. Isn't that disgusting? Grandmother has only been dead a few months.'

'Yes, I know,' giggled Anna, relieved that Christine knew.

'What are you laughing at? I don't think it is very funny,' stormed Christine, 'and anyway, how did you know? My grandfather has only just told me.'

Anna stopped laughing and stared at Christine. 'You don't know, do you?'

'Know what?' replied Christine irritably.

'It's me he's marrying. Me. Me and your grandfather.'

'I don't think that's a funny thing to say when I'm upset, Anna. I thought you were my friend.'

'But I am marrying him, Christine. My father has fixed it up with your grandfather, that I am to marry him.' Christine stared at Anna, absolutely appalled.

'Never, he can't. That's disgusting,' she said. Anna tried to reach out to her but Christine knocked her hand away and ran off back to her home. Anna sat on the grass and contemplated what her life would be like without the love and support of Christine. She shook her head. It didn't bear thinking about.

After a while, Anna returned to her home. As soon as she walked through the door, her mother called to her.

'Anna, come and see this material. I think it will be just right for your bridal dress.'

'Oh mother, I feel awful; Christine is really upset about the marriage.'

'Did Christine know about it?' her mother asked.

'She knew that her grandfather was getting married again so I thought she knew that it was to me.'

'Oh dear. What did she say?'

'She said it was disgusting and ran away home. How will I bear it if Christine isn't my friend anymore?'

'I'm sure she'll come round again. I suppose it was a shock for her. Now, come and look at this material,' said Jane, trying to distract Anna from her mournful train of thought. 'It's a beautiful shade of dove grey. It will be very becoming and will be useful afterwards when you are entertaining.'

'Whatever you think, mother. You choose.'

'But surely you want a say in your marriage gown? You've always had very definite ideas about what your wedding day was going to be like.'

'But that was when I thought I was choosing the groom. I can't pretend to be happy at marrying Christine's grandfather.'

'Feel the material, it's the finest, softest wool imaginable,' coaxed Jane.

'Lovely, that will do,' replied Anna with hardly a look.

'You'll also need some extra dresses, befitting your new station in life as Lady of the Manor.' But Jane got no comment, which was unusual as Anna usually complained that she didn't have enough dresses.

'You've probably got enough kirtles, as you've just got all new ones before you went to your Aunty Judith's,' said Jane. 'And we'll have to get you all new underthings. We don't want Jack to think we're too poor to provide a trousseau for you.'

The name Jack penetrated Anna's brain. She would have to call him Jack, not Christine's grandfather in future. She gave a big sigh and then told her mother she was going for a walk.

'You can't go for a walk; you need to make some decisions about this marriage. We haven't got much time.' Anna stopped halfway to the door.

'What do you mean? Not much time? Usually there is a period of engagement isn't there? And anyway, they are still in mourning.'

'Jack doesn't want to wait. He wants to arrange the marriage as soon as possible.' Anna's heart sunk.

'So when is the marriage?' she asked in a tiny voice.

'Next Wednesday,' replied Jane.

'Next Wednesday?' screamed Anna, 'but that's only six days!'

'That's why I'm trying to get you organised. We haven't got long. Now come, we will take these piles of material to Sylvia in the village. She can make your new clothes.'

'You take them, mother, I'll go for a walk.'

'You'll do no such thing. What would that look like, if you didn't go to order your wedding garments? Besides, she will need to measure you and know what style you want.' Anna sighed again, and then followed her mother into the village to be measured.

They arrived at Sylvia's hut and shouted hello. Sylvia came out and invited them into her hut. It was a very superior hut and had two rooms, and a large strip of land outside. Jane did most of the talking, whilst Anna stood sullenly at the side of the room.

Sylvia was delighted to be asked to do the whole marriage trousseau and became quite chatty.

'And who are you marrying, Miss Anna? A young man you met at your Aunty Judith's?'

Anna didn't reply. Her mother nudged her.

'Anna, answer Mistress Sylvia.'

'I'm marrying Christine's grandfather,' she said sullenly, 'next week,' she added as an afterthought. Sylvia didn't hide the shock on her face quick enough for Anna not to see. And for once, Sylvia lost her chattiness, and got on with measuring Anna, and looking at the material.

Jane explained what garments they would like and what styles and asked if Sylvia could complete them before the wedding. Sylvia replied that she could, and asked them to return on Saturday for a first fitting. All the way home, Jane grumbled that Anna had been rude, but got no response. Anna was away in a trance, thinking of how different her marriage was going to be compared with her lovely dreams.

Normally she would have been ecstatic to get all these new clothes, but she just couldn't drum up any enthusiasm at all. Less than one week, she thought grimly to herself. By next Wednesday, she would be a married woman, and she hadn't even spoken to her groom, not that she wanted to particularly. Why couldn't he have waited a little longer? Anna thought. I've only just got used to the idea of marrying him at all.

Eventually, they got home and Anna went straight up to her bedchamber, as she didn't want to talk to her mother. She was summoned downstairs during the evening by Flossie.

'Miss Anna,' she said, 'your father's home and wants to talk to you. You're to come down now.'

Anna got slowly off the bed and followed Flossie downstairs, taking her time rather than dashing down, as she would normally do when her father arrived home.

'Anna, I'm so pleased about your decision, you won't regret it,' beamed her father. Anna gave him a wan smile. 'Jack is coming round tonight to speak to you,' he continued.

'No, not tonight, I don't want to see him tonight,' Anna cried.

'Why not?' asked her father. But Anna could give no reason. Too late, there was a hammering on the door and then the door was thrust open, as Jack de Ribbleside marched through the door. Anna shrank back against the fireplace and looked at this man, who was to be her husband. He was not a pretty sight, she decided. He was tall in height but too fat, his belly sticking out like a woman with child. He wore his hair long but it was greasy and uncombed, and receding at the front; his beard was straggly and streaked with grey. He had a large nose and tiny eyes that looked mean.

'Is this her, then?' he asked, pointing at Anna.

'Yes, this is my Anna, who thanks you for your generous offer of marriage. Don't you Anna?' but she was too frozen to respond and just stared at the man.

'Here's a trinket for her, as an engagement gift. I know girls like these baubles,' he sneered, throwing a ring down on to the table. 'I'll see you next Wednesday at our house, then?' he said. Anna was shocked enough to respond.

'Your house? Why not at the church?' she asked boldly.

'Don't hold with this new-fangled idea of getting wed in church. Never did it when I was a lad. It's just a ruse by those greedy priests to get more money out of us poor people. No. We'll just affirm our vows at home in the old-fashioned way. Why waste time and money?' Anna didn't reply.

'Well, I'll be off then. See you all next week,' said Jack, and then left the house, slamming the door as he went.

Anna burst into tears.

'I can't do it, I can't do it,' she cried in anguish. Her mother cuddled her and made hushing noises.

'Now Anna, it's all arranged,' said her father. 'We can't change our minds now, can we?'

Jane tried to change the subject. 'Look Anna, here is your lovely ring. Do put it on,' she said, waving the ring towards her.

Anna gasped as she looked at the heavy gold ring, with diamonds encrusted on it. It was Christine's grandmother's ring. He hadn't even bothered to buy her a new ring. She dropped the ring back on to the table.

'I can't wear that! It's Christine's grandmother's ring.'

'Anna, you must. It's your betrothal ring. He'll be very offended if you don't wear it,' said her father.

'But Christine was always promised that ring. I heard her grandmother tell her many times. What will Christine think?'

'She probably got some other new ring instead,' reassured Jane. 'Come child, it's time for bed. Leave the ring off until tomorrow. You'll soon get used to it. It will be a symbol of your married status.'

'Mother, could I take Flossie with me?' asked Anna hopefully, 'she would be such a comfort to me in my new home.'

'No, I'm sorry child, we've already suggested that to Jack, but he felt that you didn't need your own servant.' What he had actually said was that he wasn't prepared to have extra mouths to feed just to please a young chit of a girl, and she'd have to get used to it. And besides, she was only next door to her family. It wasn't as if he was taking her a long way away. But Jane wisely kept that information to herself.

Anna went to bed but sleep was a long time in coming; her heart too painful and heavy. She reflected also, on how different her father was in Jack's presence. In the past, he hadn't really cared for him, and didn't go out of his way to meet him, but now he was being almost obsequious to him. It was all very strange, she thought, as she eventually fell asleep.

The next few days went by in a blur for Anna. Normally, she felt that time dragged, but now it seemed to be hurrying in indecent haste towards the wedding day. Two days before the wedding, Anna brightened a little when visitors from Yorkshire arrived for the wedding and filled the house to overflowing. Richard's two older brothers and their wives arrived, complete with seven children between them, and also Richard's sister, husband and three children. Anna's room was more like a dormitory in the convent; there were so many straw mattresses on the floor. She also had to share her bed with three of her cousins, Helen, Doris and Alice. Mealtimes were chaotic and noisy, as the family didn't get together very often.

The very next day, even more visitors arrived. Jane's cousins came from Yorkshire and Aunty Judith arrived with Rupert. Sadly, the house was full to overflowing and as it had been on first come basis, the new visitors had to go and sleep at the convent in the hospitality rooms. They still came back to the house for meals however, so it got even noisier.

At the first opportunity, Anna slipped away for a walk with Aunty Judith.

'You don't seem to be a sparkling bride, my little Anna. What's the matter?' asked Judith.

'I'm so unhappy; I can't bear the thought of marriage to this man. What can I do?' Anna replied.

'Unhappy? Why? I thought it was a marriage you had wished for. What has happened?'

'My father arranged it. I'm marrying the grandfather of my friend Christine.'

'The one who's grandmother had died when you came to stay with me?' Anna nodded her reply.

'But do you wish this marriage?'

'No, he's an old man, and horrible also,' replied Anna, 'but I have agreed because it is what father wishes. It's necessary for the family, he says.'

'I'm so sorry that you are not happy, Anna. But just remember this, if ever I can help you in any way, you must come to me. Promise?'

'Promise, Aunty Judith, and thank you.' The two women hugged each other and walked slowly back to the house.

Chapter 6

The day of her marriage dawned far too soon for Anna's liking, but she resigned herself to the inevitability of it all and allowed her mother to dress her in the fitted new gown, made of the pale grey soft wool. It was more fitted than her kirtles, and the sleeves were longer, as befitted the latest fashion. There was a neat little hat made to match the gown. As she finished dressing her, her mother tried to reassure her, but Anna refused to be cajoled. Just before the time of the wedding ceremony, Anna was led by her father and mother, with all the family following. At the rear of the procession, Peggy and Flossie and the other servants followed, across the way to Christine's house.

They arrived in the large hall and were amazed to see that there were no special preparations for the wedding. No garlands of flowers, no special arrangement of the furniture, no musicians, no table laid with food, and no gay atmosphere.

Anna reflected dully on how she imagined her wedding to be. It would have been in the church, for all to see, with the local children and women coming to see her. Musicians would have played her to the church and then been available for dancing afterwards. There would have been a handsome young groom. It would have been the best day of her life and yet she felt that this was the worst day of her short life so far.

The young servant, Ethel, walked into the room. Anna came alive.

'Where is Miss Christine?' she asked Ethel.

Ethel looked at Anna with a blank expression, then said 'But she's gone, Miss. Didn't you know?'

'Gone?' said Anna, 'gone where?'

'Gone to her aunt's house in Ripon, Miss Anna.'

'When? When did she go?' demanded Anna.

'Why, two days ago, Miss Anna.'

'Before my wedding? She didn't stay for my wedding?' said Anna.

'No Miss, said she wanted to get away quickly like,' stammered Ethel. Anna's heart sunk. Christine's presence was the only thing about this marriage that she was looking forward to and now that was denied her. She fell on to the chair, breathing heavily, feeling even more miserable than she had been before.

Suddenly, the front door opened and in burst Jack, looking hot and dishevelled. He stopped in his tracks when he saw the hordes of people in his main hall.

'What's all this then? Who are you lot?'

'Jack,' replied Richard, 'these are Jane's family and mine. They have come to watch the wedding. Are not your family here?'

'No, didn't see the point. Not set eyes on that harebrained son of mine in years and the girls aren't much better. Besides, I'd have to put them all up and I don't want a lot of strangers in my house at present.'

'But they're your family, not strangers,' replied Richard, aghast at Jack's callousness.

'It's only a wedding. It's not such a big deal,' said Jack.

Anna had kept her head down during this altercation, but even she could sense the disgust that her family were feeling.

A voice rang out in the silence. 'It's a big deal to the bride, Sir.' said Aunty Judith in an icy voice. Jack just laughed at her.

'She'll learn,' he said, 'she's only young. Now lets get on with it and then you lot can get home.'

There were a few gasps amongst Anna's family but nothing further was said.

'Isn't the priest coming?' asked Richard.

'No, he's away on business. Wasn't waiting until he came back. We can manage without him. He'd only want a fee anyway. Another waste of money. No, we have enough witnesses here, I think,' he said sarcastically. He drew some papers out of his pocket and thrust them at Anna.

'You can read, I believe? Just read out the vows and then I'll do the same and then it'll all be over with.'

Anna mumbled her vows in a tiny scared voice, whilst he shouted them out with confidence. In a short time, the marriage was over. Anna looked down at her wedding band, but only saw it as Christine's grandmother's ring. It felt as though it was burning into her finger; as if it had no right to be there.

'Right, that's it, then,' laughed Jack. 'I'm a married man again, thank goodness. Terrible being without a wife, I can tell you,' he leered at the assembled congregation. 'Ethel?' he roared, 'bring some ale for these people.'

'But I thought you said that we were having a wedding breakfast, Jack?' said Richard. 'I offered to supply one and you said that there was no need.'

'Ethel? Bring some bread and cheese with that ale as well. A lot of it,' Jack yelled.

Ethel soon returned with platters of bread and cheese and then went back to get the ale. She returned with Martha, the cook, and together they distributed the food and drink. Anna could see that her family were unhappy, but couldn't bring herself to say anything. Jack sat on his own by the fireside, not making any attempt to converse with his guests.

Anna still stood where she had made her vows, but she could hear her father telling the family quietly that he would provide a meal for them later. Anna could tell that her father was mortified and her mother looked extremely sad. Her Aunty Judith looked livid; in fact Anna had never seen her appear so upset before, but the oldest brother was keeping her by his side and trying to calm her down. How Anna longed to go back with her parents to her own home and with her own family, but her fate was now sealed and she could no longer call next door her home, more's the pity she thought. That short miserable ceremony had tied her to this oaf of a man for life. It was an uncomfortable thought.

After half an hour, her family left, each hugging Anna tightly as they left. Nobody congratulated or spoke to Jack at all and he didn't speak to them. It was all very miserable.

Eventually, they were left alone. Anna was still standing in the middle of the room.

'Well, wife. You'd better get your things taken up to the bedchamber. Do you know which one it is? You've spent enough time in this house over the years.' Anna nodded and went to get the parcel of her belongings that Flossie had brought round earlier. Nobody had bothered to move them from the corner of the room where they'd been dumped. Jane had brought quite a few things round during the week prior to the wedding so it wasn't a large bundle.

It was the same bedchamber that her mother and father had in their house but it was a lot more sparsely furnished. She looked round to see if there was a clothes chest and found it at the bottom of the bed. Anna carefully placed her belongings in the chest.

There was an old curtain hung across the corner of the room and Anna looked inside but it was just an empty space. This would make a great place to hang some of my clothes up, she decided. It would only need a few nails on the wall to hang them on. There was also a small cupboard mounted on to the wall, with a lock on the front, framed by a curtain, which was open.

The bedchamber itself smelt fetid, and the sheets looked old, with signs of bedbugs. He hadn't even bothered to make sure that there were clean sheets on the bed, thought Anna with disgust. Christine's grandmother had always been so precise in her cleanliness. Not being sure what to do, Anna returned to the main hall to her husband. Husband, the word stuck in her throat, but husband he was.

Jack looked up as Anna entered the room.

'I've got to go out now. Got to see some lazy workman. Reckons he's too ill to work. I'll be back in an hour. Make sure there's some food ready for later.'

Anna nodded as he left without waiting for a reply. She saw him through the window; jumping on his horse and riding off at great speed. Anna went into the back kitchen to find Ethel and Martha. This house was different from her own, whereas Richard and Jane had an integral kitchen in the main hall; Jack had built an extra room, to make a separate area for the preparation of food. The servants lived and slept in this back kitchen, rather than the main hall that was traditional in most homes.

Ethel and Martha both jumped up when she entered the room.

'Er, he . .er. . Master de Ribbleside said to tell you that he wanted a meal ready for later,' said Anna nervously. Ethel nodded but Martha merely sniffed and muttered under her breath.

'Yes M'lady, is there anything you prefer?' asked Ethel.

'No, whatever you like,' suggested Anna, trying to be amenable.

'I've cooked a piece of beef,' said Martha grumpily, 'like it or lump it.'

'Oh, I'll like it, thank you,' said Anna. 'But I've just realised, it's Wednesday, it's a non-meat day. We can't have beef to today. Should we have some carp?'

'No, we'll have the beef,' said Martha. 'Master doesn't hold with non-meat days. Says the Holy Father in Rome should mind his own business and not try to tell him what to eat and when in his own house. Says it isn't in the Bible that we shouldn't eat meat, so who made it up?'

Anna gasped. Her family had always observed the non-meat days of Monday, Wednesday and Friday, dictated by the church. They were also careful to avoid meat in Lent and Advent as well. But in all truth, she had had these very same arguments with the sisters on more than one occasion. It didn't say it in the Bible, so why should they have to forego meat on so many occasions in the year? But she kept her mouth shut, as she didn't want to further antagonise Martha or her husband.

So many things were different in this house. No wonder Christine was morose at times. Anna could now empathise with her. She needed to get away from the house for a while, to chat to her mother and talk through some of the things that she had encountered already.

'I'm just going to go to my own house, I mean my mother's house,' she said.

'Wouldn't do that if I was you,' muttered Martha, 'Master won't like it. Best wait here for him.'

'Oh, I see,' said Anna, but didn't really understand why she shouldn't go next door. She would talk to him about that when he got home. She sat herself down in the main hall by the fire and reflected on how strange this wedding day had been; nothing like the one she had planned and dreamt about for so long. Why, the groom had even left her alone within an hour of her wedding. And yet she was glad, because she didn't know what to say to him or how to behave as a wife.

Anna sat in the chair, daydreaming about her life. She hoped that some day, she would still be able to train as a physician, but at this present moment, she couldn't see how that would happen. She sighed deeply and longed to talk to her mother, but didn't dare go to see her, after the warning that Martha had given her.

The hours slipped by into two hours before Jack arrived home. He was not in a good mood. Anna noticed that all the servants and workers kept silent during their meals, not like her own home, where mealtimes were a noisy affair, even when no family was visiting. Also, the candles were of a very poor quality and the rancid smell made her gag. She tried to disguise it by coughing or making noises in her throat.

'What's the matter with you woman?' Jack shouted at her. 'Coughing and spluttering, you fair put a man off his food.'

'I think it's the tallow candles, sort of catching my breath,' she explained apologetically.

'Well, they're not making anyone else cough, are they?' sneered Jack. 'I suppose you're used to better than these, aren't you? Your father's always been a wastrel. No wonder he never has any money.' Anna was shocked at this taunting of her father and the mention of money. Anna had always believed that they were comfortably off and yet Jack hinted that her father had no money. It was all very strange.

After the meal, Jack and Anna sat in silence by the fire, the servants having retired to their back kitchen. Eventually, Jack said 'Time for you to go to bed. Go on.' Anna jumped up to do as she was bid. Jack made no move and Anna was grateful for that. He was letting her sleep on her own, just as her mother had said.

Anna said goodnight but he didn't reply so she went upstairs with a tallow candle to light her to the bedchamber. Placing the candle on the floor by the bed, she got out her night undergarment that she slept in. Her mother had insisted on her having a new one made, which Anna thought was silly, as her other ones were satisfactory, but Jane insisted that all brides had new under things as well as new night things, so Anna had agreed.

Kneeling by her bed, Anna said her prayers, praying that she would be a good wife to Jack, because that was what her father wanted, and that Jack would be a good husband to her. The door flew open and Jack strode into the room.

'You can stop that mumbo jumbo right now and get into bed,' he said, 'I want no prayers said in this house.' Anna was shocked. She didn't know anyone who didn't say their prayers. Indeed, the church ruled every aspect of their whole life.

'Come on, girl, get into bed,' he barked. Anna scrambled off the floor and crawled into the other side of the bed from where he was stood. Jack proceeded to take his outer clothes off. Anna quickly averted her gaze. She had never seen a man undressed before. She would wait until he had his night under things on before she looked round, but he jumped straight into bed before getting changed.

Anna could feel his bare skin touching her arm and she tried to surreptitiously move it away, but he grabbed it and pulled her towards him. He leaned over her and pressed his sloppy lips on to hers and pressed hard. It was awful. Anna felt herself pulling away but Jack wouldn't let her. His hands started to move over her breasts and he took one of them in his hands and squeezed very hard.

'Ow,' shouted Anna, as she sat up, 'that hurt. What are you doing?' Jack pulled her back towards him again.

'What do you think I'm doing, you spoilt brat, didn't your mother tell you anything about marriage?'

'Yes she did, but she said that because I was so young that you would wait until I was older,' Anna pleaded.

'Did she indeed? Well, she was wrong. You're my wife now and a proper wife you'll be to me or else you'll be sorry. Now come here.' He dragged her nearer to him and started kneading her breasts again. The pain was excruciating and Anna started whimpering.

'Shut up, girl, you're beginning to annoy me, and get this silly garment off. My wife doesn't need night garments. They get in the way.' With that, he ripped the garment off her, leaving her frightened and vulnerable. He looked down at her body and Anna felt sickened by the look on his face.

'Can I blow the candle out?' she pleaded.

'No,' he replied, 'I want to see what I've paid for.'

Anna closed her eyes and couldn't believe what Jack was doing to her body. He was touching her everywhere and hurting her. Then he forced her legs apart and did even worse things to her. Anna started to fight but that seemed to make him more excited, and he started slavering. Eventually he got on top of her and forced something inside her and was moving up and down on top of her. The pain was excruciating, she thought she was going to be torn apart, and she could barely breathe. Anna blanked her mind out and went into her trance world. It was the only way she could bear the pain. After a lot of grunting and groaning, Jack suddenly stopped and rolled off her.

'That wasn't much fun,' he said to her. 'You've a lot to learn.' He turned over away from her and within seconds, he was sound asleep and snoring heavily.

Anna lay quietly crying by his side, her whole body aching and the area between her legs felt as if it was on fire. She lifted the blankets and saw that she was bleeding, just like her monthly curses. Climbing gingerly out of bed, so that she didn't wake Jack, Anna crept to the bottom of the bed, thankful that the candle was still burning. She got out one of her monthly rags, and after wiping her legs on some old cloth that she found in the bottom of the chest; she tied the rag between her legs and round her middle.

Getting back into bed, she blew out the candle and lay at the far side of the bed away from Jack. She couldn't believe what had happened to her. Her whole body ached. She couldn't understand why her mother said that the marriage act was enjoyable. That was awful; she could never enjoy it, ever. Eventually, with many quiet tears, Anna slipped into a fitful sleep, tortured by strange dreams of people chasing her.

71

Jack rudely woke her next morning by rolling her over to face him. 'What's this thing you've got on round your waist?' he said.

'I started my monthly curses last night,' said Anna blushing. She had never mentioned them to a man before, it was an absolute taboo.

'Don't be so naïve, girl,' he roared. 'Now get it off.' Anna numbly took off the rag and hid it under the bed, until she could remove it later. Jack pulled her to him and started the same procedure as last night.

'But you can't do that,' Anna pleaded, 'it's against the church's rules to have relations with your husband when you have your monthly curse.'

'Oh is it? Well, what the church says, doesn't apply to my house so shut up and get on with it.' He continued to maul her as he had done the night before, before getting on top of her. Although the pain wasn't as bad this time, it was still equally distasteful and uncomfortable. Anna just let her mind go in to her private place where he couldn't invade and thought pleasant thoughts of walking in the country or playing with her animals.

As soon as it was over, he got dressed quickly and went downstairs and Anna was glad to be left alone. She lay in bed wondering how she could cope with her new life. If this happened every night and morning, she could hardly bear it. But at least it didn't last all that long, even though it was too long an event for her. She turned over in bed, conscious of her aching body, and the soreness, especially between her legs.

After a while, she got dressed and went downstairs. Jack had already gone out on business. Ethel offered her some porridge and she ate it thankfully. It was a little thin and didn't have the honey that she usually had with it, but she was glad of something to eat.

Martha came in and said in a sullen voice, 'Master wants you ready by midday. You're going out riding with him.'

'Out riding? Where to?' asked Anna, amazed that he would want her to go out with him.

'Not for me to know, I'm just giving you the message,' she replied.

Anna thanked her and asked her if there was anything that she could do to help in the house.

'Do you think I'm not capable of running the house for you then?' barked Martha.

'Oh yes indeed,' replied Anna, 'I just wanted to be useful.'

'There's nothing you need to do. Just amuse yourself,' she said with a sneer, and went back into the back kitchen.

'Don't fret yourself, M'lady,' said Ethel kindly. 'She was very fond of the old mistress. Came here as a girl when the mistress did. She wasn't happy about the Master's marriage.'

'Neither was I,' blurted out Anna, and then put her hand to her mouth. 'I'm sorry Ethel, I shouldn't have said that.'

'Don't worry M'lady, can't say as I blame you,' Ethel giggled. 'Now I shouldn't have said that, either.' The bond between the two young girls developed from that moment and Anna felt that Ethel was sympathetic to her cause.

'Would it be possible to have a bath then, if I'm to go out with my husband?' she asked Ethel.

'We don't have a bath, Mistress,' replied Ethel, 'Master says it's a waste of time and water.'

'How do you get washed then?'

'Just a bowl of water from the well.'

'Cold water?'

'Usually.'

Anna's heart sunk. Loving her baths, she could think of nothing worse.

'Could you heat up a little water for me, please Ethel? I'll take it upstairs myself.'

'Well, I don't know whether I should,' Ethel dithered.

'Aren't I the Mistress of the house now? I say I want some hot water. Oh never mind, get on with your business; I'll do it myself,' said Anna crossly. She put the pan on to the fire and waited until the water was warm, and then took it upstairs to her bedchamber. Although it was only a small amount of water, she was able to wash herself adequately, but she would have loved a bath. Perhaps in future she could go to her mother's house to have a bath, but her husband seemed to be in control of her going out, so she would have to wait and see.

After the wash, she felt better, although still sore down below. As she was to go out with her husband, she put on her marriage gown from the day before and sat by the bedside waiting for him to arrive home.

By midday, she went down to the main hall to await him, hoping it would please him that she was ready and waiting, but he didn't even notice. He didn't even enter the main hall but sent the groom in to get her.

Anna walked carefully out to the stables. Jack was astride a horse, and there was no carriage or cart around. A smaller horse was ready next to Jack.

'Come on then, get on the horse, I haven't got all day,' he barked.

'You want me to ride a horse?' Anna said with horror, thinking about the soreness between her legs.

'Unless you want to walk behind the horse. Of course I want you to ride. Now get up and hurry up.'

'But husband,' Anna whispered, inclining her head towards him so that the stable hand couldn't hear, 'I'm a little sore from last night so riding would be uncomfortable. Could I be excused?'

'Sore?' Jack roared, 'don't be so soft. Get on the horse.'

Anna cringed that he had mentioned it out loud for all the staff to hear. She saw the stable hand, Jem, smirking as he walked away. Nobody helped her on to the horse, and although she was a competent horsewoman normally, she mounted with difficulty. Sitting astride the horse was agony.

As soon as she was on the horse, Jack set off, shouting over his shoulder that he was going to take her round to all his tenants, to introduce her. Anna thought that it was a daft idea as she had grown up round the village and knew most of the tenants anyway, but she kept her thoughts to herself.

'How many tenants do you have?' Anna asked to try and make conversation.

'Forty two farms, thirty five cottages in Ribbleside and twenty six cottages in other hamlets,' Jack replied.

'And how far are they spread over?'

'Up to the Forest of Bolland, over to the Yorkshire border, and past Clitheroe towards Mellor,' he replied. Anna's heart sunk. That would take at least a day or two of travelling, without having to stop and visit anyone, but she said nothing.

They started in the village. The first house they called at was the priest's house. His house was in the centre of the village, next to the church and had been built in stone, like the church. A previous ancestor of Jack had built them both, in the last century. The priest was allowed to live rent-free in the house, but was expected to give some of his tithes to Jack for the privilege. At the back of the house, there was a big tithe barn, where he kept his produce and animals.

Jack shouted to the priest as they arrived and got off his horse. 'You can stay on your horse, if you like,' he said to Anna. Anna thanked him, amazed at this rare show of consideration.

The priest came out of his house and gave a curt bow to Jack, ignoring Anna.

'I've come to introduce my wife to you, Father John.'

'Wife? You didn't wait for me to get back to conduct the marriage service then?'

'No, when did you get back?'

'Early this morning. Anything else happen whilst I was away?'

'Nothing of note. We affirmed our vows at the house as you weren't here.'

The priest scowled. 'You know the Holy Father in Rome wants marriages to be held in church now. You should be setting an example to the village, M'Lord,' said the priest.

'I'll do as I like and you'll do as I say, or get out of this house,' replied Jack.

The priest sighed. Jack was a very difficult master to obey and caused him no end of trouble, but at the end of the day, what he said was true. It was up to Jack who was priest in the village and so Father John had to toe the line.

All through this conversation, Anna had been ignored. The priest suddenly turned to Anna.

'Welcome, M'lady to our village, although you are well acquainted with it,' fawned the priest to Anna. Before she could reply, Jack butted in.

'Sorry she can't get down off the horse, but she's a little sore after last night. Fulfilling my husbandly duties in accordance with the church, you know,' Jack laughed. Anna was mortified. And in front of the priest. So this is what this trip was about. To show off to the village that he was married again and to further humiliate her in front of all his people and tenants. Despite feeling embarrassed and wanting to cry, Anna remained sitting firm on her horse, merely looking the other way and ignoring the men.

Soon, they were on their way, and moved to the next household. At each house, Anna was introduced and she could tell that people were embarrassed for her, both at the fact that she had married Jack, and for his uncouth and lewd language.

After two hours, they had passed round all the villagers. Most of them had given a small gift and Anna made a point of thanking people gratefully for their tokens. She knew that many of them could ill afford anything, but felt honour bound to give a present to their master, to keep in his good favour.

Jack never mentioned any of the presents or thanked anyone for them. He simply took them off Anna and put them in his sack on the side of the horse.

'Do they own their cottages?' asked Anna, trying to show interest as they headed back to their own house.

'No,' he said brusquely. 'I do. In return for my largesse, they have to work on my farms for two days a week, or more as I require it, during busy times like harvest.'

'And do they all have a piece of land to go with their cottage?'

'Yes, but the amount of land they have depends on their importance in the village, their trade and their status. Some day I will take you to the church where we finalise all these things and let you see how the Manor works.' Arriving at the house, Anna was left to dismount and go into the house herself.

They set off again towards Yorkshire, after having left the presents at the house and having a bite of bread and cheese and a mug of ale.

There was little talk between them this time as they rode, but Anna was thrilled to be out in the open air, despite her discomfort. She had felt hemmed in by the last week of preparation, and more especially since she had married yesterday. Dear God, was it only a day since she had got married, she thought to herself. It already felt a much longer time, and a lot of her firm beliefs, values and habits had been challenged or disallowed.

The routine of introduction remained the same as they met the tenant farmers. Jack strident; Anna embarrassed. She noticed that the tenants were respectful to Jack but none of them seemed warm towards him, as if they knew they had to be respectful to stay in their homes, but they weren't putting any extra effort into it. Many of the women present gave Anna welcoming or sympathetic looks, whilst the men were engaged in discussing seeds, hay, milking and various other farming topics.

Jack was quick to notice any farm buildings that were sub-standard and gave strict instructions that they should be repaired immediately. The tenant farmers sometimes tried to explain why something was as it was, but Jack wouldn't listen to them, merely repeating the instructions to make it better.

After they had visited six farms, Jack decided that it was time to go home. He was hungry, he said to Anna, so again there was no consideration for her needs, but only his own.

Anna was relieved to get off the horse at last; Jack left her to it, not waiting to help her. She got down and went into the main hall behind Jack. It was almost dark and the meal had been waiting for some time. Martha had allowed none of the servants to eat and she had made them wait until the Master got home. The meal was served almost immediately and as soon as the meal was over, Jack told Anna to go upstairs, and he would be up shortly. Anna's heart sunk. She was hoping for a respite from his attentions tonight. After being on the horse all day, she was even sorer and stiffer than she had been this morning.

On arrival at the bedchamber, Anna started to slowly undress, wondering what he would do to her tonight. She had taken her new marriage gown off and was standing in her under things, when Jack came into the room. He never seemed to walk quietly anywhere, but always seemed to crash into rooms, making a lot of noise.

'Stay as you are,' he ordered, as he walked towards her. 'I want to watch you undress.'

Anna gulped but did as she was told, keeping her head averted. She had barely finished undressing when he grabbed her hand and threw her on to the bed and took her harshly again. As soon as he had finished, he said that they would be going out again tomorrow, and every day afterwards, until they had finished touring all the tenant farms. Anna nodded, and then turned over in bed, away from him. Fortunately he was soon asleep, and as she was so exhausted and sore, Anna soon followed him.

Chapter 7

The next morning, Anna woke to the sounds of heavy rain. She started getting out of bed to open the window and look out, but Jack caught her arm and pulled her back.

'Where are you going to?' he asked.

'I was just going to look outside at the rain,' she replied.

'Well, get back in bed. You're going nowhere until I've had my needs met.' The ritual started again and Anna let her thoughts drift to her faraway place of dreams. It was the only way she could stand the assaults on her body. Afterwards, they got up and had breakfast, but Jack went straight out without saying where he was going. Anna took the opportunity to get some hot water and go upstairs to wash herself.

As she was finishing getting dressed, Jack came into the bedchamber.

'What are you doing?'

'Getting washed and dressed,' replied Anna.

'Is this hot water?'

'Yes,' replied Anna simply.

'And who gave you permission to have hot water?'

'Me,' said Anna.

'You! You!' shrieked Jack, 'and who are you to decide anything?'

Anna was fed up of him and decided that enough was enough.

'I'm the Lady of the Manor, as you made a great deal of telling everybody yesterday. You have given me nothing that I wanted yet, or even let me do the things I want, but this one thing I'm telling you, I will have my hot water,' replied Anna quietly, shaking all the time she was speaking. There was silence for a few seconds and then Jack walked out of the bedchamber, slamming the door behind him.

Anna didn't know what to do, so sat on the bed, still shaking with the mixed emotions of fright and elation that she had stood up to him. She was just a little worried what he may do in retaliation. She didn't have long to wait.

Ethel appeared at the door of the bedchamber and asked Anna to go downstairs. She found Jack sat by the fire.

'As we can't go out riding very far today, we will go to the one village house that we missed on our trip yesterday,' said Jack, with a steely glint in his eye. 'We'll go to your parent's house. You were pestering about going yesterday, Martha tells me. Come on, let's go.'

Anna followed after Jack but couldn't keep up with him. He walked straight in to the house without even knocking. Peggy dropped the jug that she was holding when she saw who it was.

'Sir, Miss Anna,' she mumbled.

'She's not Miss Anna anymore and the sooner you remember it, the better,' growled Jack. 'Where's de Rexar?'

'They're in the solar,' stammered Peggy. 'Shall I get them for you?'

'Yes, you stupid woman. I haven't come here to pass the time of day with you.' Peggy looked at Anna, but went upstairs to get Richard and Jane.

Jane arrived first and ran over to Anna and hugged her. 'Anna, my dear girl, how nice to see you.' Anna grabbed Jane hard and didn't let go, until her father came in.

'Father,' cried Anna and ran towards him, sheltering under his arm.

'Hello little one,' said Richard softly, 'how's married life?'

'She's loving it, 'cos she's married to a real man, aren't you?' said Jack glaring at her. Anna tried to smile to please him, but it came out more like a grimace.

'We're going to visit all our tenants this week,' Jack continued, 'but as the rain is too heavy to go to outlying farms today, we thought we'd come and visit you instead. We did all the village houses yesterday.'

'I'm not a tenant,' said Richard sharply.

'No not yet, but it could be arranged, or it might come to that one day.'

'Never,' replied Richard with force.

'That's up to you, then, isn't it,' Jack replied with some menace, but Richard didn't reply. Anna was puzzled. There was obviously something going on between her husband and her father and she hoped that one day she could get to the bottom of it. Anna looked to Jane to see if she could get any inkling from her, but Jane was just twisting her hands in her kirtle, like she did when she was nervous about anything.

'Well come on, wife, we've better things to do than stay here, especially with us being newly married,' Jack leered.

'But we've only been here a few minutes,' Anna protested.

'Long enough,' said Jack, 'you wanted to see your parents, well now you've seen them.' Jack grabbed hold of Anna's arm and pulled her towards the door. Anna cast a tearful glance back to her parents as she was pulled through the door, leaving her parents standing powerless, with their arms beside their sides, and looks of sheer anguish on their faces.

Once they were back home again, Jack had several mugs of ale with his bread and cheese at midday and then announced that they were going to bed.

'What? In the middle of the day?' asked Anna.

'Why not? I need a son, so I have to put a lot of effort in to getting one. Besides there is nothing else to do in this relentlessly bad weather.'

'But all the servants will know what we are doing,' said a shocked Anna, but Jack only laughed.

'None of their business, is it? What's the good of having a wife if I don't use her, she's there to be used,' he jeered.

Used. He'd actually said the word used. That's a good word to describe how I feel, thought Anna to herself as she went upstairs to endure another session with Jack. During the evening meal, Anna hoped that this afternoons session would have slaked his thirst, but she was wrong, as it was repeated at night and again, first thing in the morning.

On the Sunday, Jack decided to go to church, to the surprise of the entire household, but Anna knew that it was just to show her off

81

again. They walked to the front of the church as befitted the Lord of the Manor and stood for the service. They were served first for the mass, before anyone else. Jack made it very clear that he was in charge, rather than the priest. But Anna didn't let her humiliation spoil the beauty of the mass and she let her mind drift as she heard the familiar words; Christe Eleison, Kyrie Eleison.

After the mass, Anna was introduced to some people that she hadn't met before, but only those with any status. They all appeared very interested in this new bride of Jack's but muttered to themselves afterwards, when they were out of Jack's hearing. Anna would have loved to hear what they were saying. She wasn't introduced to any peasants from the outlying villages.

The days went slowly by in a round of visiting farms and being abused in bed. Anna got more and more tired as each day went on, and her natural bounce and sparkle was long gone.

One thing that Jack did allow her to do was sell some of the butter and cheese that she helped make and the eggs that were collected from the hens and weren't needed by the family. Ethel was dispatched into the village and sometimes to Clitheroe market to sell these. Anna would have dearly loved to go with her, but was never allowed. Apparently Christine's grandmother had sold butter, cheese and eggs all her life.

The good thing was that Anna was allowed to keep the money, a tradition that Christine's grandmother had started, so she decided to start building a little nest egg in her bedchamber, so that she would always have some money of her own if she ever needed to get away. That was after she had given some of the money to Ethel for her trouble. Ethel refused at first but Anna insisted that she deserved it; it was to be their secret.

Out of her first egg and butter money, she got some new blankets and sheets for the bed. Jack didn't even notice when she changed the bedding, so Anna washed the dirty bedding herself, and put sprigs of wormwood in the bed to help repel the fleas. It was one small victory that she introduced without him throwing his weight about or refusing. Anna reflected ruefully that there was only one thing on

Jack's mind when he got in to bed, so that was probably why he didn't notice the clean bedding. But it made her feel better to know that she was lying on clean bedding.

About eight weeks into the marriage, Anna asked if she could rest the next day as she was feeling particularly tired. Jack said no, but on the next morning, Anna was sickly and unable to eat her porridge. The feeling passed off during the afternoon and Anna thought that she might have eaten something that had disagreed with her. It didn't excuse her in bed though, as Jack relentlessly demanded his rights.

Next morning, she felt sickly again and Martha gave her a knowing look at the table as she served her.

'You with child, then?' she asked brusquely.

'Me,' said Anna, with a look of astonishment, 'with child? Could I be?'

'With the length of time you spend in that bed you could well be,' remarked Martha to a blushing Anna.

'How would I know?' asked Anna.

'Have you had your monthly curses lately?'

Anna thought for a moment. 'No, not since my wedding night.'

'How long did it last for?'

'Just the one night,' replied Anna.

'And what's your usual number of days?'

'Six.'

'You're probably with child, then, but you'll have to wait and see,' said Martha.

'But how do you know?' persisted Anna.

'Did your mother never tell you anything? First your curses stop, then you get sickness in the morning when you get up, then when that stops, your belly swells,' explained Martha.

'Oh,' said Anna, a little dismayed. Could she be with child? Did she want to be with child when Jack was the father? Could she ever love a child that was from him? If only she could talk to her mother, but Jack had made that patently clear that he didn't want her going visiting with her mother all the time, even though they only lived next door.

83

As another month passed and no curses came, Anna realised that she probably was with child but she didn't tell Jack. She didn't need to. When she had missed her second monthly curse, Jack asked her if she thought she was with child. Anna replied that she might be, but she wasn't sure, to which Jack said that Martha had told him she probably was. Anna couldn't believe that Martha had discussed such an intimate thing with Jack, without her being there, but the two of them seemed to have a special relationship. Or more likely, Martha was just a tell-tale.

Jack told Anna that he wanted a boy, as if she could arrange it herself. Anna dreaded to think what would happen if it was a girl; it just had to be a boy. Jack continued to demand his rights, even though Anna had tried to remind him that the church said that a woman with child should refrain from relations with her husband, but she got the usual nasty reply about the church.

Anna was sure her soul would be condemned for all eternity for the many sins that she was committing, but she didn't dare go to confession with the priest, as it would get back to Jack and there would be trouble, and she was more frightened of Jack than she was of the priest. No, she would just ask forgiveness from Jesus himself for her sins, and that would have to do. Surely he would forgive her when she was forced to do things that she didn't want to? The priest preferred them to go to confession but Anna knew that Jesus was the only one who could forgive sins, not a mere priest.

The constant sickness and weariness was getting her down and she became more and more introverted, finding it difficult to get any enthusiasm for doing anything.

One morning, Anna woke up and slowly got out of bed. Jack had already gone out. Only after she was dressed and downstairs did she realise that she hadn't felt sick. She tucked into a large bowl of porridge and felt better than she had for some time. She moved around the house gingerly at first, sure that the sickness would return. But it didn't, for which she was very grateful.

As the days and weeks passed, Anna felt much better in herself and started to gain weight. Whilst she was sitting in the solar one day, she felt something flutter in her stomach. At first she thought it was wind, or indigestion, but then she realised that it was her baby moving. Anna held her hands over her tummy and cradled it. Up to now, it had just been Jack's baby, one that she didn't want, but now that it had moved, Anna was aware of the miracle of creation that was growing in her stomach.

Whilst she could never love the father of her baby, or even like him, come to that, Anna decided that she would be a good mother and do her best to care for this baby.

As Anna's stomach began to swell, she was paraded around the villages and farms again, to show off that she was with child. But Anna was used to such humiliating behaviour by now, and it didn't affect her as much as before. In fact, many of the women talked to Anna about babies, birthing and childrearing. Anna felt accepted into this sisterhood and didn't feel as excluded or uneasy about meeting the tenants and farmers. Drinks of ale or bread and cheese were offered in many houses, which all helped Anna to feel welcome.

Christmas came and went, with virtually no difference in their routine. No presents were bought by Jack; no yule log brought in; no Mummers encouraged to come; no family visited; no carols sung; no visits to church to celebrate the birth of the Infant Jesus. Anna missed all these traditional occasions and happenings, but Martha said that they didn't celebrate Christmas. Anna was not surprised!

Anna didn't care about what Martha said. She bought presents for her parents and Peggy and Flossie, and took them round on the eve before Christmas, whilst Jack was out. For Martha, she had bought her a new mixing bowl, as the one she had was cracked, and also some comfortable slippers for her feet. For Ethel, she gave her a new fine wool gown. She was at a loss what to buy for Jack but felt that she couldn't leave him out. In the end she bought him a new blanket for on his horse. She couldn't have bought any presents at all if it hadn't been for her egg and butter money.

Anna was touched when Ethel gave her a present, very secretly. It was a bag of lavender and the bag had been hand sewn by Ethel at night. Anna told her how much she appreciated it and kept it in her clothes chest to keep her clothes smelling nice. But she was also thrilled with the present from her parents. Richard and Jane had bought her a wooden bath, like they had themselves. They brought it round the eve before Christmas, when they knew Jack was out. It was in the bedchamber behind the curtain before Jack returned. He didn't get a chance to argue.

Soon after Christmas, Jack came home in a very foul mood and started shouting as soon as he arrived in the house. It emerged that he had been ordered over to Lancaster to see Sir Henry.

'What a stupid time of year to send for me,' he raged to Anna. 'Why couldn't he wait until the Spring?'

'Couldn't you tell him that you can't go for some reason?'

'Don't be stupid, my life depends on it,' Jack replied.

'Your life?' queried Anna, not understanding.

'Well, perhaps not my life, but my livelihood,' he explained. 'Sir Henry allows me to keep this Manor, even though I inherited it. One word from him and I can lose it all, so I have to jump when he tells me to.'

'Can't you tell him that I'm with child? Wouldn't that be enough reason to let you stay?' asked Anna.

'With child? Of course not. That's no reason for non-service. I'll be away at least a week. Martha will look after you.'

Anna tried very hard not to let her face burst into an enormous grin. A whole week without him. A whole week without being abused. A whole week where she could lounge in bed on her own. A whole week when she could wallow in her new bath. A whole week where she could go and visit her parents without any objection. A whole week when she could walk about the village. She couldn't wait!

'Do I need to prepare anything for you to go?' she asked in as solicitous a manner as she could.

'No, Martha will prepare some food and Jem will prepare the horses and clothes that I will need. I'll go at first light tomorrow and then we might get there before dark fall. Don't want to have to pay for a hostelry.'

That night, with thoughts of the impending separation, Jack woke Anna several times during the night and early morning to demand his rights. Anna was exhausted by morning and was glad when he went. She tried to wave him off without an expression on her face, but as soon as he had gone, she grinned to herself, being careful that Martha did not see her. She went back upstairs and did a little dance round the room, and then went back to bed for another few hours of uninterrupted sleep. It was sheer bliss.

On waking, she asked Ethel to prepare her a bath. Martha wasn't happy about it, but she hadn't had the chance to use her new bath since Christmas, and it wouldn't be long before she was too big to get herself in and out of it. She had a luxurious soak in the bath and then dressed in clean clothes. Once dressed, she changed the bedding and made the bed. Next she went downstairs and told Martha she was going to feed the hens. Taking the seed, Anna set off to the back of the house and fed the hens as quickly as she could. Looking surreptitiously round to see if Martha was watching, she ran into her parents house and up to the solar, throwing herself at her mother when she got in.

'Mother, he's gone away for a whole week,' she cried, 'I'm so happy.' The two women hugged each other and Jane stroked her hand over Anna's stomach.

'The baby is really growing now, isn't it? Are you quite well? Have you stopped being sick?'

'I'm really well, now. The sickness and the tiredness have gone. I feel like I could do anything now,' laughed Anna.

'Do you want a boy or a girl?' asked Jane.

'For me, I'd just like a healthy baby, but Jack insists I have a boy,' Anna laughed.

'To be hoped you do have a boy, then,' replied Jane.

'Don't even think about it being a girl, although I would love one myself.'

'Well, to be sure, one of you will be pleased,' laughed Jane and Anna agreed. Oh, it was so good to be with her mother and chatting again.

'When is father home?'

'It should be tonight. Why don't you come round for the evening meal if Jack is away?'

'I'd love to, but I'd better check with Martha first.'

'Oh blow Martha, it's ridiculous that I can't have my daughter to visit when I want to, especially now that I'm going to a grandmother. Just go and tell her you are coming here.'

Emboldened by Jack's absence, Anna laughed and said 'Send Flossie round to tell Martha that I won't be requiring an evening meal, tonight.' She would deal with Martha and Jack later, she decided, if they were unhappy about this visit. But for now she didn't care. It was worth it to have some normal family life. Jane hurried away to give Flossie the message and then came back to the solar.

That evening, Anna had the best night of all with her parents and it was almost like before she was married. The conversation stayed on a light note, and much as Anna would have liked to ask questions about her marriage, she didn't want to upset the tenor of the evening.

Anna had a whole new routine whilst Jack was away and did what she wanted to do. Martha's face was growing more dissatisfied daily, but Anna didn't care what repercussions there would be, she was enjoying herself far too much. Besides, Jack wouldn't dare harm her; not when she was carrying his precious child.

On the fourth day he was away, the sky became heavy and wooden looking. Martha prophesied that it would snow before morning and she was not wrong. By morning, when Anna looked through the opened bedchamber window, there had been a heavy fall of snow. The whole village looked beautiful. Pendle Hill looked like a white mountain. She decided that she would go for a walk in the village, after her breakfast. But she had reckoned without Martha. There was no chance of Anna going out in the snow, Martha said, because she may miscarry if she slipped in the snow, and she would be in trouble with the Master when he came home for allowing it. Anna suggested that it would be her fault if she slipped in the snow, not Martha's, but Martha was having none of it, so Anna had to admire the snow encrusted trees from the house.

All through the day, the snow continued to fall and over the next night too. Martha said that it was the worst snowfall that she ever remembered and Anna had to agree. Martha shook her head sadly, and said that the Master wouldn't be able to get home in this weather, and Anna had to really concentrate not to give a whoop of joy. Long may the snow remain, she prayed.

Her prayers were answered. The snow stayed for three weeks and it was another week after that before Jack returned home, very disgruntled.

'What a waste of a month. Stuck in Lancaster in Sir Henry's household. A very poor table he keeps as well. I tried telling him I was to be a father and needed to get home, but it didn't work. I set off once to get home and got stuck in a snowdrift over the Trough of Bolland. Stuck there in a hostelry for a week. Mind you,' he grinned, 'the landlady's wife was very obliging. Much more idea than you, girl. She could have given you some lessons.' Jack laughed raucously, whilst Anna sat in horror, realising what he meant about the landlady's wife. Here he was freely admitting that he had committed adultery and enjoying telling her. She looked at him with disgust, and didn't realise he was speaking to her, and had to ask him to repeat himself.

'Are you deaf?' he roared. 'I said, let's see if you can be so obliging as the landlady's wife. I bet you've missed me in our bed, haven't you?' Jack leered.

Not one second have I missed you, thought Anna, but made a small grimace as if she had. But then Jack caught hold of her hand and dragged her up to standing. He looked down at her stomach.

'Well, it's good to see the brat's growing. I'll be having difficulty taking you in a bit, if you get any bigger.' He roared at his own joke and pulled Anna towards the bedchamber, even though it was just after midday. He took her savagely and then got up and went downstairs, demanding food. Anna lay on the bed and sighed. It had been a wonderful holiday without Jack, but now it looked like it was back to the normal routine.

Strangely, Jack didn't mention about her having been to her parent's house, even though Anna knew that Martha would have reported all her misdemeanours to him. Even stranger, he seemed glad to be home. It's a shame it's not reciprocated, thought Anna. And the next morning, he didn't even complain when she had a bath after she got up. Anna was worried. Was this the calm before the storm?

Once the snow was clear, Jack decided that he should go and visit all his outlying farms again. He said he was sorry that he couldn't take Anna, but due to her condition, it wasn't safe. He didn't want his unborn son to be put at risk, he said. Anna was glad not to have to go. She knew that he would be crowing to all his tenants about the forthcoming child, and would probably have embarrassed her again if she had gone. Hopefully, it would snow again and Jack would have to stay away for longer.

As her baby grew bigger, she started to prepare small garments for the baby. She prepared the swaddling bands that it would require in the first few months and made some linen squares to use as napkins. Whilst Jack was away, Jane had brought Anna a chest to put the baby's clothes in. It was a beautifully crafted piece of furniture, and Jane showed her a small drawer hidden at the bottom of the chest. It was intended to put the baby's keepsakes in or christening presents but Anna decided it was a perfect place to keep her egg and cheese money, too.

Chapter 8

Easter came and went without any special events at the house. Anna did, however, manage to persuade Jack to visit church on Easter Sunday. But she knew in her heart that it wasn't because he wanted to worship God, or confess his sins, or partake in the mass, but to flaunt his wife whilst heavy with his child.

As she got nearer her time, women from the village brought little gifts of mittens or bonnets for the baby to wear. Anna carefully laid them in her chest to await the baby. She was getting very big now and finding it difficult to walk very far. Not that it stopped Jack's activities with her, nothing would stop that, Anna thought ruefully.

On May Day, Anna decided that she would go down to the village to watch the maypole dancers on the village green, as Jack had gone to visit a tenant. As she came out of the house, she slipped on a piece of rotting vegetable outside the house and fell on the floor. Ethel had been right behind her, but didn't manage to catch her before she went down.

'Are you all right?' Ethel cried.

'I'm fine,' Anna reassured her, but in truth, she was quite shaken. As they got to the village, Ethel asked one of the villagers if she could have a chair for Anna to sit on. A chair was quickly brought out and Anna was glad to sit down. Although she'd told Ethel she was all right, her back was aching. She sat and watched the dancers, dancing round the maypole but after a few minutes, she started hitching around in her chair.

It was Matthew Fox's mum who asked her if she was all right this time. 'Begging your pardon, but are you at your time, M'lady?' she asked.

'More or less, Mistress Fox, why do you ask?'

'Well, you are fidgeting on your chair and your stomach's tightening.'

'I suppose I do feel a little uncomfortable, but I fell earlier and thought I was just sore from that. Do you think I could be starting with the baby? I don't know anything about it at all really.'

'I'll get Mistress Cobb to help, but I suggest you go home, just in case,' replied Mistress Fox. Anna looked longingly at the young maypole dancers, but knew that it was more sensible to go home. As she stood up, water gushed out from her and flooded the ground.

'Oh, how embarrassing, what's happened,' said Anna, in obvious distress.

'It's your waters, M'lady,' said Mistress Cobb who had just arrived, 'sure sign that you are in labour. I'd get home now if I were you,' and took hold of Anna's arm to guide her homewards.

'Shall I get your mother?' Mistress Fox asked.

'Yes please,' asked Anna as she was led home.

By the time they got home, Jane had arrived and Martha had got the pan on to boil over the fire. Martha had got some old blankets to spread on the bed and moved Anna's new ones. Ethel brought in the crib that had serviced generations of de Ribbleside babies. Physicians now recommended that newborn babies were put in a separate crib, rather than lie in with the mother, as some parents had accidentally smothered their babies. Martha had also got some pieces of twine ready to tie off the cord when the baby was born, and a sharp knife to sever the cord.

As Jem had gone out with Jack, one of the younger stable boys was sent out to Clitheroe to get the physician to come. Mistress Cobb looked round the bedchamber and was satisfied with the preparations.

'Do you have a birthing stool?' she asked Martha.

'No, we don't,' Martha replied.

'Can we send someone to my hut to get mine?' said Mistress Cobb. Ethel volunteered to go and soon returned with the vital piece of furniture. 'Where's the father of the baby?' asked Mistress Cobb.

'Away on outlying farms,' replied Jane.

'Is he expected back today?' she asked but Anna replied.

'No, he'll be away at least tonight, possibly two.'

'Good,' said Mistress Cobb, 'we're better off without the men; they only get in the way. Now then, let's have a look at you. Just lie on the bed, please. Are you having any pains yet, M'lady?'

'Just a few, and they aren't too painful yet.'

'They will be, don't you worry. As sure as eggs is eggs, they will be painful very soon,' Mistress Cobb laughed, nodding at Jane and Martha.

Mistress Cobb's manner was a little brusque, but Anna had every confidence in her. She had been delivering babies in the village for as long as Anna could remember and was generally thought to be very good at her job. Anna lay down on the bed, whilst Mistress Cobb carefully palpated her stomach, then put her ear down on to Anna's stomach.

Mistress Cobb moved away and spoke quietly to Jane and Martha.

'Sometimes I can hear the baby's heartbeat but sometimes I cannot. Today I cannot, but that is no matter as the baby is still stirring at my touch. The baby's head seems to be well down in the birth canal, which is a relief, with her being so young. At thirteen, their hips aren't always fully formed, but this girl's hips seem to be wide enough, thank God.'

Anna let out a cry. 'Oh that was quite painful,' she gasped when it was over.

'Let's get you off the bed then, and keep walking around. It helps the baby to go further down the birth canal,' instructed Mistress Cobb. 'Keep walking round for as long as you can.'

Anna nodded and started to get off the bed. She had just managed to sit upright when another pain came along, longer than the last one.

'Oh, that's quite close together, your labour is moving on, young lady. Perhaps you are going to be quick in labour.' Anna fervently hoped so. The pains were getting strong now, and she felt like screaming, but was aware that there were other people in the room. In between pains, she looked at the bed where she would lie in after the birth. It suddenly dawned on her that it was the same bed where Christine's grandmother had lain. In all these months of her marriage that fact had never struck her. But now it did, as she realised that it was the same bed where Christine's grandmother had died. In childbirth.

With the next pain, Anna began to panic.

'I don't want to die, I don't want to die,' she wailed. The other women in the room all rallied round and chivvied her, saying that she was young and healthy and there was no reason why she should die. Anna was not so sure, but the pains were so relentless, that her mind was diverted.

'Have some feverfew tisane to drink,' pressed Mistress Cobb. 'That's always helpful in labour.' Anna thanked her gratefully; glad of anything that would help her through this trial. Sipping it gently, Anna hoped it would work quickly.

The pains seemed to be coming one on top of the other now, and Anna felt as if she had been in labour for days, she was so weary and yet it was only just going dark, so it hadn't been very long. The hours dragged on.

Suddenly, Anna realised that the pains had changed in nature. Although still excruciatingly painful, they felt to be dragging down, making her want to bear down, as if she was going on the chamber pot. She said as much to her attendants.

'Time to get you on the birthing stool,' said Mistress Cobb, and eased Anna into a squatting position on the stool. The stool was placed at the bottom of the bed, where the clothes chest usually was, so that Anna could rest back against the bed when she needed support. 'Now push down into your bottom with each pain,' said Mistress Cobb. 'You'll need to push harder, but stop now, if your pain has gone. Just rest between pains, then push with all your might. Is the pain coming back again? Well then, push, harder, harder, that's the way, keep going. Good, keep going and rest, if your pain has gone.'

Anna felt as if she was pushing a cow out, not a little baby, so vast was the pressure inside her. She was sure she was going to split in two. The pushing went on for nearly two hours. Anna was exhausted, and felt as though she just couldn't go on with it anymore. Death would be welcome, she thought to herself. Then Mistress Cobb shouted 'Stop pushing, don't push, the baby's head is coming.'

'I can't help pushing, my body wants to push,' Anna gasped, but managed to stop herself pushing. The baby's head slowly appeared between her legs. Ethel gasped in surprise, as this was the first birth that she had seen. She was even more astonished when the baby's head started to turn part way round on its own.

Mistress Cobb explained to an amazed Ethel that that was because the baby was turning itself round in the birth canal, to let the shoulders be born easily.

Anna cried out with another pain. 'Now start pushing,' instructed Mistress Cobb. Anna pushed with all her might and felt the immediate release as the baby was born. Gasping for breath, after this final push, Anna lay back against the end of the bed, exhausted.

Nobody spoke whilst Mistress Cobb wiped the baby over and tipped it upside down. The baby cried out; a sharp vigorous cry that brought smiles to all the women in the room. Anna opened her eyes at that point, trying to focus on her baby.

'It's a girl,' exclaimed Mistress Cobb, 'and she looks very healthy. She's a lovely colour and has everything she should have. Now we'll just have to wait for the afterbirth.'

'A girl,' said Anna weakly, 'let me see,' as she reached her hands out.

'Not until you are back on the bed,' said Mistress Cobb. The women all helped Anna back on to the bed and then propped her up with the pillows. Mistress Cobb had wrapped the baby girl in a soft linen cloth and wiped her eyes before giving her to Anna.

Anna looked down at the baby and felt a surge of protective love overwhelm her. Her baby. Jack was forgotten for the present. This was her baby and she would look after it for the rest of her life. She would never love anyone else again. Her eyes filled with tears as she looked at the tiny fingers peeping out of the cloth. The baby's hair was dark brown, like Anna's and she looked just like Anna. Anna was relieved. She didn't want the poor baby to look like Jack, she thought to herself with a smile. Her pain was forgotten; it had all been worthwhile.

But her pain soon returned. A niggly pain started in her stomach.

'I've got another pain,' remarked Anna. 'You don't think there is another baby in there? Why am I still having pains?'

Mistress Cobb laughed. 'I don't think there's another one, M'lady. It'll be the afterbirth. You have to push it out like you did the baby. Here, Ethel, take the baby, whilst we sort the afterbirth out.'

Ethel came and gingerly held the baby and put her in to the crib, whilst the other women sorted out the afterbirth.

'What was that?' exclaimed Anna, as she got a glimpse of the afterbirth, 'was that inside me?'

They all laughed.

'Yes, that's what's been feeding your baby inside you. So you have to get rid of that as well,' replied Jane. It reminded her how young Anna was, that she didn't know about afterbirths. Mind you, she had still been at the sisters a year ago, so it was hardly surprising that she didn't know about childbirth.

'What are you going to call the baby?' asked Ethel, still looking down at the baby in the crib.

'I think I'll call her Jane, after my mother,' replied Anna.

'Oh thank you, Anna,' said Jane. 'That's really kind of you. But don't you think Jack might want to decide on a name?'

Anna suddenly remembered Jack telling her he wanted a boy. Oh dear, he wouldn't be too happy that she had had a girl.

'He might want to name her, but he'll be sorry it's a girl,' said Anna bitterly.

'Oh Anna, don't be so sure. He'll be so pleased that you have delivered safely,' replied Jane. 'Your father was delighted that you were a girl.'

'Yes, but you'd lost so many babies that he was just glad to get a live healthy one,' replied Anna. 'It was really important to Jack that he got a boy.' This conversation had put a small dampener on the previous gaiety so Mistress Cobb started rallying everyone round.

'Right, Martha, we all need food and drink,' said Mistress Cobb. 'Ethel, Your mistress wants a good wash down. New grandmother, you can start getting the swaddling bands ready, and new mother, you can just lie there and watch me, whilst Ethel washes you.'

96

'What are you going to do,' asked Anna.

'I'm going to wash the baby with medicated ointments and put salve in her eyes, as all good birth attendants should to ensure a healthy baby,'

'Where did you learn your trade, Mistress Cobb?' asked Anna.

'From following my mother round, learning from her. She was the birth attendant in our village, where I lived as a girl.'

'I want to be a physician when I'm older,' said Anna, 'and I'd like to learn about helping mothers in childbirth.'

'That is good, but for now, your first priority is to get some rest, so that you can feed your baby, or should I arrange a wet nurse? Some of the gentry ladies seem to be having them now, mind you, I don't really hold with it myself.'

'No, no wet nurse. I want to feed my baby myself,' replied Anna.

'Would you like a try now? Little Jane seems to be stirring.'

Anna smiled. Little Jane; that sounded lovely. Mistress Cobb brought the baby over to Anna and positioned her in the bed so that she could put the baby to the breast. Anna wasn't sure what to do, but with Mistress Cobb's advice, Little Jane was soon sucking merrily at the breast.

'Well, that one knows what to do,' laughed Mistress Cobb. Anna was overwhelmed at the feeling of closeness that she felt as the baby suckled at her breast. She gently stroked Jane's head and spoke soothingly to her. Little Jane ignored her mother's voice and didn't stop feeding until she was full, then after a large burp, she promptly fell asleep at the breast. Mistress Cobb and Anna were laughing so much at the sound of the burp that they didn't notice the door opening and a man coming in.

'Well I see I'm too late,' said the elderly gentleman. 'Mistress Cobb, I hand it to you. No woman needs a physician when you are around. I take it all went well?'

'Yes, all went well. She's a strong girl, is M'lady.'

'And you Mistress de Ribbleside?' said the physician turning to Anna. 'You are feeling well? Already feeding the baby yourself I see? Good. I'm sorry to be late for your great event, but it is quite a distance from

Clitheroe, and although I hurried, I was informed that Mistress Cobb was here, so I knew that my patient would not be in danger. May I look at the baby and then I'll look at you?' Mistress Cobb took Jane away from Anna and put her in the crib. The physician examined the baby, and then Anna, and pronounced them both to be fit and well.

'I will visit again in a few days time, or sooner if you should require it. Now where is the happy father?' asked the physician.

'Gone to visit remote farms. He should be back soon,' replied Anna.

'Do give him my regards and congratulations, when he returns. I will leave you in the capable hands of Mistress Cobb. Good bye.' He bowed to Anna and Mistress Cobb, and then took his leave. Anna was suddenly very tired and started yawning.

'I'm really tired now. Can I go to sleep?' asked Anna.

'Of course, you've worked hard for it. I'll take baby Jane downstairs and I'll get grandmother Jane to help me with the swaddling bands. Sleep well.'

'Thanks. And Mistress Cobb? Thank you for all you have done for me. I was very frightened, being so young, but you made me feel really safe.'

'I'm glad you felt like that. But you were a good patient as well. You did just what I said and you didn't make a song and dance about it, not like some I have to deal with,' Mistress Cobb laughed.

But Anna's eyes were nearly closing, so Mistress Cobb slipped from the room, and left her in peace.

The next two days were a comfortable female existence, where baby Jane's needs were paramount. On the third day, Jack returned and made his presence felt immediately.

He dashed up to the bedchamber, where Anna was still lying in.

'I see you've had the brat?' he demanded. 'Where's my boy then?'

'It's a girl,' replied Anna quietly.

'A girl? What good is that to me? I wanted a boy,' Jack fumed.

'At least it's a healthy girl,' said Anna, 'we should be thankful to God for that.'

'God? If God had been listening to me, he'd have sent a boy. I need a boy. Never mind, the next one had better be a boy.'

Anna gasped. She could no more think of another child than she could of killing herself. She decided not to answer. Oh how pleasant it had been without him, and now her peace was shattered. Back to the old routine, she thought to herself. Little did she know how soon her predictions would come true. That night Jack joined her in the bed and immediately started groping her.

'You can't, I've just had a baby!' said Anna disbelievingly.

'I can and I will,' he said, 'besides, that was three days ago now.' and continued with his activity, not caring that Anna was crying out in pain, because of her sore body.

After he had finished, he fortunately fell asleep. Anna crept out of bed and washed herself. On return to bed, she sobbed her heart out, but Jack didn't even stir. Eventually she cried herself to sleep.

The baby's cries woke her in the middle of the night and she got out to feed her. As she put her to the breast, Jack shouted out for her to be quick and shut the brat up, some folk were trying to sleep. Why she couldn't have a wet nurse, he didn't know. Then he could have peace at night.

'Hush Jane, hush,' Anna crooned to her baby. Jack was awake instantly.

'Jane? What sort of name is that? We haven't discussed a name yet.'

'It's my mother's name,' replied Anna meekly.

'Well it's not my mother's name so why should I have it? It's not my baby's name.'

'I like the name Jane,' replied Anna defiantly.

'I don't. So it is not Jane. Edwina, we'll call it Edwina. That's a good name.'

Anna was horrified. 'But that's your late wife's name,' she said.

'Nothing wrong with that. Good wife she was. Far better than you. Knew what to do in bed. No Edwina, that's what I'll call her.'

'What about Edwina Jane, then?' braved Anna.

'If you must, but she'll be known as Edwina, and that's the final word on it.'

Anna was pleased that she had won her little victory about Jane as a second name, but still deeply unhappy that she had to call the baby Edwina. But it didn't matter what she was called, she still loved her with all her heart.

After attending church for her purification ceremony, Anna started to go out and about a little. As long as she took little Edwina with her, Jack seemed to be more lenient about her visiting people, even her mother, for which Anna and Jane were truly grateful.

Caring for the baby was the only thing that kept Anna sane during the next few months. It was a delight to watch her growing and developing new skills. By six months old, she was gurgling and laughing and sitting up without having to be supported. Anna thought there was never a cleverer baby in the whole world, like all new mothers do. However, her gurgling was getting on Jack's nerves, so Edwina had been relegated to sleeping in the bedchamber next door, which had been Christine's previously.

Anna didn't mind. Sometimes, if Edwina woke her in the night, she would put the crib next to the bed in the child's bedchamber and lie on the bed watching her sleeping. And quite often she fell asleep on the spare bed, much to Jack's disgust, who wanted her always in his bed, to be eternally available.

When Edwina was about nine months old, Anna realised that she might be with child again. It was not surprising, but she was horrified to realise that she would have two small babies. Edwina wasn't walking yet and the new baby would be born in about five months, according to Mistress Cobb.

Also, at the back of her mind, was the worry that she couldn't love another baby as much as she loved Edwina. Would she have enough love for both of them? Would she prefer Edwina to the new one that was coming? She knew that Jack took hardly any notice of Edwina, so she knew that this thought wouldn't have entered his head. Only if she had a boy would he show any interest.

Anna went regularly to church and prayed to the Holy Mother

fervently that this one would be a boy. Perhaps then Jack would leave her alone. This time, carrying the baby was not as easy as the first one had been, as she was tired coping with the excessive demands of a husband and a small baby.

Her body looked larger than the first time, too. Jack made caustic comments about her shape, but it didn't stop him taking advantage of her at night and morning, right up to the end of the nine months. But he did seem to be going out more, and staying overnight, for which Anna was grateful. She didn't ask him where he was going. She just enjoyed the occasional reprieve from her wifely duties, and the freedom of having the bed to herself.

This time her labour was shorter, albeit just as painful. But she had chosen a time when Jack was at home. His shouting and creating trouble, made all the staff and Mistress Cobb uneasy and Jane, of course, was barred from being in attendance this time.

Anna eventually pushed her second baby out and demanded to know what it was.

'It's a boy,' said Mistress Cobb.' Anna almost swooned with relief, but not before thanking the Holy Mother for giving her a boy. As the baby cried, Jack came into the bedchamber.

'Well, what is it?' he demanded.

'A boy, Sir,' replied Mistress Cobb.

'About time, too,' Jack replied. 'We'll call him Jack,' and walked out of the room, without even speaking to Anna. Anna didn't care. She was too exhausted and relieved. But when Mistress Cobb placed little Jack into her arms, her heart contracted with love for this little boy. She realised that her worries had been unfounded. She had enough love in her heart for both her children, and knew that she would love all her children, however many she had in the future. As Anna fell asleep, she thought that perhaps Jack might leave her alone, now that he had got his boy. But she was wrong. Within days of the birth, he was abusing her again.

Chapter 9

The next three years passed quickly for Anna. Fortunately she hadn't conceived again since Little Jack's birth. Her time was too taken up with the two toddlers to think about having any more children anyway. Not for want of her husband's trying though. Her days passed pleasantly, caring for her two babies and taking them out to show them the world around their house. She also loved taking them to see their grandparents next door, although Jack still remained unhappy if the visits got too frequent.

Making her cheese and looking after her hens also took up time, and the children liked to come and feed the hens with her, in fact, Little Jack's first word was 'egg'. Little Jack was a softer version of his father, but looked very much like him, with the large face, but not as large nose, fortunately.

Ethel and Anna were making quite a profit from the sales of eggs and cheese. Anna never asked what Ethel did with her small share of the profit, but Anna suspected that it went to help her mother and father who only had a small piece of land in a nearby village, and several children to feed. Anna's pile of money was steadily growing, as she had little to spend her money on. She never got chance to go to Clitheroe. The only time she spent money was when Tom the pedlar called in, or at Christmas time.

One day, when Jack was away with Jem, Ethel was unwell and was unable to go to Clitheroe market to sell the eggs and cheese. Anna decided that she would go to market herself. Asking her mother to care for the children, she then asked young Arthur from the stable yard to help. Also, Matthew Fox had left the sisters and was learning to be a stable hand at the Manor. Even though he was older than Arthur, he was far less experienced. Martha tutted about the expedition, but Anna was adamant.

The three of them set off in the older cart as Jack had the best one. The children looked on disconcertedly as she left them, but grandmother Jane soon diverted them. Anna was in her element, driving the cart and looking around her with interest. She had never been so far on her own before in this direction, and she loved the rolling countryside and deep valleys and steep hills. Within an hour, they were approaching Clitheroe; the castle keep of the de Lacy family and the church that they had built, dominating the landscape; and Pendle Hill to the left dominating them all. They made their way to the market.

Arthur went off to the animal feed store, whilst Matthew stayed close by Anna; seemingly aware of the importance of his duty in caring for the Mistress. It was strange to reflect that they had played and been taught together at the sisters, only a few short years ago, but now she was in a position of authority over Matthew. Not that she lorded it over him when they were together, rather they chatted about everything under the sun. It felt good for Anna to chat with someone nearer her own age, as apart from Ethel, she had no one to talk to. Not that she would have let her husband catch her talking to Matthew. It was more than his job was worth.

Clitheroe market was grand, Anna reflected. Not as grand as Brun Lea, but good nevertheless. She sold all her eggs, butter and cheese to a hostelry that Ethel regularly visited, so didn't need to stand by a stall. The three of them met up together, once Arthur had completed his purchases. Anna decided to treat them all to a meal in the hostelry where she had sold her produce. Realising whom Anna was, the owner treated her like Royalty and provided the choicest cuts of meat and vegetables. After a splendid meal, the three of them set off back to Ribbleside, in great spirits, keeping Pendle Hill always at their side.

As they got nearer home, Anna wondered if Jack would be home tonight and dearly hoped that he wasn't. She was disappointed. He was already home when she arrived, and not best pleased.

'Where do you think you have been? Swanning off to Clitheroe, just because Ethel can't be bothered to go; dumping your children on your mother; going with two men; and coming back here laughing like a kept woman. I've a good mind to whip you,' he said as he prodded her in the chest as he made each point. 'Now get upstairs and do your wifely duty.'

Anna's heart sunk. It was the middle of the afternoon. All the servants would have heard what Jack had said. It was too embarrassing.

'Hadn't I better go and get your children,' she asked Jack, slightly emphasising the 'your'. It was too much for Jack. He slapped her across the face, dragged her upstairs in to the bedchamber and took her savagely. Anna blanked her mind off as usual, thinking about what a lovely day she had had in Clitheroe. It was worth having to put up with this, just to have had some time away from him, and all her heavy responsibilities for one so young.

It was not long after this, that she suspected she was with child again. The sickness was very severe this time and so Jack noticed it quite early.

'Are you with child again?' he demanded.

'I think so. The signs are there,' she replied.

'Whose is it, then?' he said.

Anna was dumbfounded. 'What do you mean? It's yours of course.'

'Are you sure? What about when you went gadding about into Clitheroe with two men. You could have easily slipped behind a hedge with one of them, or with both of them for that matter. We'll know if it has red hair, won't we? Or was it the landlord in the Swan? I heard that he was very pleased to see you.'

'How dare you,' rasped Anna, 'I've not been near another man like that. I wouldn't dream of doing. Which is more than I can say for you.'

'What I do is my business. Besides, it's different for men. They have their needs. Especially when they don't get it at home.' Anna thought of all the times she'd had to endure his body on top of her, hating every minute of it. She exploded.

'You do get your needs fulfilled at home,' she shouted, 'morning, noon and night. I never get a moments peace.'

'That's it; tell the entire household our affairs,' he snarled. 'Well, one thing's for sure, you won't be going out again without me. You can stay at home and be available for me at any time of morning, noon and night, as you so rightly said. In fact, you can get up there now.' Anna's heart sunk. Why had she said that last retort? Now she would pay for it, she thought as she slowly climbed upstairs.

The following months seemed to bear heavy on Anna. She was constantly tired with looking after the children and being with child, and Jack's demands seem to have increased even further, if that were possible. He was also drinking much more heavily than he had done before and often stayed out at the hostelry in the next village until the early hours.

Eventually the baby was born. The labour was even quicker this time. Jack didn't let her have the physician for her second and third children, as he said it was a waste of money. Fortunately, Mistress Cobb managed fine without him. It was another little girl. Anna gazed at her and fell immediately in love; her capacious heart easily expanding to accommodate another child. She was absolutely beautiful and was the image of Christine, Jack's granddaughter. The same fair hair that swirled into a widow's peak at the front and the same round face and features.

Jack was disappointed that it was another girl.

'Look Jack,' Anna said animatedly, 'she looks just like Christine. Shall we call her Christine?'

'No, not Christine. She's never been near here since she left. Why would we want to use her name? Call her what you will. I've no interest in another girl. Now if the next one is a boy, then I'll think of a name.'

Anna despaired. She had three children and yet was only eighteen years old. How many more years of child bearing would she have to endure? How many more years of abuse? Why, she could bear children for another twenty or even thirty years yet. Hopefully Jack wouldn't be able to perform for so long, she giggled to herself, but knowing her luck, he would carry on for years. And where will that leave me? she thought sadly. Worn out or dead with too much child bearing, like Christine's grandmother.

But the joy of having the little girl's name to choose overcame her maudlin thoughts. She decided on Isobelle. And Isobelle was a delight; an extremely good baby, except when she was teething. Anna kept saying that she was the easiest, but her mother said that it probably got easier with each child, as you had more idea what you were doing. Anna was also glad that Isobelle didn't have red hair, or Jack would probably have murdered her. Perhaps it was as well that she looked so much like Christine, as Jack couldn't throw any aspersions round.

Soon after the birth, Jack was notified that he had to travel to the courts of Sir Henry of Lancaster again. All Lords of the Manors had to visit on a regular basis and assist at the court cases in Lancaster or Preston. This time, he decided to take Anna with him. Whether that was because he had been told to bring his family, or because he didn't trust her left behind in Ribbleside, after the escapade at the market, Anna didn't know. But she felt sure that it wasn't to give her an exciting experience. If Jack had known how excited she was, he would have probably stopped her going, just to spite her.

Just in case, Anna pretended to be lukewarm about the visit. She argued that she couldn't go without Isobelle as she was still feeding her. Jack was more interested in taking Little Jack, so Anna suggested that they take them all.

'Three brats? You must be joking,' he said, 'I like to go there for some fun. What fun can I have with three brats round my ankles? It's bad enough having to take your wife.' Anna realised then that he must have been told to take his family.

'We'll leave Edwina at home then. Just take the younger two,' he said.

'That's not fair,' argued Anna.

'It's not fair that I have to take any of you. That's my final word on it. We go on Friday.'

Anna reeled at the cruelty of her husband. To leave one child at home and take the other two was so nasty. Anna didn't know how she could tell Edwina that she was to be left behind, but in the end, her mother invited Edwina to stay at her house, because she was now a big girl. Edwina was ecstatic and preferred to stay with grandmother Jane and grandfather Richard any time. Anna was relieved and knew that Edwina would be happy with them.

On the Wednesday, Donald came to the house from the forge. As Jack was out, Jem brought him into the house to speak to Anna. They were both glad to see each other and had a good chat, which they couldn't have done if Jack had been there. Eventually, he told her the purpose of the visit. Jack had ordered a new carriage to be made.

It was a lightweight frame that Donald and his father had made, and then they had taken it down to the carpenters in the village. Roland the carpenter had put strips of wood over the frame, so that it looked like a box on wheels. At the front of the box, there was a seat big enough for three people. There was also a special harness to fix on to the horse's collar to pull the carriage.

Anna's eyes glowed when she saw it. It would mean that she and the children would be safe and warm whilst they were travelling, and wouldn't have to ride. How thoughtful of Jack to ask for this to be built, thought Anna with surprise.

'Why, that's marvellous, Donald. That will be wonderful for our journey to Lancaster. Just perfect, thank you.'

'Well, best be getting back to work, M'lady. Glad you're pleased.'

'Oh Donald, fancy calling me M'lady. Aren't I Anna any more?' she teased.

'No M'lady. Was told not to call you by your first name anymore, begging your pardon.' Donald bowed to her and left the house. This saddened Anna. She could guess who'd told him to stop using her first name. It was ridiculous. They were childhood friends. What harm would it do? But she knew that Donald and his father depended on Jack's good favour to keep the forge. However her sad thoughts didn't stop her delight in the new carriage.

When Jack come home, Anna ran to tell him that the carriage had arrived and been put in the stable.'

'Goodness, wife. I thought you were glad to see me for one minute. Should have known it was only the carriage. All the other Lord of the Manors travel in carriages and besides, I was freezing cold last time I went on the horse, especially when I got snowed in.'

Typical, thought Anna. Selfish to the last, but never mind; I get the benefit of the carriage for the long journey. On the Thursday, Anna packed the bottom of the carriage with straw palliasses and lay blankets over them. She packed all the things that she thought she might need for the journey and explained to little Jack that they were going on a journey.

Friday dawned fair for once and after a hearty breakfast, the family and stable servants set off early; the servants following on horseback. Edwina proudly waved them off, whilst clinging tightly to her grandmother Jane's hand. Isobelle slept throughout the journey but little Jack needed more entertaining. However, all the people and villages they saw on the way delighted both him and Anna.

Once they left the villages, the horse had to climb up the steep path through the picturesque but rugged Trough of Bolland. They stopped several times, to let the horse have a rest, and for them all to eat.

Eventually, they arrived at Sir Henry's house in Lancaster. As it was going dusk, Anna only got an impression of the house, but it seemed enormous. They were taken straight up to their room and told that the evening meal was just about to start.

'Splendid, I'll be right down. My wife will have to settle the children, so you can bring her something up here,' he commanded. The servant nodded and left. Jack took off his travelling cloak and slipped on a new overgown and went downstairs to the main hall.

Isobelle was fractious, as it was time for her feed, so Anna fed her first and settled her down in the crib for the night. The food duly arrived and she and little Jack enjoyed the food, although little Jack kept asking for an egg instead. He soon fell asleep, tired out by the journey and all the new vistas that he had seen.

Anna sat for a while by herself in the room. It was a pleasant room, with china bowls of water so that she could wash at any time. There was also a cubicle at the corner of the room with a closet in. Anna was impressed by the opulence of having an inside closet room. As time went on, Anna started to think about her hosts. Should she go downstairs to meet them? Would it seem rude if she didn't go down? Would Jack expect her? He hadn't told her what to expect and she had never been in an high-ranking household before and didn't know any of the rules that applied.

A knock at the door diverted her thoughts.

'Come in,' she gently said. It was the serving girl.

'Have you finished with your food?' she asked, with a curtsy.

'Oh yes, thank you. I wonder if could you help me, am I expected downstairs? Is it polite to go downstairs? I've never been here before.'

'No M'lady, you are not expected downstairs. Your husband has told everybody that you are fatigued with the journey and with the children as well, and are going to have an early night.'

'Thank you. That's correct. I am tired,' Anna replied with a smile. The servant left the room and the door closed. Early night indeed! I bet he wakes me up when he comes to bed tonight. But she was wrong. As soon as her head hit the pillow, she fell asleep. Waking next morning, Anna realised that Jack hadn't been to bed at all. She fed Isobelle and got little Jack and herself washed and dressed, and then found the way downstairs, leaving Isobelle asleep in her crib.

The main hall was a busy bustle of activity. Several servants were clearing a large table of old food and then replacing it with new food. Anna asked if she could have some breakfast for little Jack.

'Certainly M'lady,' murmured the servant, a different one from last night, 'come through into the proper dining room. This is just for the servants.'

Anna was taken through a side door into a large room that had long cupboards down each side, which were full of serving dishes, silver tankards and plates. A long table ran down the middle of the room, with a white tablecloth on it.

'Help yourself, M'lady. There are hams, larks, cod, bread and cheese, porridge and eggs.'

'Eggs,' piped up little Jack. 'I want an egg.' Both women laughed at him and the servant showed Anna where the eggs were. Little

Jack was soon happily peeling his boiled egg, so Anna took the chance of having something to eat in peace, whilst Isobelle was still sleeping. She couldn't fancy larks or fish at this time in the morning, but she settled for some porridge, which was thick and creamy, not like the miserable stuff she got at home, and there was honey to pour all over it.

Just as they finished their breakfast, an elegant lady came in and served herself some breakfast.

'Good morning. I'm your hostess. You must be Jack's wife.'

'Yes, I'm Anna, your Ladyship,' replied Anna curtsying.

'Oh please call me Isabella,' she replied. Anna looked up sharply.

'My baby is called Isobelle. I am pleased that you share a similar name.'

'I am honoured that we have the same name, too. I must look out for my little namesake tomorrow. Well Anna, your husband is a comedian. He had us all laughing out loud last night.'

'Yes, your Ladyship,' said Anna, totally bemused. Jack? A comedian? He'd never made her laugh in six years of marriage, more the reverse. Perhaps her Ladyship was mixing her husband up with another Jack.

'The men have gone off hunting this morning, but I bet they've all got bad heads. The wine flowed rather merrily last night. Did Jack say that when he came to bed? He didn't disturb you, did he?'

'No, your Ladyship, he didn't come to bed last night. I was wondering where he was. Gone hunting, have they?'

'Oh,' said Lady Isabella looking a little embarrassed, 'perhaps he fell asleep downstairs after all. He was quite inebriated.'

'Probably,' replied Anna, wondering just what Jack had been up to.

'We usually have a meal of bread and cheese around midday and then the evening meal about six hours later. The servants can look after your children whilst you come and dine.'

'Thank you, that would be most pleasant,' replied Anna.

'Walk in the grounds or come and sit in my solar at any time and bring the children. It will amuse us all, as there are no other small children here this time. We're very civilised, my husband and I have a solar each and I have many books to keep you occupied.'

'Oh, I'd love to read. I never get chance at home,' replied Anna, not admitting that Jack didn't like books in the house, and wouldn't let her have any.'

'Then feel free to borrow any of them, and I'll see you later,' smiled her Ladyship, gliding out of the room.

Anna didn't see Jack until it was time for the evening meal. She had had a busy and happy day with the women of the party. They had all marvelled at her children and couldn't believe that she had a child of nearly six at home. One of the other ladies had taken little Jack out for a walk for over an hour so Anna had managed to do some reading, whilst Isobelle was asleep.

Whilst she was getting dressed, Anna was worried that her clothes wouldn't be of the standard of the other ladies. She was right. As she went down into the large dining room, she felt very parochial and under-dressed. Velvet and lace, feathers and ruffles were very much the order of the ladies clothes. Even the men were fussily dressed. Anna's brand new gown that she thought was quite fashionable looked like a working dress, when compared with the other ladies.

The gowns were close-fitted and had very long sleeves. The ladies wore headdresses rather than simple hats or scarves. Anna spent quite some time looking at all the fashions that were displayed around the room: it was easy, as Jack had left her as soon as they got in to the room and had gone to talk to a group of men.

The men all seemed to be wearing shorter tunics, over heavy hose. Some of the tunics were more fancy than the ladies, with their very decorative sleeves and collars.

She knew that the easiest way of telling rank was by their shoes. The longer the pointed toes; the higher the rank. And there were some ridiculously long pointed toes in the middle of the table. Jack didn't go in for fashion statements, as did very few of the people deep in Lancashire, as they weren't at an elevated household very often.

The other people started to sit down at the table, so Anna hung back. She wasn't sure of the protocol of where she should sit. Jack, as usual, was no help. He had plonked himself down with a group of men. Anna decided to sit at the far end of the table from Lady Isabella. In that way she wouldn't be offending anyone.

The table looked beautiful. All the linen was immaculate, the platters and mugs were polished silver and the table was piled high with food. Flagons of ale and wine and even cider were on the table at various points. Edible platters made of bread were also provided, so that when the courses had gravy, it could be soaked up and eaten without spilling any. Anna thought that this was a novel idea and decided that she would take this idea home with her. Small dishes of salt, sugar, powdered mustard, crushed herbs and spices were also available at various points on the table.

The first course was brought in following a fanfare from a band of musicians. A server, who was wearing a very short tunic and hose, introduced the dish. He announced that it was a potted meat course. Dishes of several different potted meats were brought in as an aperitif for the rest of the meal. The next course was fish; again with a fanfare of music. Several stuffed pike were carried to the table, Sir Henry and Lady Isabella being served first.

Anna eagerly ate the fish, hoping she was using the correct fingers. Jack had hurriedly told her whilst they were dressing that in polite circles, different fingers were used for different courses. Looking surreptitiously at her neighbour, she noticed that she was using the same fingers. Good, thought Anna with relief. She didn't want to be thought of as a country bumpkin. She was also grateful that the conversation was held mainly in English, although it did change to French at times. Anna was thankful that the sisters had taught her French so well, as she was able to keep up with the conversation. She was also glad that Latin was rarely used in company anymore, being used mainly in church.

The third course, again with fanfare, was chicken cooked in herbs and covered in a light pastry cover. The next course was the roasted meat and there were a variety to choose from; beef, venison and swan. Following this was the desserts. Here there was a choice of baked quince, fruit compotes, fruit potage or damsons in wine. As well as the main courses, there were dishes of nuts to nibble in-between courses.

Between courses, Anna got talking to the lady who was on her left side. As she had sat at the end of the table, she had no one on her right. Although older than her, the lady called Julia, had only been married three years but already had two children and whispered to Anna that she was with child again. The two of them chatted happily about childbirth and childrearing. Anna was glad to be able to talk to her as Jack had just abandoned her all night. Also, it was easier to make sure that she was using the right fingers for each course. Anna couldn't believe that Jack thought the house kept a poor table, as she thought the food had been overwhelming, and far better than any they had at home.

After the food was taken away, the musicians took centre stage, instead of being at the back of the room, making the fanfares for the courses. Some were singers, and others played fifes, flutes, shawms, drums and stringed instruments. They sang mainly of courtly love and heroes in battle and Anna recognised one or two of the tunes. She had missed hearing musicians, as they didn't come to Jack's house and she wasn't allowed to visit her parent's when they came. Having said that, Anna reflected, they hadn't been to her parent's house for some years now.

Anna noticed that Jack was getting drunker and more flushed. She hoped that he wouldn't disgrace himself in this fine company. He had moved seats now and was sitting next to a young woman who also seemed to have had too much to drink. The pair of them had their heads together and were whispering to each other, then laughing out loud.

At the end of one of the songs, Sir Henry called for the loyal toast to His Majesty King Edward III. Everybody stood up and taking a mug in their hand, proclaimed their loyalty to the King. This seemed to mark the end of the formal festivities. Julia announced that she was going up to her bedchamber and said goodnight to Anna. Anna went over to Jack and asked if he was ready to go upstairs. It was the wrong thing to say.

'Ready for me, are you? Can't wait to get me in bed?' he said in a raucous voice that everyone else heard. Anna blushed and started to walk away.

'I'll come when I'm ready and not before, but you be ready for me when I do come,' he shouted as she walked away. Anna hurried upstairs and got ready for bed. After checking the children and feeding Isobelle, she curled up in a ball in the bed and hoped she would be asleep before Jack arrived.

Anna awoke next morning to realise that she had had a second night alone in their bed. Not that she was complaining, but she was a little annoyed that he was probably making a fool of her, in front of all the other Lord's of the Manor, and Sir Henry and Lady Isabella.

The servant knocked to remind Anna that the house would all be attending church, and could she breakfast early, so that she could be ready. Getting the children ready, Anna went downstairs to breakfast, and heard that the women would be taken to church in carriages, whilst the men would ride or walk.

Not being able to find Jack, Anna went to church in a carriage with Julia and her children. They stood in the middle of the church, leaving the front empty for Sir Henry and Lady Isabella. Anna was thrilled to be attending Mass and her heart soared as she heard the familiar words of the Mass. After taking the sacraments, Anna waited whilst the other people all took their turn. Jack was at the back of the church and was one of the last people to take the sacraments. At least he's here, thought Anna to herself. Most of the time, he refused to go at home. But she supposed that he couldn't be seen not to attend in front of Sir Henry.

A day of quiet reading and eating large meals ensued, as befitted the Sabbath. No party games or musical interludes were held either. This time, Jack came to bed, as alcohol had been in short supply all day, he complained. Besides, he said that he had a bad headache, so was glad of the rest. He even forgot to abuse her.

Chapter 10

On the Monday morning, all the men were expected to have a meeting with Sir Henry, after which, six of the lords were chosen to stay an extra week, to go to the law courts in Lancaster and Preston. Jack was not chosen. So early on Tuesday morning, they prepared to go home. Anna had mixed feelings about going home. She had enjoyed her first taste of high living, but she was embarrassed by Jack's behaviour, and also his suspected misdemeanours.

On the way home, Jack told her about the meeting that they had had with Sir Henry. The war in France looked as if it was going to be a long one, so Jack had to find some more soldiers from his tenants to send to Sir Henry to become part of his regiment.

'How will you chose them? Will you ask for volunteers?' asked Anna naively.

'No, I'll send all the lazy one, all the ones I don't like and all the troublemakers,' replied Jack with a laugh.

'So whom shall you send?'

'I have my ideas. I'll decide when I get home.' From that, Anna deduced that Jack wasn't going to tell her. All of a sudden, she had a panic stricken thought. Was her father young enough to go to war? Would Jack get his revenge because of this so-called feud that seemed to exist between them by sending him to war? Anna's heart was beating fast, but she didn't dare ask Jack outright, in case he hadn't been thinking that, and she put the thought into his head.

'Are there restrictions on age or fitness, or what trade the person does?' Anna asked idly.

'Yes,' Jack replied, 'they like young men, with no ties, preferably with their own horse, and a trade that is useful to the King's army. Somebody like young Donald from the forge would be ideal,' he smirked, watching Anna's reaction.

So that was his plan. To send Donald away because he dared to call Anna by her first name. What a petty tyrant Jack was, Anna fumed.

'Well, well, that's quietened you. Afraid I'll send your little friend away, are you?' Anna's heart had sunk, but she managed to keep her voice firm.

'I'm sure you'll send the best people you can to represent Ribbleside,' she replied. Jack simply laughed.

'You can be sure I'll send the best, as you say, and Donald will be one of them. He'll be very useful to Sir Henry with his knowledge of metal and forge techniques. And he's a strong young man too. Yes, one of my better decisions.'

Anna didn't take the bait, as she knew that Jack wanted her to argue, but she had learnt to keep quiet at certain times. Soon they were home and Anna had a joyful reunion with Edwina, who was very full of herself and what she had done with Grandmother Jane. Jack barely spoke to her, but went to bed as he still had a bad headache. Even several doses of feverfew had failed to alleviate it.

Not long after they got home, Jack drew up a list of all the young men who would be required to become soldiers. Anna looked at the list when he wasn't watching and saw that Donald was at the top of the list. Also on the list was Jonathan, who had recently got married and his wife was expecting their first child. How cruel was that? thought Anna, then remembered that Jonathan was a bow maker, so would be useful in the army.

Within the week, the men and boys had been notified and were ready to go off to Lancaster to join the army. Many of the villagers had been to see Jack during that week, pleading that their son should be released from the conscription, but Jack was merciless. All the original list of males had to go.

On the day of their departure, the whole village went out to see them off, waving and wishing them 'God Speed' on their travels and a safe journey home.

Anna was saddened to see not just Donald, but many of her childhood friends from the sisters. The village would not be the same without them, and many families would struggle to manage without their strong young sons. It was almost as if Jack had picked the most vulnerable of families to give up their sons. Knowing Jack, Anna thought bitterly, he would have done that deliberately.

The day after the soldiers went, Jack went out to visit a tenant. He hadn't said when he would be back, but had complained that he wouldn't be long as he was extremely tired. He wanted an early night, he said, but without its accompanying leer. Anna thought no more about it and got on with looking after her small family.

About midday, there was a commotion in the front of the house. It was Jem, looking extremely agitated.

He ran up to Anna, and shouted 'Master's had a turn; they're bringing him home on a gate. I'm going to Clitheroe to get the physician.' Then he jumped back on his horse and set off at a great speed. Anna hurried into the house and told Martha and Flossie. Flossie went out to tell young Arthur and Matthew, and then took the children round to their grandmother Jane's house next door.

'What sort of turn?' demanded Martha.

'I've no idea. That's all Jem said. Oh, and they're bringing him home on a gate.'

'A gate?' exclaimed Martha, 'that's not very dignified for the Lord of the Manor.'

'No, it doesn't sound it, but come on Martha, we need to be ready for all eventualities. Do you think we should send for the sisters?'

'The sisters? What can they do?' replied Martha indignantly.

'They may be able to give us some advice before the physician gets here.'

'That's up to you, I suppose,' mumbled Martha.

'Yes, it is, isn't it, Martha,' Anna replied icily. 'Arthur, go and get one of the sisters from the convent hospital,' Anna shouted. Arthur scurried off, whilst Anna and Martha got some blankets and extra bedding together in silence.

An hour later, everyone was ready to receive Jack when he arrived home. He was carried on the door by four farm labourers and looked a sorry sight.

'Take him upstairs to our bedchamber,' Anna ordered and she and Sister Agnes from the convent hospital followed the men upstairs. Martha and Ethel followed behind them.

They put Jack on to the bed and Anna got a good look at him. She thanked the men and told them to go downstairs and get some refreshments, but to wait just in case they were needed again. Sister Agnes said 'He looks like he's had a seizure.'

'What makes you say that, Sister?' asked Anna.

'Look at his right side. It's all twisted. His arm is hanging lifeless, his mouth is drooping and he's drooling, and he doesn't seem able to speak. And he appears to be unconscious.'

As if to contradict them, Jack opened his eyes and started making noises, but they were more like grunts and were unintelligible. As he tried to talk, his drooping mouth seemed even more pronounced.

'Hush Jack, let us look at you to see what can be done,' chided Anna, leaning over to him. His left hand reached out and grabbed her arm sharply. Anna tried not to react in front of Sister Agnes, but she paled with the pain of his grasp.

Sister Agnes took Jack's hand and removed it from Anna without comment. She had seen everything.

'I suggest he is put into his night clothes, so that it will be better to deal with him,' said Sister Agnes. Jack again started making his weird noises and pointing at Sister Agnes.

'I think he is trying to tell you to go out before he is undressed, Sister,' laughed Anna. 'Perhaps he has become modest in his old age.' Jack gave Anna a look that could have turned water to ice; his twisted face seeming even more menacing than usual. But at long last, Anna was suddenly not fearful of him. In this pitiful state, Jack could no longer hurt her. It was a blessed relief.

'I'm used to seeing men in varying states of undress, despite me being a child of God,' said Sister Agnes, and as she spoke, she whipped the clothes off Jack before he could protest. She bundled him into his night wear with some difficulty, trying to get the weak side to manoeuvre into the clothes. Then she took off his hose. He had soiled them. Cleaning him up without comment, Sister Agnes fashioned a large napkin round his bottom, in case of further accidents, then covered him up with the blankets. Jack continued to glare at them both.

The physician from Clitheroe arrived at this point. He looked at

Jack and examined him, and conferred with Sister Agnes, at the side of the room, then spoke to Anna.

'I agree with Sister Agnes. He seems to have had a seizure. The next day will be the most important. Sometimes, they have another seizure soon after the other one, so he mustn't be allowed to get too hot, or the heat will go to his brain. If you can get some weak gruel into him, that will be good, but it is all in the hands of God and the position of the stars and planets now. What has been ordained will happen. Some recover, some don't. You will need help to nurse him.' With this grim prognosis, he left the room, telling Anna to call for him at any time, day or night. He hadn't spoken once to Jack himself. Jack's face mirrored this insult to him, but he was powerless to make himself known.

'We can send a sister round to you each day, if you like,' offered Sister Agnes.

'No thank you, although your offer is kind. I will be doing all the caring myself,' said Anna to a stunned room.

'But it will be very hard,' interjected Martha, 'you're only a little thing.'

'Nevertheless, he is my husband, and I will nurse him,' said Anna resolutely. 'But you can ask in the village if there is a young girl who can come and help with the children.'

'My sister Eloise could do it, M'lady,' whispered a frightened Ethel. 'She looks after our young ones very properly.'

'She'll do fine,' replied Anna. 'Can you go and ask your mother now? I need someone as soon as possible to help with the children.' Ethel nodded and left the room.

If life had been hard before, Anna's life became even harder now, as she cared for Jack, with no thanks at all. The following morning, he had a further seizure, and lost the ability to make noises, or even to grasp Anna. All he had left was his venomous looks, but they couldn't hurt Anna any more.

A small bed was made for Anna, which she placed by the side of their bed, so that she didn't disturb Jack. Each day, she carefully washed him and cleaned him when he soiled, even though sometimes she felt that he soiled deliberately, especially when she had just put clean bedding and clothes on him. But she supposed it was the only way he could force his will on her. Washing him became harder, as his arm was twisted up and wouldn't stretch out

Each day was a burden to Anna and she sometimes wept with tiredness at the end of the day. One sad result of this extra work was that her milk dried up and so Isobelle had to be weaned earlier than she would have been, but she didn't seem to take harm from it.

The children rarely visited their father, as they were frightened of him in his changed state, so Anna had to make sure that she spent lots of time with them, when Jack was asleep. Between Eloise, and her mother, the children thrived and weren't unduly disturbed by their father's illness.

A summons arrived from Sir Henry during Jack's illness, for Jack to attend to his duties at the courts. Although Anna would dearly loved to have gone, she sent his apologies and explained about Jack's illness. She also informed him that she was managing the estate for him at present. Sir Henry sent her a message back, commiserating with her about Jack's illness and confirming her right to manage the estates. Not that she was doing much for the estate, as she was so busy with Jack and the children. She was relying heavily on Jem to get on with the day-to-day management of the farms and livestock.

Soon it was time for Edwina's first day at the sisters, and Anna allowed Martha to care for Jack that morning, so that she could accompany Edwina on this important day. Edwina loved it straightaway and was full of her own importance with little Jack when she got home.

After Edwina had been at the sisters for one week, she cried when there were no lessons at the weekend, so Anna made up a game for her outside with the chickens and she was soon soothed. Going back to check on Jack, she found him choking and going purple in the face.

'Jack, Jack,' she cried shaking him, but there was no response. After a sudden tremor of all his limbs, where he almost sat up, he suddenly relaxed and fell back against the bed. With a big sigh, and a final glare at Anna, his breath left his body and he was still. Anna moved towards him and held her hand before his nose to see if she could feel any breath, as there was no movement of his chest, but there was no breath. She sat on the side of the bed and wept. Not with sorrow, but with sheer unadulterated relief that he had gone. A little later, that was how Martha found her.

'Has he gone then?' asked Martha. Anna nodded. 'I'll get the sisters, they'll come and lay him out for burial.' Anna nodded again, unable to speak. 'Shall I get the priest as well?' Anna nodded. 'Although I suppose it's too late for him to be shrived isn't it? Should have thought about that before, but he couldn't talk anyway, so he couldn't confess his sins. No, he'll have to go and meet the Almighty as he is, sin and all, although I suppose we could get a sin-eater,' said Martha, shaking her head as she walked out of the room. Anna watched her go and thought that was probably the longest conversation she had had with Martha in six years.

'Martha,' Anna called, 'thank you for all you have done for the Master. You have always been very good to him.'

'Didn't deserve it, though, did he?' came the surprising reply from Martha. 'Mean old goat, wasn't he?'

'Martha, is that any way to speak of the deceased?' said a shocked Anna.

'I only came for the Mistress's sake. Mistress Edwina, not you. I loved her and served her happily. I came when her milk dried up, as the wet nurse, when she was poorly. And I just stayed. When she was dying, I was ready to up and go and find myself a new position, but she says, "Stay and look after him, Martha," so like a fool, I did. Not that he's ever thanked me for that.'

'So you had a baby? I never knew that,' said Anna softly.

'Yes, but it died, and so did my husband, so I was glad to nurse the little one. Mine was a boy, but this was a girl. Brought her up I did, like my own. She died in childbirth when she was fifteen. It fair broke my heart.'

'Martha, you've never told me all this. Why not?'

'Ancient history. Have to move on in life. But now that he's gone, begging your pardon, I'll be off as soon as I can. I've a sister who lives in Chatburn hamlet. There's room there for me anytime.'

'You are welcome to go Martha. And I thank you for all the faithful service that you've given to this family. You will be rewarded before you go.'

'I'll go and send someone for the priest. Would you like something to eat and drink M'lady? I'm sure you'll need to keep your strength up in the next few days.'

'Thank you, Martha. I don't know what I'd have done without you all these six years,' said Anna, but Martha was already going out of the door, as if she didn't want to have any more discussion. It's all very strange, thought Anna. I've found out more about her in the last ten minutes, than I've ever known. But perhaps I've been at fault as well, thought Anna, because she had always felt in awe of Martha, and reluctant to talk to her beyond what was necessary.

Events happened very quickly after that. Jane arrived shortly afterwards and held her daughter in her arms for a long time. She promised to tell the children later, but asked if there was anything that she could do to help.

Anna was at a loss what to say, as she didn't have the first idea what she should be doing. No doubt Martha would guide her along. The priest was the next person to arrive and he made the arrangements for the burial in the church graveyard, two days hence. Jack's body was taken to the convent and got ready for burial. The sin-eater was sent for and performed his grisly ceremony; eating bread to take Jack's sins into his own soul, thereby giving Jack the absolution he hadn't been able to ask for himself. Anna wasn't sure about this procedure, but let it happen anyway. If the nuns accepted it, perhaps she should too, she reasoned with herself.

That night, Anna still slept on her little bed; she couldn't bear to sleep in the bed where Jack had died. As she lay in bed, her thoughts went over the last six years. They had been hard years and she had been very unhappy, but out of those six years, she had won minor victories, and she had her three precious children, who were healthy and strong. And she had her little hoard of money.

At long last, she was free. Free to do what she wanted to do, without fear of reprisal. She couldn't mourn for Jack; that would be hypocrisy, but she looked eagerly towards the next stage of her life as a widow. She would fight for her children and see that they had a better life than their parents. She would make sure that little Jack was known as the best Lord of the Manor for miles around when he grew up. And she would never force one of her daughters to marry where they didn't want to. They would all be happy. Life was good.

Chapter 11

Next morning, Anna began reorganising the house to suit her. She changed the bed that Jack had died in for one of the spare beds in another bedchamber. All the bedding was changed and washed and she ordered new mattresses for both beds. The bedchamber next door was made into the children's bedchamber and she ordered an adjoining door to be made, so that she could have easy access to them in the night if need be.

Martha tutted at these changes, but it gave Anna something to do with her time. So much had been taken up by caring for Jack, that time now hung heavy for her. It was a sort of limbo between the death and the funeral. Anna remembered to give thanks to Saint Wylgeforte. She knew that Saint Wylgeforte watched out for women with bad husbands, and Anna was grateful that her prayers had been answered.

Anna carefully explained to the children again that their father had gone to live with Jesus and the angels in Heaven. The children didn't seem unduly perturbed about the loss of their father, but then he had never been special to them, as Richard had been to Anna, and like most other fathers were.

Searching through Jack's clothes chest, Anna gathered together all his clothes and asked Martha to give them to the poor. After she had finished, it was as if Jack had never lived in that bedchamber, and Anna felt better for it. She made the bedchamber wholly hers, even to picking some wild flowers and putting them in a mug on top of the clothes chest; a thing that Jack would never allow.

Having found the keys to the manuscript chest, Anna opened it up and looked inside. There were several large books that seemed to be accounts. There were also several small bags with coins inside, quite a lot of them in fact. Anna decided to transfer the money to the closet in her bedchamber, that was let into the wall. It seemed a better place than where it was. She would count it later. At least she knew that she would have no money worries. After the funeral, she would look at all these accounts and start to understand how the estate ran.

The following day was the funeral. Anna dressed carefully and after taking the children to her mothers, walked to the church with Martha, Ethel, Jem, Arthur, and Matthew. Her father linked arms with her to assist her during this difficult time. Six of the estate workers carried Jack from the convent to the graveyard surrounding the church. Anna and her entourage followed behind.

The priest gave a short eulogy following the mass, and then intoned the prayers for the dead. The body was lowered into the grave and it was soon all over. Anna let out a sigh of relief. Now that he was buried, she felt truly free and able to get on with her life. She had served him well, despite not really receiving anything in return. But at least she had done her duty; she hadn't had much option not to, she thought grimly to herself. His threats and occasional acts of violence saw to that.

Anna looked round the graveyard, smiling at and registering all the villagers that were present. She doubted that any of them were sorry that Jack had gone. Most of them had felt the brunt of his anger or cruel deeds at some time in their lives. Only Martha was crying. Very few people from outside the village had attended either. Only two other Lords of the Manor had come from nearby. None of Jack's family had come, although they had been notified.

'Please all come back to the house for some refreshments,' said Anna. 'Martha and Ethel have prepared enough to feed the five thousand, so please don't waste it.' Anna turned and set off back to the house, but nobody followed. Eventually Sylvia started moving and it was as if that gave everyone permission to go to the house as well. They had been waiting for the first person to move.

The house was soon full, and Anna enjoyed herself for the first time as a hostess. There had hardly been any dinners whilst she had lived there, so she was glad to entertain the villagers. Much food and a lot of drink were consumed, and some of the villagers went home a little merry.

A lot of Jack's finest wines and cider was drunk; he'd be turning in his grave if he knew, thought Anna. She turned away to hide the laughter that bubbled up inside her. Laughter. She hadn't had a good laugh for years, except when the children did or said something funny. She felt years younger in herself already. Why, she felt like dancing, but perhaps she'd better wait; the guests at the funeral meal might be a little shocked to see the supposedly grieving widow throw up her skirts and dance.

At the end of the meal, Anna pressed food on to all the villagers to take home and she still had enough food left to last the household a few more days.

'Martha,' said Anna, 'you have done me proud. What an amazing funeral meal. Thank you so much. And Ethel too. Are you sure you want to leave Martha? I would be so happy for you to stay.'

'No Mistress. I've served my time, I've kept my promise and now it's time for me to have a good rest. But I do have a favour to ask you?'

'Anything, Martha, what is it?'

'Could my niece come and work here? She's a willing body and tries to please. Ethel will need more help in the kitchen when I've gone.'

'By all means, that would be excellent. Is she the daughter of the sister you are going to live with?'

'Yes, the youngest one. All the rest are long married with children of their own.'

'When can she start?'

'Tomorrow, if you like.'

'Good. Will you stay another week to get your niece settled in here? You can teach her your high standards and way of doing things.'

Martha beamed at Anna. 'That's most kind of you and a good idea. Shall I send one of the lads with a message?'

Anna laughed. 'Not tonight, Martha. I think they'd be likely to fall off the horse tonight, with all the ale they've supped.'

Martha agreed and after clearing away, she and Ethel settled down for the night. Anna went round to her mothers but the children had already settled down to sleep, so she left them there overnight.

Early next morning, Anna went for the children, but talked to her mother before they were awake.

'Why did you make me marry Jack, Mother? Why was it for the good of the family? Didn't you know I would be unhappy? I've always wanted to ask, but was frightened of hearing the answers. But now that Jack is dead, I want to know.'

Jane held her head low, as if she wasn't sure what to say. 'I don't know whether I should tell you or not,' she said.

'Why not?' asked Anna. 'I'm a grown woman, a widow even. Why can't I be trusted to know?'

'I'll ask your father first, it's his story really.'

'Ask me what first?' asked Richard as he came into the solar.

'I want to know why you had to marry me to Jack, for the good of the family. It certainly wasn't good for this member of the family,' said Anna bitterly.

'I suppose you ought to know. But it's not a pretty story and I'm ashamed of it,' replied Richard.

'Tell me,' demanded Anna.

'Well, it happened whilst you were at your Aunty Judith's. I had invested quite a lot of money in an ocean going vessel and the ship sunk with all hands and the entire cargo of expensive spices. It was going to make my fortune, but instead it bankrupted me. We were going to have to sell the house and I owed money to people who were pressing for it. In desperation, I talked to Jack about it and he agreed to give me some money but I had to pay him back on a regular basis, and if I reneged, he would take my house. I had to sign to that effect.'

'So why did I come into it?'

'I hadn't quite got myself back on to an even keel and couldn't meet the first payment, so he suggested I give you to be married instead of the first payment.'

'You sold me?' screamed Anna.

'Not sold you, my dear.'

'Oh yes you did,' Anna replied vehemently. 'I was thirteen, and he gave me no allowance for that. He raped me on the first night

127

and every night after that. And mornings come to that. He was a beast. How could you?' Anna burst into tears, and then noticed that both her parents were sobbing too.

'We are so sorry, Anna. We didn't know what to do,' said Jane. 'We hated it that you were unhappy and yet he wouldn't let us come near to you, to give you any comfort at all.'

'I bitterly regretted being so weak and allowing it to happen,' replied Richard. Eventually, the three of them clung together and that was how they were when Eloise and the children came in from their bedchambers.

'Mummy, are you crying?' asked Edwina. Little Jack and Isobelle looked close to tears as well.

'Yes, we're all sad because your father has died. We were just talking about him,' said Anna, praying for forgiveness for such a blatant lie.

'Don't be sad, you've still got us three,' replied Edwina, 'and we're not dead.'

'No, you're not, my lambs, and we're going to have some fun times together now. Eloise, could you take the children to see if there are any eggs, so that we can have eggs for breakfast?'

Eloise took the hint and persuaded the children that that was what they really wanted to do, rather than watch their mother and grandparents crying. Off they all trooped and the adults pulled themselves together.

'And have you finished paying off what he lent you?' asked Anna.

'No,' said Richard sadly, 'it will take many years yet.'

'It will not,' said Anna. 'The debt is cancelled from this day forth. I've paid with my body for all the money he lent you.'

'Anna, that's not a very nice thing to say,' said a shocked Jane.

'True, nevertheless,' said Anna. 'We'll say no more about it.'

Richard and Jane clung to their daughter, thanking her.

'I think you've more than made up for it in babysitting, especially these last few months whilst Jack's been ill,' Anna laughed, and harmony and forgiveness was restored.

When she got home, Anna took the books that Jack kept his

accounts in, and set herself up at the table in the solar. It made interesting reading. The first book was about the cottages and farms that he owned. Each tenant had a page to themselves. Every payment or work on the land was recorded and every lapse in payment or failure to attend for work on the estate. Harsh punishments were meted out to those who didn't keep their agreements and Anna was amazed at how cruel Jack had been, demanding payment off people who had no money in the first place. But then, was she surprised? Jack was not known for his mercy.

Anna couldn't believe how much income Jack had and yet he had pleaded poverty at all times. Every time there was a famine, he had used that as an excuse to tighten the household finances, but he gave no respite to his tenants. In land alone, Jack was a wealthy man, far richer than many of the other Lords locally.

In the next book, Anna found the accounts for the buying and selling of livestock. Again, this was a revelation as to the amount of money he made at the cattle markets and wool markets. He had even sold her father some wool at full price. Not even a discount for a family member. In fact, the wool had been sold to her father at an inflated price after her marriage. No wonder her father was in dire straits. Oh, what an evil man Jack was, thought Anna again.

Looking through the papers in the back of the accounts book, Anna found an agreement between her father and Jack. It made chilling reading. So merciless that Anna shivered as she read it. There was no way her father could have managed to repay the high rate of interest, never mind the original loan. She tore the papers up and burnt them in her fire. At least she could do that to help her father.

The third book was the household accounts and wages. Anna was appalled. Nobody had been paid for nearly two years. Not staff or tradesmen. His illness had only lasted for a few months, so why had he not been paying the bills? It certainly wasn't through lack of incoming money. So where was all the money going? Anna went to her bedchamber to check the amount of money in the little closet. She tipped it on to the bed. There were hundreds of pounds worth of guineas and other coins. Without counting them, she put them back in the closet and locked them up again.

Walking straight down stairs, she went into the kitchen and asked for all the staff to assemble, even the estate staff. They all looked a little worried when she summoned them and shifted uneasily, the men curling their hats in their hands.

'I have been checking my husband's accounts and find out that none of you have been paid for two years. Is that correct? Or did my husband pay you without recording it?' Nobody answered.

'Well, I'm waiting? What has been happening?'

Eventually Martha answered. 'No, we've not been paid. Neither have the tradesmen. It's embarrassing. You can't look them in the eye when they deliver goods.'

'Why didn't you say? And why do the tradesmen carry on delivering if they don't get paid?' asked Anna, completely astounded.

'It was up to the master to pay us, not you,' replied Martha. 'And the tradesmen had to continue delivering as most of their homes were owned by the master.'

'I am sorry to all of you. I will pay you back immediately. Come back here at dusk and I will give you all your pay. Do you know which people we owe money to, Martha?'

'Not really, although I know the candle maker hasn't been paid, as he came and asked me recently, but with the Master dying, it escaped my mind.'

'Right, tomorrow, I will visit everyone in the village and find out who is owed money. Thank you, you can all go back to work, now. Hopefully things will be better from now on,' Anna promised.

Next morning, Anna sent word round the village that she would be in the church around midday and if anyone had money owing to them, they should come and see her. She arranged with the priest to have a table and chairs taken into the church and sat and waited. She didn't have long to wait. Martha was worried that a lot of villagers would say they were owed money just to get something out of the Manor, but it didn't seem that way. There were only a handful of people, who all arrived together.

Young Jonathan's wife, Lois, was the first in the queue. She was near her time now, Anna noticed, and looked weary and thin.

'Do we owe you some money, Lois?' asked Anna gently, after making sure that she sat down.

'Yes, Jonathan wasn't paid for the last two lots of bows for the archery ground. He did ask the master for some money before he went to war, but the master said that he couldn't have any 'cos he hadn't paid his rent. But he couldn't pay his rent until he got paid. So we lost the hut and I've gone back to live with my mother and father. It's a little cramped, but we manage.'

Anna checked her records and found that what Lois said was true.

'I'm sorry about that Lois. Now go back to your own hut. There'll be no rent due until Jonathan is back working again. And here's the money owing to you.'

Lois beamed her thanks, too overcome to say much. She waddled away, to tell her mother the good news.

Next was the candle maker. His bill was quite large, but Anna knew how many candles they went through as a household, although not as many as her parents. She paid him gladly.

'I thank you, M'lady. I was beginning to get worried about money. I'm sorry I asked Martha about it.'

'Think nothing of it. We should have paid you promptly. I was never aware of how bills were paid, but as I am now in charge, until my son is old enough to take up his place as Lord of the Manor, I will ensure there is a better system of payment.'

Next in the queue was Roland the carpenter. He told Anna how much he was owed and was delighted to receive the money in full. Anna thanked him for his service. Donald's father came in next. The only amount of money he had owing was for the carriage frame that he made for the trip to Lancaster.

Another couple of villagers came in; the saddler and the wheelwright, both with small claims. Anna waited a while longer, but it was as if they had all come together. Perhaps they were frightened that the money would run out, so wanted to get there first, Anna mused.

On walking home, Anna planned how she could best manage the money in future. She could really do with someone who was better at sums than her to keep the books. It was never her best subject! With that thought in mind, she veered towards the convent instead of home. On entering the classroom, she asked if Sister Bernadette had anyone in mind who was good at maths.

'You've already got my best mathematician,' she joked.

'Who is that?'

'Matthew Fox. Don't you remember? He took longer with reading, but he was always quick with sums.'

'Of course, I never thought of him. I'll approach him later today, and thank you for your help.'

'And if you need someone to replace Matthew on the land, young Roger needs a place soon.'

'Young Roger? Old enough to work? My goodness, time is moving on. Yes, send him round to me.'

Anna said goodbye and went home. Even more changes were afoot at home. Martha's niece had arrived and was being shown round the main hall and back kitchen.

'M'lady, this is my niece Ghislane,' said Martha.

'Pleased to meet you, Ghislane, I'm glad you could come and join us here. I'm sure your aunty will settle you in and show you round.'

'Thank you, M'lady,' replied a nervous Ghislane, 'I'll do my best.'

'And now where is Ethel?' asked Anna. 'I need to see Matthew Fox. Ethel, there you are, could you get a message out to Matthew that I want to see him?'

Ethel nodded and went outside. A few minutes later, a worried Matthew came through the door.

'You wanted to see me, M'lady?' he asked nervously.

'Yes, Matthew, don't look so worried. I've got a proposition to put to you,' said Anna.

'Me, M'lady? What sort of prop . . . er thing?'

'Do you still like doing sums?'

'Yes, but I don't do them very much now.'

'I need some help doing the books. Could you help me?'

'Do you mean after I've done my work on the estate?' he asked.

'No, help me instead of working on the land. I need someone who can keep the books correctly and start going out with me to collect rents and see what repairs want doing on the farms.'

'I'd love that, M'lady. I really would. And I'd protect you anytime we went out.'

Anna laughed. 'That's what I need, Matthew. I need someone like my Aunty Judith's Rupert. You can start tomorrow.'

'But who'll do my work?'

'Don't you worry about that. We'll find someone else to do your work. Now, come here tomorrow, and put your best clothes on, as befits your new job.'

'Yes M'lady' replied Matthew, walking away with a beaming smile.

When Martha left, Anna found out that Jack had owned Martha's sister's hut in the next village, so Anna gave them the hut as a thank you present, with no ties to serve on the land, plus a cash gift as well. Martha was overwhelmed, but secretly felt that she had been treated well, after all the hard work she had put in for the family.

The next few months were busy ones for Anna. The Manor settled down and ran more smoothly under her direction. Ghislane proved to be every bit as reliable as her aunt and soon found her feet and made friends with Ethel and Eloise, and the men in the stable. Matthew responsibly paid all the bills each month so that no one was left in financial straits because of the Manor House.

Anna reinstated the non-meat days and allowed any of her staff to go to mass on Sundays, or every day if they preferred. She herself took to going to confessions regularly and attending mass at least twice a week. She even planned to go on a pilgrimage the following year, when the children were a little older and could understand what a pilgrimage was for.

Anna and Matthew became a common sight together on the farms and highways, visiting the tenants. Matthew quickly took to the book keeping and the money seemed to be growing in her wall closet. Jane gave Anna a beautiful black velvet cloak with a hood, with satin fastenings, which she wore all the time, and soon came to be recognised by her cloak. The villagers laughingly called her the black widow.

Life was happier for everyone in the house, and Anna instigated harvest suppers and feast day celebrations, for which she always offered food and drink for the villagers. Some of the oldest villagers said that it reminded them of the olden times, before Jack was Lord of the Manor; his own father had been a much better Lord.

The children were growing steadily and seemed to have more confidence, now they weren't expected to be always silent, like they were forced to do in front of their father. Jack had joined Edwina at the sisters and Isobelle was running round and chattering twenty to the dozen, even though nobody could quite understand what she was saying most of the time.

It was around dusk one evening; Anna was sat in her solar having a few quiet minutes to herself, whilst Eloise was giving the children their tea. Ghislane came running into the solar, quite agitated.

'M'lady, there is a lady come, asking for Jack. She won't be sent away. Can you come and talk to her?'

'Yes, I will. Where has she come from?'

'Don't know M'lady. She just keeps asking for Jack. I've told Eloise to keep Master Jack out of the way, just in case.'

'And very sensible too,' replied Anna calmly, although her heart was pounding, wondering who could want her son. She went downstairs and found a poor looking woman, with a baby in her arms and two small children clinging to her skirts.

'Can I help you,' asked Anna in her best Lady of the Manor voice.

'I want Jack,' she repeated. 'I know he lives here, he told me. He hasn't been near for months and I want to see him now,' shouted the woman.

Anna was stunned. This woman wanted her husband, not her son.

'Why do you want Jack? How do you know him?' Anna asked.

'I've told you why I want him. He hasn't been near for months and I've no money left. He's never left me this long before. Now where is he? Are you his granddaughter?'

'No,' said Anna quietly, 'I'm his wife.' The woman was visibly shaken, pulling the children close to her.

'Wife? He never said he had a wife. Told me she'd died. Said he'd marry me, now I've got the children.' The woman was crying and twisting her clothes. Anna felt sorry for her.

'Here, sit down, what's your name?'

'Kate,' was the monosyllabic reply. It was obvious the woman was in shock. She sent Ghislane to get some ale for her to drink.

'And you say my husband used to come to you?'

'Yes.'

'How long has he been coming for?' Anna couldn't help asking.

'Six years.'

Six years, thought Anna, the whole of my marriage to him. How could he? No wonder he had started staying away from home more frequently. No wonder some money couldn't be accounted for. She was furious with him all over again, but first she had to deal with this woman. She steeled herself to ask the next question.

'Are these his children?'

'Yes.'

'How old are they?'

'Big one's six, middle one's five, and baby's one.' Anna's heart contracted. They were all similar ages to her own children.

'I have some bad news for you Kate. I'm afraid Jack died six months ago. He had a stroke before that so was ill for quite some months. I'm sorry he deceived you. Do you have family?' but the woman had collapsed in tears and was distraught. She seemed genuinely to care for Jack. Anna couldn't understand that.

'What am I going to do without him? How will I live? How will I feed my babies?' she cried desperately.

'Did Jack pay for your cottage?'

'He said he owned it. I think he must have done, 'cos no landlord has been round for money.'

'Where is the cottage?' asked Anna.

'Gisburn.'

'Right, well you can keep that cottage and I'll give you some money for the children now. Then I will send you some money regularly to keep you going. But now, I'd like you to leave. How did you get here?'

'Walked with the children. They are very tired.'

'I'll get you all some food, and then you can sleep in the stable tonight, but tomorrow, I want you gone from here and I don't want to see you or your children ever again. Is that clear?'

'Yes,' said Kate. 'Can I see the grave? I'd like to see his final resting place.'

Anna was shocked at that, but after a moment's hesitation, she agreed. 'I'll get one of the estate workers to take you down and show you,' she said with as much grace as she could muster. 'Now leave,' Anna turned her head away from the woman and hoped she would leave quickly.

After she had gone, Anna sat and thought for a long time. Besides bitter thoughts about Jack and his duplicity, both to her and Kate, she wondered how many more of Jack's women were going to turn up demanding help. She sighed heavily and then decided to go and see her mother. Jane would help her and give her advice. Jane was horrified at Anna's tale and said much the same as Anna had.

'I think you've been very gracious with her, Anna. I don't know that I would have been so calm if someone had turned up asking for your father.'

'But my father wouldn't do that sort of thing, would he? Besides, you love my father and really care for him. I never cared for Jack. I didn't even like him, so I'm not as bothered as I would have been if I'd really loved him. No, I felt sorry for her really. She seemed to genuinely care for Jack. She asked to see his grave.'

'No,' said a shocked Jane, 'and did you let her?' Anna nodded.

'Why not? I don't want to go and see the grave, so if it gives her comfort, then let her. It won't harm me. I'll just make sure the children don't see her, that's all. You know, the only thing that bothers me about this whole episode, is how many more 'Kate's' are going to turn up? He could have had women all over the county.'

'Don't even think about it. This is probably the only one,' reassured Jane. But it had upset the enjoyment of her new life. Now there was a small cloud on the horizon, that wouldn't go away, even though Anna was the happiest she had been in her adult life. Putting it behind her, Anna started planning a Midsummer feast. She would hold it on the day of the summer solstice. That would cheer her up.

Chapter 12

It was an excuse to have a big party and instead of holding it in the church, she decided to hold it in the house. Days of planning and preparation went into the event. The whole village was invited, plus many of the farm tenants.

'What will you do if they all turn up, M'lady?' asked Ethel, 'the house won't be big enough.' But Anna only laughed and said the more the merrier.

'Besides Ethel, as it is summer, we can spill out in to the courtyard.'

'But what if it rains?' persisted Ethel.

'Then we'll get wet or be squashed in the main hall. Rain is a way of life in Lancashire; we just have to live with it.'

The arrangements went ahead. The day dawned and Ethel's grim prognostications were unfounded. It was a glorious summer day, so they set up tables and chairs all round the courtyard. The party started at midday; all work was cancelled for the day, after the livestock had been fed and watered. There was every imaginable kind of food to eat and lots of ale to drink, and the villagers wasted no time in tucking in to the spread, and playing riotous games afterwards.

Most of the children had fallen asleep where they were playing and some of the villagers had started to go home, conscious that they would have to be up early to do their work on the morrow.

With all the noise going on, Anna didn't see the horseman arrive and stand watching all the merriment that was going on. It was only when the stranger stood in the doorway and shouted that Anna noticed him.

'Is this my homecoming?' he shouted in a very unpleasant voice. 'That's strange; you didn't know I was coming. Just what is going on here? I come back to find a cavorting mass of imbeciles eating and drinking with gay abandon. Who can tell me what is going on?' The noise stopped instantly and the villagers were looking frightened.

Anna stepped forward. 'I can tell you what is going on, Sir,' she said icily. 'This is my house and my villagers and tenants. And who might you be, stranger?'

'You? You're only a child. What right have you to say that it's your house?'

'Every right, I was married to Jack de Ribbleside,' she said in a haughty manner. The man burst out laughing.

'Were you, indeed. Well, I've got to admire the old goat, wedding a chit like you. Well, your worries are over, I'm here now.'

'I have no worries,' replied Anna, with a strange feeling of trepidation in her heart, 'and what do you mean by the fact that you are here? What can that have to do with me?'

'Because you no longer own this place. I do,' he said to the stunned audience.

'How come you think you own my house?' demanded Anna, 'what right have you to this house?'

'Birthright, girl. I'm Max de Ribbleside. I've come to claim my inheritance.' There was silence in the courtyard, but Jem was sober enough to realise what was going on.

'Come on folks, party's over, get off home now,' Jem chivvied, waving his arms at everyone. The villagers and tenants all slunk off quietly, whilst Anna and Max just stared at each other.

'You'd better come inside,' said Anna quietly, the servants all having scurried away into the back kitchen.

'That's rich. You are inviting me into my house,' replied Max.

Anna gave him a glassy stare, 'Until you can prove who you are, it is still my house and my son will still inherit it when he is of age.'

'Your son?' hooted Max. 'You have a brat? So there was still life in the old dog.'

'I have three children. And you? Have you got a wife and children?' asked Anna, trying to stall for time and appear polite.

'No, not any more,' he snarled. 'Wife's just died and the brat with her.' Anna shivered. She could see now how like Jack he was. Not just in his looks but also in his evil manner. 'Thought I'd come and claim my inheritance now. Haven't got anything else to do. Yes, I'll be on the lookout for a new wife. Perhaps I can inherit the wife as well as the estate,' he leered, looking at Anna suggestively, 'you look as if you could warm a man's bed on a night.'

139

Anna fought to quell the rising nausea that was threatening to erupt. Instead her anger surfaced. 'I could think of nothing worse than marriage to you. I was married to one pig, and certainly wouldn't want to marry another one,' she spat at him.

'Oh, what a temper! I like a woman with a bit of spirit,' he replied eagerly.

'Why didn't you come before?' asked Anna. 'Why didn't you come to the funeral or send a message?'

'It wasn't convenient. I was busy,' he replied leaving Anna no wiser. 'Now, I'm tired and hungry. I want to go to bed. We'll talk about this in the morning.'

'Ethel? Get our visitor some food and drink, and then show him to the guest bedchamber. Goodnight Sir, I am going to speak with my parents.' Anna held her head up high and walked out of the house, giving him no further opportunity to talk or make ribald comments.

As soon as she got to her parents house, Anna broke down in tears. Her parents tried to comfort her, but Anna felt that her whole new world had just collapsed round her feet.

'What am I going to do?' she kept wailing but couldn't think straight.

'Wait until tomorrow, things will look better then,' her mother soothed. 'He may be ready to make good arrangements for you and the children.'

'More likely throw me out,' said Anna mournfully.

'I don't think he'd be allowed to do that. You were Jack's legal wife. You must have some rights, and he must have some responsibility to his step-mother.'

Anna grimaced. 'Don't call me that. It was bad enough being Jack's wife without being this oaf's stepmother.'

Together Anna and her parents talked until long into the morning, without coming to any conclusions except that Richard and Jane promised to help her in any way they could.

Anna slipped into the house quietly and went to bed, but her mind was going round and round in circles, and sleep evaded her. Eventually she got up and moved all the money from the wall closet on to the bed. She wrapped up most of the money in the children's clothing and put it in the bottom compartment of the clothes chest that her parent's had bought her when Edwina was born, with her hoard of egg and cheese money.

She carefully left a couple of coins in each of the bags, so that it looked as if not much money was kept in the house. If Max did throw her out, she wasn't going without some money to ease her passage until she could work. Feeling tired, she lay down on the bed just as dawn was breaking.

After a few hours sleep, Anna got up when she heard the children playing.

'Somebody shut those brats up,' called a male voice, strangely reminiscent of Jack, 'can't a man have a lie-in in his own house.'

Anna shuddered. He was calling it his own house already. She knew without doubt that her future at the Manor House was precarious. It was then that she remembered her Aunty Judith's last words to her, before her marriage. If ever you need help, I'll be there, she had said. I wonder, thought Anna. Would Aunty Judith take me in and train me as a physician?

With the stash of coins I've got, I could pay her for our keep, until I was trained, she thought. The idea was appealing to her more than ever. But what about the children? Who could care for them? Would Eloise come with her and look after the children? I'll go and ask her, thought Anna, hurrying downstairs. Eloise was in the Main Hall with the children. They had had an early breakfast and the two older ones were getting ready to go to the sisters.

'Eloise, I need to talk to you urgently. I'll come with you to the sisters and then talk on the way home,' said Anna.

'Is there something wrong M'lady?'

'No, it's just an idea I've had,' she said, 'come on, let's go.'

Anna hustled the children and Eloise out of the house and marched them to the sisters. Poor little Isobelle's feet hardly touched the ground; they walked so fast. Waving goodbye to the older children, Anna started talking straightaway.

'Eloise, you can't have failed to hear all that went on last night. Max has made it very clear that he is now the owner, and there will be no provision for me and my children.' Eloise's mouth opened in shock. 'I feel that my life will be in danger if I stay here, and possibly that of my children too, so I've decided to go to my Aunty Judith's in Brun Lea and live there. Will you come with me?'

'Just for the journey, do you mean?' asked Eloise.

'No, to live there with me. How do you feel about that? Do you have anyone here that you wouldn't like to leave?'

Eloise laughed. 'No, I can see my family anytime. It sounds like a good adventure. I've always wanted to live in a busy town.'

'It's not that big, it's not really a town, but it is bigger than Ribbleside. And the market is much bigger than Clitheroe,' said Anna with a grin.

'Then how can I resist? Of course I'll come.'

'I may not be able to pay you very much until I am earning myself, but you will have your bed and board.'

'I don't mind that. When are we going?'

'I don't know yet, it might not come to that, but I'm pretty sure that we will be made to leave, and we may have to be ready in a hurry. Could you go and see your family today and tell them?'

'Yes, I will, but I'll tell them not to say anything yet.'

'Good idea, you're so sensible for one your age. I'm so glad that you came to work for me, Eloise.'

'So am I. I love the children as if they were my own, and I enjoy living here, but not if that man is in charge in the future. He seemed awful.'

'Worse than that. Well, off you go and make it right with your family.' Eloise hurried off, leaving Anna to entertain Isobelle, which she thoroughly enjoyed.

Going back into the house, Anna noticed that Ghislane and Ethel both looked nervous.

'What's the matter?' Anna asked.

'He wants us to move his things into your bedchamber and move yours out. He says he should have the best bedchamber now,' said Ethel dully. Anna didn't need to ask who 'he' was.

'Where is he?'

'In the solar. He wants the keys for all the manuscript cupboards. He's looking for them,' replied Ethel.

Anna hurried upstairs to the solar and caught Max trying to force the door of the manuscript box.

'What are you doing?' she demanded.

'Trying to look inside here,' he replied angrily, 'what does it look like?'

'It won't open without the key,' said Anna.

'Well, give it me, you silly woman,' he said, still riving at the door.

'Why should I? I don't know you from Adam. You could be anybody pretending to be Max,' replied Anna, even though he was just like his father, she wasn't giving in without a fight.

'There are lots of people who know me. Jem for one, and the priest, and some of the old villagers. And where's Martha? She always knew how to run a good house. What have you done with her?'

'Martha left after your father died. Her niece Ghislane is here in her stead.'

'Is that the tall dark buxom wench? Very young?' asked Max.

'Yes,' said Anna, her heart sinking at his description.

'Mmm, that's a shame. I wouldn't dare interfere with one of Martha's lot,' smirked Max.

Anna shivered. 'And what do you mean by telling them to change our bedchambers over? I'll decide if and when that happens.'

'Oh no you won't, woman. You're coming to the priest with me now. When he has verified who I am, I'm taking charge. By nightfall, I will be in the main bedchamber, and if you insist on staying there, well, all I can say is on your head be it. But you will be in there with me as well. Think about it,' he said, looking her up and down very slowly, with a leer that was very familiar.

Anna swallowed, trying to control both her temper and her tears. She knew she had lost. He was never going to give her a position in this house, which she could be satisfied with. And she would be eternally frightened for herself and her children.

'Come on; let's go to the priest. Then I can get my bedchamber sorted out before bedtime,' Max added.

Anna reluctantly followed him to the door, grabbing her black cloak as she left. The visit to the priest soon verified that he was Max de Ribbleside, as did several of the villagers and Anna knew that she had to get out of the house as soon as possible.

On returning from the village, Anna went to see her parents and give them an update on what was happening with Max, but found Jane alone. She told her what was happening and that she was going to stay with her Aunty Judith, as she couldn't bear to live under the same roof as him.

'But we won't see you or the children,' said Jane mournfully.

'You can come and see us any time. I'm sure Aunty Judith won't mind.'

'But does she know you are coming? Will she be able to accommodate you? What if she doesn't want you?' Anna didn't dare think about that and dismissed it from her mind.

'Aunty Judith said that I could go to her any time I needed her,' replied Anna. 'I'm sure she won't mind.'

'Yes but to take four of you, it's an awful imposition.'

'Five,' said Anna quietly.

'Five? Who's the fifth person?' asked Jane.

'I've persuaded Eloise to come with me to care for the children, whilst I'm learning to be a physician,' replied Anna.

'Well, you seem to have got it all sorted,' said Jane in a bit of a huff. 'I'm glad you bothered to come round and tell us. I suppose everyone but us already knows.'

'Mother, don't be like that, it's all happened so quickly since yesterday. But I'm going to tell Max now, and then I'm going.'

'You could have stayed here, with us,' interjected Jane.

'That was my first thought Mother. I knew you'd help me, but I don't want to live so near Max and see him in my house and running my business. It would break my heart, knowing that Jack isn't going to inherit it. Believe me, it'll be for the best, mother.'

Jane sighed. 'Well, if you're sure. We'll just have to come and visit you on a regular basis, so that the children don't forget their grandparents.'

'I'd love that Mother. I'm so sorry that Father isn't here. Will he be back soon?'

'Yes, he's just gone to the forge. I'll send him round to you.

Anna went back home and found Max pacing in the Main Hall.

'Where've you been? I needed to talk to you,' he demanded.

'To see my parents,' Anna replied calmly. 'They only live next door.'

'That's handy,' said Max, 'you could move in next door and out of my hair. I don't intend providing for my father's bastards.'

Anna swallowed to keep her temper. 'I assure you they are not bastards,' she said icily. 'Your father's bastards, as you so delicately put it, live down the road in Gisburn. He was carrying on with her whilst he was married to me. There are three of them as well. Children that is. Four with the mother.' For once, Max looked stunned and it took all of Anna's energies not to laugh out loud.

'And by the way, I'll be leaving today. I will require the carriage and when I get to my destination, I'll return the carriage to you.'

'Why should you have the carriage? Can't you walk next door?'

Oh, the arrogance of this man, thought Anna, but she stayed calm.

'No, I can't, I'm going a lot further than next door. And neither can the children walk, your father's children, your half brother and sisters,' Anna emphasised.

Max nearly choked at that, but quickly renewed his attack.

'Well, you'll leave with nothing but the clothes you stand up in,' he said nastily.

'I assure you; I will take everything that is mine. I think that the law would be interested to know that you are throwing me and my children out of this house; neglecting your duties as Lord of the Manor. Lady Isabella in Lancaster would be especially interested to hear about it. She was very taken with young Jack and Isobelle when we visited, just before your father was taken ill. Indeed, Lord Henry has told me to carry on running the estate until young Jack grows up.' For once Max was speechless, and at that point, her father walked in.

'Anna, are you all right?' he asked tenderly.

'Perfectly, father. I was just informing Max about his duties and letting him know that I'll be leaving today and will require the carriage.'

'And I've come to tell you that I will be coming with you to your destination.'

'Will you father?' asked Anna, 'that will be so good for me.'

'Good,' said Max, 'and you can bring my carriage back, de Rexar. The sooner the better for all I care. Now where's the keys?'

'I'll give them to you as I leave,' replied Anna haughtily, 'and not before.' With that, Anna swept out of the room and up to her bedchamber. She hastily gathered all the children's clothes and toys and put them in large bags that usually had the spare bedding in. Next, she got her own belongings and asked Ethel to help her with the chest. Between them they carried it down to the Main Hall. Eloise had arrived back from her family by this time and hurriedly got her own things ready when she saw the piles of belongings in the Main Hall.

Richard went home to get overnight things and then Matthew brought the carriage round, and started loading it up.

'Where do you think you are taking that chest?' roared Max when he came into the Hall.

'Away with me,' replied Anna with similar force. 'This was a gift from my parents on the birth of Edwina.' Anna held her breath whilst this altercation was taking place. All her vast amount of money was in that chest. If she couldn't have that, she was sunk.

'Yes, it was a gift from us,' reinforced Richard, 'come on Matthew, give me a hand with it,' he said as the two of them loaded it on to the carriage. The sooner I get away the better, thought Anna. This man is worse than Jack, if that's possible. Eventually everything was loaded up and Anna made a great play of handing over the keys. She explained what each one was for, and then showed him the carefully written account books. She also told him that Matthew had done all the work in maintaining the accounts for the last year, and that he was very competent.

'Huh,' Max sneered, 'I bet he was. Kept you company did he, whilst he was feathering his own nest?'

'No, to both of those things,' said Anna with dignity, as she climbed on to the carriage with her father, Eloise and Isobelle. 'Good bye Max, and I hope you can live with yourself.'

Anna said a personal word to each of the staff and left, her head held high. They drove to the sisters and collected Edwina and Jack and set off. She had deliberately left them at the sisters until the last minute, as she didn't want them to witness any unpleasantness.

'We're going on a visit to see Aunty Judith,' said Anna, trying to keep her voice as light as she could. 'Grandfather is coming with us to make sure we are safe and Eloise is coming as well.'

'Oh goody,' chimed in both Jack and Edwina. 'Didn't want to stay at the sisters. We were doing sums,' said Jack mournfully. A boy after my own heart, reflected Anna as she laughed at them both. The carriage set off towards Pendle Hill and Anna looked back at the house as they left the village, which had given her the best of times and the worst of times. It had certainly changed her life whilst living in that house. Never mind she thought, turning towards Pendle Hill, look to the future, it could only get better.

Chapter 13

The journey was slow and plodding as the rain started nearly as soon as they set off. The children started bickering and falling out, despite Eloise doing her best to amuse them. They called at Tom the pedlar's sister's house on the way up Pendle Hill. She was glad to see Anna and provided some ale, bread and cheese for the travellers. It was also useful to visit her earth closet, particularly for the children.

Eventually, they arrived at Brun Lea, weary and wet, the children having fallen asleep by then. Judith's household looked as if it had settled down for the night, so Richard knocked tentatively on the door. After a while, Rupert answered the door, with Judith's voice being heard in the distance, asking who was calling at this hour.

'It's Master Richard and Miss Anna,' shouted Rupert, beaming at them all, 'and some others,' he added, not sure who they all were.

Judith arrived on the ground floor and was amazed to see the entourage.

'What are you all doing here at this time of night?'

Richard spoke first. 'It's Anna. She's in a terrible mess. Jack's son turned up and claimed the estate and was very nasty to Anna. He wanted her out of the house and refuses to provide for her and the children.'

'Oh Anna, that's terrible,' said Judith, 'but why are you here?'

'You once said if I needed you, you would be here for me. Well, I need you now,' said Anna in a small voice.

'You've come to stay?' asked Judith, trying not to sound too surprised.

'Yes please. And my children and my nursemaid. I've got money. I'll pay my way, but I want to learn how to be a physician. You did say I was too young before, and that I'd to go away and be married and have babies. Well, I've done all that. So now, can you teach me?' said Anna in a pathetic voice.

Judith swallowed, thinking about the enormity of all that Anna was asking. But one look at Anna's sad face made her mind up. How could she refuse her precious niece?

'Of course you can stay, Anna. All of you. Just come upstairs and we'll bed you down in the main hall tonight and sort everything out tomorrow.'

The look of sheer relief on Anna's face was enough to convince Judith that she had made the right decision.

'And who's this young woman?' asked Judith.

'This is Eloise. She is very good with the children, and I thought she could look after them, whilst you teach me to be a physician.'

'You've certainly thought of everything, Anna, and welcome Eloise,' laughed Judith. 'Come on, we'll get you all fed and watered upstairs and then talk tomorrow.'

Judith provided mattresses and blankets and after a meal, everyone settled down to sleep. Next morning, the children were up bright and early, wanting to explore their new surroundings. Rupert kept mixing the children's names up and they had great fun together. The children were amazed that they lived upstairs in this house, and that the animals lived downstairs. They were used to having the animals in the fields or stables, but Aunty Judith explained that it was a very old house, and that was how people lived in those days.

After breakfast, Judith set about sorting out rooms for the visitors, except for Richard, who was going home again the same day.

'It's a good job I've got plenty of bedchambers,' joked Judith.

'I am grateful to you, Aunty. Shall I go and buy new bedding for us all?'

'No, there is no need. I have plenty. And I think you can drop the aunty bit. Just call me Judith. It makes me feel old having a niece as old as you, with three children.'

'It doesn't seem right, it sounds like I'm taking advantage,' replied Anna.

'Not if I've told you to, it will make life much easier.'

Anna agreed, and went back to sorting things out for sleeping. For now, all three children were to go in one bedchamber together. Anna would have another bedchamber, next door to Judith, so that if Judith got called out to a case in the night, it was easy to wake Anna up, without disturbing the rest of the house. Eloise would have her own bedchamber next to the children, at the other end of the house so that she could have some privacy yet be near the children if they needed her.

The beds were all made up quickly, with Judith, Anna, Mary, Fanny and Aggie all working hard. They then sorted out some clothes chests so that everyone could have one each.

'Judith, I forgot to give you my money last night. I want you to have it all,' said Anna, rummaging in her children's clothes chest that she had brought with her. 'Here, there is lots of it. I made sure I left Max very little money in the house. I think I've earned a secure future for my children, and I've earned most of this money myself anyway, so I wasn't leaving it for him.' She tipped the money on to the bed, leaving Judith gasping.

'Anna, there is a fortune here,' said Judith.

'I know,' giggled Anna. 'If you can just pay Eloise's wages for me, you can have all the rest.'

'No Anna. You keep it. If ever I need it, I'll let you know. But some day, you may need to set up a home yourself and you'll need it then. I'll keep it safe for you, if you like?'

'Are you sure? That's so kind of you. Taking us all in and not taking any money off us.'

'Don't worry, Anna, I'll get my money out of you in work. Believe me, it's not an easy option training to be a physician. It will take at least three years for you to learn enough to satisfy the board in Lancaster.'

'Lancaster? Is that where you have to go to be examined?'

'Yes, but that's a long way off yet. Now, to more practical matters. If you pay Eloise her wages, I won't want another penny. How much do you pay her?'

Anna laughed. 'I told Eloise that I might not be able to pay her anything beyond bed and food, but she still wanted to come with me, as she said it would be an adventure living in a bigger town.'

'I wouldn't call Brun Lea a town, just a large village,' replied Judith.

'That's what I said, but compared to Ribbleside, I suppose it is an exciting metropolis,' laughed Anna. 'I'm sure she'll be ecstatic to get any money at all. By the way Judith, is there an abbey or convent in Brun Lea? I don't remember seeing one when I was here before.'

'No, there isn't. Why do you ask?'

'The children have enjoyed going to the sisters for their learning and I'd like that to continue.'

'No,' replied Judith. 'The nearest abbey is at Whalley, but I don't think they teach children. Besides, it's about ten miles from here, too far for them to go. Let me ask around and see what I can find.'

'I would be grateful. Both Edwina and Jack are bright and I wouldn't want them to lose their skills.'

'Right,' said Judith. 'Let's get down to work. I can see a patient coming up the road to see me, so let's go down into the back room. Go and check on the children and Eloise, to see if she has everything she needs, then join me in the back room.'

Anna did as she was told, then went outside to the special back room in the garden that Anna used to see her patients. As she entered, Anna was introduced to the patient, and told to sit down and listen. The patient had a cough, and after asking her some questions, Judith listened to the patient's chest by putting her ear on her back. Once satisfied that it was not too serious, Judith prescribed her a bottle of medicine containing lungwort leaves, which were good for people with breathing problems. She got a ready-made bottle off the shelf in the preparation room next door.

This room was lined with shelves that held all sorts of bottles, herbs and potions. There was a wooden table, with different sizes of pestle and mortar and a chopping block. Judith said that she would explain everything to Anna later, and just grasped the bottle off the shelf and gave it to the patient. The patient gave her a few small coins and left, after thanking her.

Several more patients came and went and Anna observed closely what Judith did with each patient, noted the questions that she asked, and watched how she examined them. When the last one had gone, Judith told Anna that for once, she had no visits to do, so they would spend time together outlining what her training would entail.

'First of all,' said Judith, 'I need to tell you about the different ways of becoming a physician. And also about the different types of medical people you might meet. As well as physicians, there are barber-surgeons. Now we have one in Brun Lea called Robert. And we are lucky, some are rogues but he's a good man, and we often work together, even though barber-surgeons don't have a very good reputation. Next year, I'll send you to work with him for a few weeks. It's important to see the whole picture of making people better.'

'Right,' said Anna, 'and will I learn to do surgery?'

'Yes, it may come in handy sometimes. Now, other people that you might meet are herbalists, midwives, and wise women. And if you're really unlucky, you might meet a witch!' laughed Judith. 'But all these people have their own role to play and sometimes we can help each other, so don't despise the other people who haven't got as much training or education as yourself. Well, except for the witches. Avoid them like the plague!'

'I've certainly met the midwife,' joked Anna, 'several times, although I couldn't quite see what she was doing as I was a little distracted at the time.'

'I suppose you were, but at least you're familiar with her work.'

'Yes,' replied Anna, 'I used to greatly admire her skill. She was very helpful in other cases as well as birthing.'

'They usually are, because people ask them to help with any illness. Now that leaves physicians. A lot of physicians train by going to university, and some maintain that that's the only way to learn the job, and are very precious about it. They don't think much of people like me.'

'But Judith, I couldn't go to university as a woman, could I?'

'Definitely not. Women will never be allowed to go to university. In this modern age, we are able to do many jobs the same as men, but university? No, that'll remain in the hands of the men for always. Like the church. Who would ever think of having a female priest?' The two women laughed together at the impossibility of women going to university or being priests.

'But how is the training different at university to what I'm going to learn?' asked Anna.

'A lot of it is based on the moon and stars, and their interaction with each other. Also the signs of the Zodiac. They do learn about patients and illnesses, and they study anatomy, but they don't have as much hands on experience similar to what you'll get here. And what possible cause could the sign of the Zodiac have on how an illness affects them? No, they look down on us, but we have much more practical knowledge than them, usually. Now the first thing I need to teach you is about the humours. You know about the four basic elements? '

'I think so, are they water, fire, earth and air?'

'Yes, that's right. Well at university, they teach that the four elements are mirrored in the four basic humours in the body. Those are choler, or yellow bile; phlegm; black bile and blood.'

'What's important about them?' asked Anna.

'The body has to keep these humours in balance or they become ill. But as a person gets older, the humours are more likely to be out of balance, along with miasmas and old age, so the person becomes sick,' replied Judith.

'Right. So how does the humour affect the person in sickness, then?'

'Well, if you take someone who has too much yellow bile, or choler, they become choleric in temperament. The same goes for phlegm, you become phlegmatic.'

'What about too much black bile?'

'That causes melancholia,' explained Judith, 'and too much blood can make you sanguine.' Anna thought these facts over carefully, and then asked another question.

'Did you say I'll need about three years to learn?'

'At least. I took three years, so you should be able to do it in the same period. In your final year, I'll send you to Lancaster where I trained. If you hadn't got the children, I'd have sent you there for the whole period.'

'It sounds rather daunting, Judith, but I'm very keen. I'm always going to have to provide for my children now so I need some kind of job, and this is the only one I'm interested in.'

'You don't know, you're still young, you may marry again.'

'Never,' said Anna forcefully. 'I would never be ruled by another man again. Marriage is not for me,' said Anna shuddering.

'Was your experience so awful, dear one?'

'Yes, it was. But that's behind me now, and all I want is to learn what I can from you.'

'Good. I'll remind you of this when you are tired and weary and don't want to get out of bed in the middle of the night,' laughed Judith.

Anna pulled a face. 'Mmm, you might be right about that,' she laughed. 'But I've had lots of experience getting up in the middle of the night with the children, so I might manage all right,' she added.

'Now let's go and eat, then we'll see what the children have been doing,' said Judith as they went back into the house.

The next day, the training began in earnest. Anna had to learn all about urine. 'Much can be learnt from the urine, Anna, it's the window of the body. Everything that passes through the body ends up being passed in the urine or the stool, so it can tell you what's going on in the inside of the body. Do you remember the first patient we saw today? He complained of reddish urine. Now that's a bad sign, usually when the urine is red, it means that there is some bleeding going on where it shouldn't be. It's often a sign that death will occur, sooner or later.'

'But you didn't say that to the patient,' said Anna.

'Of course not. You don't want to frighten him. Sometimes, it goes away again and this could happen, but in old men like him, it usually doesn't. Medicine is a waiting game a lot of the time. And a guessing game as well.'

'So why did you tell him to drink plenty of ale?'

'Well sometimes, it seems to flush the blood out, but sometimes it doesn't work. At least he'll be happy, even if it doesn't work,' laughed Judith.

'That's true, I suppose. And what can you tell from the stool?'

Much the same. Whether it is loose or hard; frequent or infrequent; blood present or not; pale or dark; too smelly or not. Different descriptions mean different diseases. See, if it is loose and smelly, it could be the bloody flux and often the patient will die, but sometimes they recover. There's a lot we don't know. We just know that there's some element that we're missing; that we don't know about yet, so we just have to go on our findings and previous knowledge.'

'Yes, it's funny, isn't it? How two people in a family can have the same disease and one will die from it but the other will get better.'

'Precisely. Look how ill you were when you had the fever as a little girl. It killed your grandmother, yet you survived, eventually. It was a worrying time for your parents and all of us. We thought you would die.'

'Yet I didn't. It is strange, isn't it?' commented Anna.

'Perhaps God had plans for you, so He had to save you. Perhaps you are going to be a famous physician, some day,' teased Judith.

'I don't want to be famous, just to have enough money to feed my children,' replied Anna.

'It will give you an income, but it won't make you very rich, not unless you can become a physician to lords and ladies or royalty. And for that you need to have gone to a university. So no hope for us mere women!' laughed Judith. 'Come on, let's go and eat, then afterwards you can study some of my own books and notes that I learnt from.'

They went back into the house to find a riotous meal taking place. The children were making everyone laugh and Anna and Judith joined in the fun. Anna was secretly pleased to see them so happy. They had adjusted well to their new home and seemed to have no after effects of the difficult days they'd had prior to their move.

Anna's training continued and she learned far more about urine than she could ever have thought there was to know. Thick urine, urine with gravel in it, smelly urine and many other combinations, and what the implications were. And the same went for the stools.

After four weeks, Judith came home from a visit looking very pleased with herself.

'I think I've found the answer to your problem of the children not going to the sisters,' she said over the evening meal. 'You know the man I went to see whose wife died three weeks ago? Well, he was saying that he feels as though he needs something to do. Nursing his wife took up all of his time and now he's got nothing to do.'

'Yes, but what's that got to do with the children?' asked Anna.

'He was a tutor to the children in a Manor House some miles away, but had to give up the job when his wife became poorly. They moved back here to be near her family, and he doesn't think he'll be able to get another job, because of his age.'

'And does he take pupils?' asked Anna eagerly.

'He hasn't done before, but I told him about your three, and he seemed quite interested. Quite put a bit of life back into his eyes. What do you think?'

'Sounds a good idea. Why don't you ask him round to meet them? He might change his mind when he's met this lot, especially if Jack is on form,' quipped Anna.

'I already have done. He's coming tonight.'

'That was quick. You don't waste time, do you?'

'Well I know that it's something that's been bothering you.'

'It had, I'll look forward to meeting him.'

The evening went well, the children for once, were on their best behaviour, although kept giggling when they first saw him, as he had an enormous wart on the side of his nose. He was a tall middle-aged man, with neat grey hair, and slim of build. He readily agreed to give Edwina and Jack their lessons, and would take Isobelle on as well when she got old enough.

The children loved his lessons. They thought that it was far more interesting than the sisters, as Master Elliott made learning fun. He even got Jack to become interested in maths; truly a major miracle, said Anna when she heard.

Lessons continued apace for both the children and their mother, and soon Judith was letting Anna examine patients first, then asking her opinion in the preparation room before she said anything to the patient. Judith was pleased with her able student and told her how delighted she was to discuss patients with her, as that had been difficult in the past, when she worked alone.

Lessons in herbal medicine moved on apace as well, although Anna wasn't too keen about having to grind some of the herbs and plants. She said it was too much like grinding the barley for the ale. Judith taught her which herb was for which illness, and stressed on her the importance of using spring or boiled water when distilling medicine or tisanes.

'Why special water,' asked Anna.

'It works better and patients seem to get better quicker than when you use river water. Nobody is sure why, but if you think what goes in to the river, you can probably guess. As well as the animal and human excrement, there are also the dyes used in preparing woollen dyes and other chemical processes.'

'Yes, I suppose it must be full of everything. We were lucky at Ribbleside as we had a lot of streams coming into the River Ribble, not to mention the well that was in our garden.' The lesson continued, whilst the two of them prepared medicines from the herbs, carefully measuring the amounts of each herb that went into the liquid and adding some sweet substance, usually honey, to make the medicine palatable.

A year passed quickly and Judith decided to give Anna a test. Anna wasn't very pleased, but the children thought it was hilarious. After some feverish studying, Anna passed the test with ease and Judith congratulated her on completing her first year. Anna reflected how quickly the last year had gone, but also how happy she had been. She seemed to have absorbed so many facts into her brain, but it only made her hungry for more. She couldn't wait to begin her second year.

Chapter 14

In her second year, amongst other things, Anna learnt the art of bloodletting, which Judith explained was often called phlebotomy. She had watched Judith many times, but now it was her turn.

'What if it doesn't stop bleeding when I don't want any more blood?' asked a worried Anna.

'Just keep pressure on the wound, it'll stop eventually,' replied Judith.

'But what if it doesn't?' persisted Anna.

'Oh, don't worry, the patient will just bleed to death; nothing serious,' said Judith with a sober face.

'Judith, don't tease me. What would I do?'

'I've never had that happen so stop worrying unduly. You would lift the arm or leg up, wherever you had taken the blood from, and keep pressing hard,' reassured Judith. 'Now for goodness sake, don't tell the patient that it's your first time. They might run away!'

'Right, I'll remember all that,' said Anna nervously, but when she had to do it, although frightened, she'd watched Judith so many times, that she just mimicked her and released a bowl full of blood, without the patient even suspecting that it was her first time.

Afterwards, the two women discussed the procedure and Judith checked her knowledge.

'Why did we decide to take blood for this patient?' Judith asked.

'Because he had a lot of unhealthy blood due to a fever.'

'And would we have taken blood if he was an old man?'

'No,' replied Anna.

'Why not?'

'Because he would be too weak to start with.'

'Good. And who else would we not take blood from?'

'Anyone under the age of twelve; er let me see,' thought Anna out loud, 'oh yes, a newly delivered woman, or someone who bleeds excessively.'

'Good,' said Judith. 'Some physicians would also say not to take blood when the moon is full, but to wait until afterwards. And what are the benefits of bloodletting?' Judith asked.

'It clears the mind, strengthens the memory, warms the marrow, rids the blood of poisonous matters, dispels torpor, promotes digestion,' said Anna in a sing-song voice. Judith laughed.

'I thought you were going to burst into song there,' said Judith. 'Is that how you learnt them?'

'Yes,' said Anna sheepishly, 'how did you do it?'

'Much the same way,' admitted Judith. 'There are more benefits, but you've done quite well there. Now, if the patient had a sore vein afterwards, what can you do?'

'Rub a leaf of rue boiled in laurel oil and place where the wound is.'

'Yes,' said Judith, 'but what else could you use?'

Anna thought for a minute. 'Oh yes, I remember, boil a bean in wine until it dissolves, add as much grease as is necessary, then bind it hot on to the arm in a cloth.'

'And when are the best days of all for bloodletting?'

'The Feast of St Valentine in February and the Feast of St Lambert in September.'

'You've learned your lessons well, Anna.'

'I've had a good teacher,' replied Anna smiling.

Towards the end of her second year, Judith sent Anna to work with Robert, the barber-surgeon. This was a totally different experience to the work that she had seen with Judith. Robert lived near the market place and welcomed Anna into his shop. He was cutting hair, the first time she saw him.

'Good morning, Mistress de Ribbleside,' Robert said formally. He was a big jovial man, who looked as though he was fond of food judging by his girth, and had a ruddy complexion.

'Good morning barber,' replied Anna equally formally.

'Do you want to learn how to cut hair as well?' he said with a twinkle in his eye.

'It would come in useful, especially having three young children.'

'Three young children? She don't look old enough, does she?' he asked his client, who shook his head. 'Well come and stand along of me, then you can learn this as well as being a surgeon.'

'Are you learning to be a physician, then?' asked the client.

'Yes, I'm working with my aunt Judith, here in Brun Lea.'

'A good woman, your aunt,' he replied.

'She certainly is, she took me in when I'd nowhere to go and now she's teaching me a trade.'

Robert was finishing the man's haircut, so the man stood up and wished Anna 'God speed' and went on his way.

'Now Mistress, where shall I start. Do you think you'd like to be a barber-surgeon?' asked Robert.

'I'm quite enjoying learning to be a physician, but Judith says that you two work together very well, so I need to learn what you do, so that we can complement each other,' replied Anna.

'She said that about me, did she? Well, that's nice,' said Robert looking pleased with himself. 'Well, I've got a juicy start for you. I've got an old woman who has a festering boil that wants lancing. Not squeamish are you?'

'Not after three children and nearly two years as a physician apprentice,' Anna laughed.

'Good. We'll go and sort it out later. First it's breakfast time. We'll go to the Lamb Inn across the road and get us some food.' Anna followed him to the hostelry but declined breakfast, having already eaten at home.

Robert tucked into a large plate full of ham and eggs, swilled down with a mug of ale. 'Just one mug of ale thanks,' he told the landlord, 'got a job to do today. Need a steady hand,' then the two of them roared at what he'd said.

'You know never to have your haircut after supper time don't you, Mistress?' asked the landlord. 'You'd get a curl in your hair that shouldn't be there,' he added.

'You don't do too badly out of my earnings, landlord, I spend most of them here,' replied Robert. The two men were obviously old friends, thought Anna. She could see how important food and drink was to both of them.

Once replete, Robert took Anna to a small hut behind the church. It was dark and dismal inside. The old lady lay on a mattress in front of the fire, which was in the centre of the single room. There was a hole in the roof to let the smoke from the fire out, and wooden shutters instead of windows. The boil was on the side of her neck, and it was painful for her to move her head at all. Robert lit a candle that he had brought with him from the fire.

'First job is to get some light, so that you can see what you are doing. Next is to wash your hands, then wash the bit you are going to cut. Next get your blade, and slice through the centre of the boil. Like that, see?' Anna nodded. The pus started oozing out and Robert helped it by squeezing around the sides. When he was satisfied that he had got all the pus out, he wiped it again, then put a piece of linen over it, with a light bandage round that to hold it in place. 'Now keep that bandage in place for three days, and then I'll see you again,' ordered Robert. He gathered his tools up and they left the hut and went back to Robert's shop.

'What would you charge for lancing a boil?' asked Anna.

'Depends how rich they are,' laughed Robert. 'The richer they are, the more it costs.'

'So how much will you charge the old lady?'

'A mug of ale, if she can afford it, otherwise nothing. She's an old widow and poor. I make my money with my haircuts and the richer patients.'

During the next few weeks, Anna learnt a lot about surgery. Robert performed far more operations than Anna had ever imagined, some quite delicate. Eventually, he let her have a try at simple operations, such as lancing boils and sewing wounds up. She also assisted him in bigger operations of amputations or removing tumours.

The worst case that Anna saw was of a small boy who had been savaged by a wolf. Fortunately for the boy, a huntsman came past and killed the wolf and the boy only lost his arm. Amazingly, the boy survived.

Robert even taught Anna to cut hair during quiet spells, and let her cut her children's hair, which caused great frivolity between

161

them all. One day, both aspects of his work were quiet, so Anna asked him about his training.

'Where did you come from, Robert.'

'I was brought up in the country, a village not unlike Brun Lea, but I ended up in York. That's where I learnt my trade.'

'What made you come back to village life, then?'

'I didn't like York.'

'Why not? It's one of our major cities. I love York. I love going to the mystery plays at Easter.'

'Ah, but do you actually visit York, or nearby?' asked Robert.

'No, I suppose we don't go in to York very often. We came from Rexar, just outside York, but my mother's family came from York.'

'Well, all the cities I've been in have too many people in them. Houses are cramped up together, most of them have no gardens, there is no spring water available, the streets and rivers are like stinking pools, and because no one has access to fresh water, they don't seem to wash. They are dirty, some of those people. Have you ever been down the Shambles when you're in York, where all the meat is slaughtered? No, I thought not,' he replied, when Anna shook her head, 'it stinks to high heaven down there; all the blood and guts run down the middle of the street. Awful,' he added with feeling.

Anna sat reflecting on what he had just said. She supposed that when she visited her family, they lived in a better standard of housing, so weren't like the people or places Robert was describing.

'And was that the only reason you moved back here?'

'No, I lost my wife and child to plague, and I wandered around for a while, quite lost.'

'I'm sorry,' said Anna quickly, 'I'm being nosy again. I just love finding out about people and forget myself sometimes.'

'Don't worry, I'm used to people asking. I ended up here by accident really. I was making my way to Lancaster to volunteer for the King's army, when I stayed the night at the Lamb Inn. One of the barmaids had a festering finger, and I managed to sort it out for her, and I just sort of stayed.'

162

'Do you regret staying here?' asked Anna, still unable to resist asking questions.

'No, because, would you believe it, people get better quicker here. They don't die as often as they would do in a city. I'm sure it has something to do with clean water, no overcrowding and having a garden.'

'You're probably right. Someday you might write a learned paper about that and make your fortune,' laughed Anna.

'You never know, lass, you never know, but I don't think so really,' he laughed with her. And then a man entered the shop, wanting a haircut and the private interlude was brought to a close. But it made Anna have a deeper respect for Robert after that, knowing that he too, had suffered in his life, albeit in different ways to her.

On returning to work with Judith, Anna enthused about what she had learnt with Robert.

'I'm not going to lose my apprentice, am I?' asked Judith.

'No, I prefer your sort of work, but I would like to do some surgery.'

Judith smiled in reply, 'If you work in a village where there is no barber-surgeon, you might have to do both. I think it's strange that the two professions are divided. Probably in the future they will just be one post of physician and surgeon combined.'

'That would be more interesting I think. I hope it does come soon. By the way, you mentioned me working in another village. Do you not see me working here with you?'

'There may not be enough work for both of us. Besides, the people here all know that you are newly trained, so it's probably better to go somewhere new. But you've still a year to go yet, so don't worry,' replied Judith. 'And I've got a surprise for you.'

'Oh what is it?' asked Anna eagerly.

'Won't be a surprise if I tell you,' replied Judith.

As they went back into the house, Anna saw Tom the pedlar's horse and cart outside. She went inside to welcome him.

'Tom, how good to see you. What have you got for us today?' she asked.

'All my usual trinkets, Mistress de Ribbleside, but also a message.'

'Who from?'

'Your parents. They said to tell you that they are coming to stay with you at Christmas for a few days.'

'Oh thank you, that's good news indeed. I've hardly seen them since I moved here. They've only managed a few short visits. The children will be delighted.'

'I'll tell your parents that you await them eagerly,' replied Tom, 'next time I go to Ribbleside.'

'Thanks, now let me look at what you have. Isobelle seems to lose ribbons every week.' Anna asked after some of the people in Ribbleside, but the arrival of the children put paid to any more conversation as they clambered all over Tom and asked to see his wares. Anna allowed them to have a small coin each to spend and they took quite a time deciding what they would have. Once the children were satisfied with their wares, Tom was given some food and drink, before setting off to his next port of call.

The news of Richard and Jane's visits seemed to cheer the whole household up and Christmas was eagerly awaited. In the weeks coming up to Christmas, Anna started going to see patients on her own, or taking sessions in the back room whilst Judith was out visiting. It was a measure of how much Judith trusted her, as she saw a real improvement in Anna's knowledge of disease and treatments, and her ability to diagnose correctly.

One of her patients needed a purgative and Anna chose linseed fried in fat as she found it better than using mallow leaves in ale. She instructed the patient as to what would happen and advised him to sit near an earth closet or pot. If that didn't work, she would try an enema of mallow, honey, salt and soap, but she didn't tell the patient that. Time enough when he needed it. Hopefully the purgative would cure him.

It felt so good to have her own patients. On returning home, she discussed the case with Judith, and was pleased at the praise Judith gave her. How she loved her new work; she enjoyed helping people and using her new found knowledge, and knew that this was what she wanted to do for the rest of her life.

Christmas was a time of great fun for all the family. Judith went to great lengths to make it a very special festivity. It was exactly opposite to all the Christmases that Anna had spent with Jack. A great Yule log was brought in, holly and ivy was picked to decorate the home, mummers came to the house to perform their traditional activities, carols singers visited, and Judith brought a swan home for the meal on Christmas Day.

The day started early, with a visit to church and then preparing the food, whilst games were played with the children. They had invited Mr Elliott to come and join them and he seemed to take great delight in being with the family. The swan was roasted to perfection, and eaten with cooked vegetables and bread, washed down with a bottle of the finest wine imaginable, which Mr Elliott had brought for them.

The servants thoroughly enjoyed being part of the family Christmas and eating with them on this special day, although those that had family locally were sent home with a basketful of food for their families and told to stay at home for three days.

Anna also enjoyed having her parents at Judith's, and she spent many hours talking to them, when the children were in bed. For their part, they were so relieved to see Anna happy and fulfilled in her work, and were glad that she had found her calling, and yet the children weren't being neglected, as both Mr Elliott and Eloise took the greatest care of them.

Their brief visit was over all too soon, and they returned home, leaving the household a little deflated, especially when the snows came down and getting about was difficult. Eloise decided that she was going to learn how to sew better, as she found time on her hands when the children were with Mr Elliott. Judith and Anna encouraged her in this, as neither of them was very good at sewing.

Robert, the barber-surgeon, reminded Anna about the old lady who had had her boil lanced. She was the finest seamstress in Brun Lea, so Eloise had lessons with her once the snow had cleared. The first thing she made was a new black cloak for Anna, which was made in a much tougher weave of wool than her velvet one, more suited to withstanding the sharp easterly winds that tore about the village at times, and more practical than her other one.

Anna's training intensified during this final year of her training. She spent time with the local midwife and gained a lot of experience of normal and not so normal births. Judith felt that this would be a useful part of the training for her future. Anna also spent time with the local herbalist and learnt more about the herbs that occur naturally, but can be used in healing.

Another week was spent at the local leper colony as this was a large part of Judith's work, and it was important for Anna to be able to recognise the early symptoms of leprosy, and any treatment that might delay the hideousness of the disease. Whilst it was distressing for Anna to see the malformations that the patients had sustained during their illness, it also humbled her to see the dedication of their helpers, who were all at risk of developing the diseases themselves. Mostly, she noticed, the helpers were monks or nuns.

In the Spring, Anna was despatched off to Lancaster to stay with the de Caton family for a month, where Judith had done her training. Although sad at having to leave the children behind, Anna learnt a great deal whilst she was there. She met different types of patients and saw different diseases and treatments.

Being a port, Lancaster had many fishermen who got hooks caught in their hands, or were nearly drowned in the sea. She also saw people from other countries, which intrigued her with their different ways and languages.

Also, the market had far more exciting foods, especially the spices and fruits and Anna decided that she would take lots of food home with her. Soon it was time for her to go home again to Brun Lea. Mister de Caton was pleased with Anna's progress, and offered his house to her for when she came to be examined. The faithful Rupert came to collect her and soon she was back home, to see her children.

As with all children, they were more interested in seeing what she had brought them as presents, than answering her questions about what they had been doing or what they had learnt. But they were glad to see her, and she them. The evening meal was noisy as each child tried to tell Anna something that they had remembered.

The routine soon took over and the final months of her training sped by. Because the two women were often going out on visits in different directions, they found another man to chaperone Anna when Rupert was with Judith. His name was Stephen. He was a village youth, with a shock of curly hair that the other boys teased him about, and most of the girls were jealous of. But Stephen proved to be as reliable as Rupert, and was happy to work on a part-time basis as his father had quite a large plot of land with his cottage, and Stephen was expected to work on it.

Anna spent a lot of time revising her knowledge but also working with the patients and with Judith to get even more experience. The week of the examinations loomed. With her head bursting with facts, Anna set off, with Judith and Rupert to Lancaster again. Judith was happy to renew acquaintance with the de Caton family and caught up on all their news. Anna stayed in the bedchamber; her head in her notes.

Finally, the day of the examination came. The examiners were all men and Anna worried if they would be prejudiced against her because she was a woman, but they didn't make any mention of it, for which Anna was glad. Anna was put through her paces, and although it was a long session, she was able to hold her own and answer all the questions. After the practical sessions on being a physician, Anna was asked about her knowledge of anatomy. She even managed to answer some questions on the stars and the planets, but not as thoroughly as the other questions. Their question about the different types of plague was easy for Anna to answer, as she had only studied this the night before.

Next, Judith had to appear before the examiners and explain how she had taught Anna, and what practical experience she had been given. The final part of the examination was that Anna had to discuss some of the cases that she had managed and treated herself, and what the outcome had been. Then they gave her some scenarios and asked her how she would manage the patient with those particular symptoms. She was then asked to leave the room.

After a long nail-biting wait, Anna was called back into the room with Judith. Judith was asked a final question as to whether she thought that Anna was capable of being a physician. Judith replied in the affirmative and the examiners agreed that they too felt that Anna could be a physician. Anna let out a sigh of relief. All the hard years of work were over. She had made it. She was a fully qualified physician, like Judith.

The clerk made out a certificate and the examiners signed it. Anna looked at the writing on it, and was thankful that she had learnt Latin with the sisters, as she realised it was in that language. But at the bottom of the scroll, it had her name and the date, September 26th in the Year of our Lord 1345.

Going back to the de Caton's house, there was a great time of rejoicing and Mistress de Caton had made a special meal for them all.

'What would you have done if I hadn't passed?' quipped Anna.

'We had every confidence in you, after what Judith told us and from how you performed when you were here. Besides, if you'd failed, it would have been a commiseration meal,' laughed Master de Caton in reply. They celebrated long into the night and Master de Caton was glad that he had got his deputy to be in charge for that night, as he was in no fit state to ride a horse, never mind to treat a patient.

Next day, Anna, Judith and Rupert returned to Brun Lea, after visiting the market to buy more of the exotic spices that weren't always available in Brun Lea. They thanked the de Catons and set off back through the Trough of Bolland, to get to Brun Lea.

On arrival home, Jane and Richard were waiting for them. They wanted to know how Anna had fared with the examiner. So it was even more celebrations at Brun Lea. The children were very excited; little Isobelle wasn't really sure what was going on, but was happy just the same.

The following day, Robert called round with a little bouquet of flowers for Anna, to celebrate her success at the examiners. More celebrations resulted after that, as Judith invited him and Mr Elliott to come and dine that night. Jane and Richard had decided to go home, as Richard needed to go to the wool markets, so it was a smaller party than the night before.

'So what are your grand plans, now, Mistress Physician Anna?' asked Robert. 'Are you staying with Judith and working together?'

Anna and Judith looked at each other. Judith spoke first.

'Actually, we think that Anna might look round to find work in a different town or village. There may not be enough for all three of us to do, Robert.'

'Mm, I suppose not,' replied Robert.

'Will you go back to Ribbleside?' asked Mr Elliott.

'No, definitely not, I wouldn't want to go near Max de Ribbleside ever again,' said Anna with feeling. 'My mother tells me he is every bit as bad as Jack was and I couldn't live like that. No, I shall look further afield, but there is no hurry, I don't think Judith is throwing me out yet,' she laughed.

'I might just,' quipped Judith back.

'Oh,' said Robert meaningfully, without explaining it further.

'Oh what?' they all asked.

'It's just that I heard last week that the barber-surgeon in Colne has died and they don't have a physician at all.'

'Where's Colne?' asked Anna.

'About six miles down the valley, beyond Marsden. It's set on a hill, with a pretty little church. It's not as big as Brun Lea, but bigger than Ribbleside,' answered Judith. 'Anna, that might be the ideal place for you to go. It's fairly near here, so that we can keep in touch, and far enough away from Ribbleside to avoid Max, but not too far for your parents to come to. It might be worth having a visit over there and see the priest or Lord of the Manor.'

'But I'm not a barber-surgeon,' replied Anna.

'No,' said Robert, 'but you have learnt quite a bit with me and you could do the simple things and then build your reputation as a physician from that.'

169

Anna thought about it for a while, and then nodded. 'Yes, that sounds an ideal solution. Eloise? How do you fancy a move to Colne?'

'Sounds fun to me,' replied Eloise, 'is it still in Lancashire?'

'Only just,' said Mr Elliott. 'It's almost in Yorkshire. Right on the boundary.'

'Then let's go to Colne,' replied Eloise. 'It might be the start of a new adventure.'

'Oh you and your adventures,' laughed Anna, 'it's only been hard work since we came here. We haven't had many adventures.'

'Well, perhaps we will in Colne,' replied Eloise, not to be outdone, and everybody laughed.

'Perhaps we could ask Stephen if he will come and work for you on a permanent basis if you move to Colne, Anna,' suggested Judith, 'you can't really trail round a strange village without some protection. Not until people know who you are.'

'That's a good idea,' said Anna, 'do you think he will come?'

'I'm sure he'd like an adventure as well,' said Eloise, just a trifle too quickly.

'Oh, you do, do you, Eloise?' asked Anna with interest.

'I was just saying he might,' said Eloise blushing.

'Would you like to ask him for me, then?' asked Anna.

'I could do,' said Eloise earnestly. 'Shall I go now?'

'No,' laughed Anna, 'wait until tomorrow. It'll depend on his father anyway, and whether he can release him permanently.'

'Oh,' said Eloise a little crestfallen, 'I'll ask him tomorrow then, when I go to market.'

'Thank you Eloise. I'm sure you'll be able to persuade him to come with me,' said Anna, trying not to laugh.

'I will try,' replied Eloise seriously, at which everyone burst into laughter, and Eloise decided it was time for the children to go to bed, and left the room hastily, shooing the children along in front of her.

'Well, well, well,' said Anna, 'looks like we might have a romance there.'

'Only time will tell,' replied Judith.

As it happened, Anna didn't go straight to visit Colne as there was an outbreak of dysentery in Brun Lea and because it was an extremely cold winter, there were also a lot of people with bad chests. The two physicians were extremely busy and so it was late February before Anna got a chance to go and see Colne. She took Eloise with her, now that Isobelle was feeling very grown up and having lessons with Mr Elliott, along with Edwina and Jack.

It was indeed a pretty village, set on a hill. Anna couldn't see Pendle Hill from the town, but she knew that she wasn't far away from it. She and Eloise liked what they saw. They visited the priest at the church and he told her that they still had no physician or barber-surgeon and would be grateful for anyone who came to the village.

Anna asked if there were any properties for rent and the priest took her to a land agent for the local Lord of the Manor who had several properties to rent. The first two were little larger than cottages, so Anna explained that she hoped to be the physician and would ideally like a more substantial building, which had some sort of room or out-building that she could use to see her patients and make up her prescriptions.

'I've got just the building,' said the man. 'It's up the hill from the church and set back from the main pathway through the village. He showed them a brick built building, that was two stories high, but it had a small side extension of one storey. It also had a large garden at the back, which would be good for the children to play in, and where Anna could grow vegetables and have chickens.

'This used to be an hostelry,' he explained, 'but it's fallen into disrepair. The small side building would be useful for your patients, as it has a separate entrance from the main house. I must say, we could really do with a physician.'

'How much do you think it would cost to repair the house?'

'Not much, as the landlord still lives in the town and has a bigger hostelry, so it'd be up to him to get it into reasonable repair. If you are interested, I could take you round to see him now.'

'Yes please,' replied Anna.

They set off back down the hill and turned into a large, busy hostelry. The landlord was very happy to know that someone wanted to rent his building and agreed very reasonable terms for the year. Happy with their days work, Anna and Eloise returned home to Brun Lea, excitedly telling everyone about what they had seen. Anna couldn't wait to get started in her new job and Eloise couldn't wait to start her new adventures.

Chapter 15

Two months later, just after Easter, Anna, Eloise, Stephen and the children piled a cart high with all their possessions and set off for their new home. Edwina and Jack were excited about their new home, but Anna suspected that that was mainly due to Eloise's infectious gaiety about the new move and the adventures they may have.

As they were leaving, Judith gave her the pile of money that she had brought with her when she had escaped from Max de Ribbleside.

'Here take this, you'll need it,' said Judith.

'You've kept it all this time without touching it?'

'Yes, and I've added a little to it as well, to pay you for your work during the winter. You'll need it to get started before the people start paying for your services.'

'Thank you, you are so good to me. And thank you also for all the bedding and clothes chests that you have given me.'

'I could have given you some tables and chairs as well.'

'I don't need any, truly. There are plenty of good enough tables, chairs and beds in the old hostelry for me to use.'

'Take care, Anna, and I hope you will be very happy, not only in your profession, but also in your private life, too. Don't forget to bring the children to see me sometimes.'

'I won't. I will never be able to thank you for all you did for me. By taking me in, letting me bring my children, and for training me. I couldn't have done it without your help.'

'I have enjoyed it. All of it. And I shall miss you. And the noise,' she laughed, as the two of them were getting quite tearful.

The only thing that Anna hadn't sorted out was another tutor for the children. There was no abbey in Colne either. She had tried to persuade Mr Elliott to come and live with them, but he declined, saying he would prefer to stay in Brun Lea, smiling at Judith. Goodness, thought Anna, is there romance there too? The rapidity of Stephen's agreeing to come to Colne was directly due to the influence of Eloise, Anna knew now, but not Judith as well? Well, why not? She was still only middle-aged and they were both widowers. What was happening to everyone, thought Anna. I'm being left behind in love, but after her experience with Jack she wasn't really bothered and wasn't looking for love for herself.

The cart set off and they made their slow way over to Colne, the children singing songs with Eloise for most of the way. When they arrived, Anna was pleased to see that the whole place had been cleaned up and a fire lit. In the annexe, there was a small table and three chairs, which would be ideal for seeing patients. There were also two back rooms to the extension where she would make one room for prescribing and preparation of medicines. She put all the stock that Judith had given her in one of the back rooms, the second back room was going to be for Stephen to sleep in, and then he would be handy if patients came to see Anna in the night.

The large area of the hostelry was going to be their main hall and kitchen. The side room was going to be the solar, and Anna found another room at the back. It was probably where the kitchen had been, or a rest room for the landlord when it was quiet.

Eloise and Anna concentrated on making the beds, whilst Stephen showed himself to be quite adept at making a meal, albeit it was only one that Aggie had made for them, and needed warming up. After the meal, he took the children out to explore, whilst Anna and Eloise sorted bedchambers out.

Edwina had already claimed hers. She found the biggest one upstairs and said that it was hers, as she was the oldest. Not to be outdone, Jack claimed the next biggest, which left Isobelle choosing a little one, that was over the front door, which she said she liked best anyway. Having been an inn, there were plenty of bedchambers, so there was no problem. Eventually, Eloise chose a bedchamber near to Isobelle and left Anna to choose her own.

Anna decided to have the room downstairs behind the main hall as her bedchamber, so that it would be easier for Stephen to get her in the night, if there was an emergency, rather than waking the entire household up. Also she would be able to hear the door if people knocked in the night.

Eventually they all got to bed and fell asleep immediately. Anna reflected as she fell asleep that this was her first real house, and her first real job. As soon as she was accepted in the village, life would be wonderful. She couldn't wait.

Next morning, she sent Stephen off to buy some chickens and some feed for them. He offered to take the children with him, for which Anna and Eloise were very grateful. They were able to go in to the village and buy provisions, to keep them going for the first few days, although Judith had given them a lot of goods to start them off with.

It gave them chance to meet the new people and tell them that Anna was a physician, too. They were also able to see which villagers had trades to offer or goods for sale. Anna found a carpenter and asked him to come and put some shelves in the back room for her medicines. They bought a good supply of butter, to supplement that which they had brought with them, and found out where the miller was situated, for when they wanted any heavy grinding doing.

Next they visited the priest's house, to tell him that they had now moved in, and to ask what time the services were held on Sundays and during the week, too. He seemed quite friendly, more so than the one in Ribbleside or Brun Lea. Anna decided to ask him about a tutor for the children.

'Do you mean someone who will come to the house to teach your sons?'

'Yes, but I want them to teach my daughters as well,' replied Anna. 'Do you know of anyone?'

'Your daughters? That is quite unusual. What makes you want your daughters educated?'

'Because we lived in a village where we had a convent, and they were a teaching order. They taught all the children, rich and poor, male and female. Besides, I'm an educated woman, and so I would like my daughters to be educated like me,' said Anna, with just a little edge to her voice.

'Good for you,' replied the priest. 'I wish other parents felt the same as you. As it happens, I would be happy to teach all your children. They could come to the church house each morning.'

'That's good,' said Anna relaxing somewhat, 'when do you want them to start?'

'On Monday?'

'That would be fine. And please could you tell me how much you charge for teaching?'

'I'll think about that over the weekend. It's given me an idea that I've long been mulling over in my mind. Shall we say Monday morning, after breakfast?'

'Yes, and I'll send them with a snack to eat for midday. Shall I send enough food for you as well, so that you won't have to break off and prepare something for yourself?' asked Anna.

'That would be very gracious of you, thank you,' replied the priest, 'until Monday then.'

'We'll be seeing you on Sunday, won't we?' enquired Anna.

'Oh yes, you'll be at mass, I hope. Until Sunday then,' replied the priest.

Well pleased with her meeting, Anna set off back home with Eloise, only to find Stephen waiting for her.

'Mistress, the local candle maker is here waiting for you. His wife has been in labour for many hours and the local midwife can't help her anymore. Can you come?'

'Yes, where do they live?'

'Not far away, across from the market square. I've got your bags ready.'

'Where's the man?'

'I've sent him back and told him to get some hot water ready.'

'Well done, Stephen. I can see you're going to be a great help to me. Come on, let's go.' As they hurried through the village, Anna told Stephen that it was always a good thing to tell a family to get some hot water ready, as she almost always needed it. Besides, she said, it gave the family something to do instead of rushing around and panicking.

As they approached the door of the cottage, Anna heard a shriek coming from the back room. She followed the direction of the cry.

An elderly middle-aged lady was encouraging the girl to push but she was getting tired and her cries were going weaker. The girl was tiny and the big mound of baby looked enormous compared to her size.

'Glad you've got here,' said the midwife, 'can't get her to push it out. Think it's stuck somewhere.'

'Let me have a look,' said Anna, moving the midwife to one side. She quickly examined the woman and realised that the baby's head had not engaged into the birth canal at all and no amount of pushing would get it out.

'It's lying across the abdomen, instead of head first. I'll have to try and turn it inside.' The midwife nodded, and watched Anna at her work. Anna tried to push the baby back up into the abdomen and turn it, so that it was coming head first. She managed to get the baby turned, but it wouldn't come down the birth canal.

'Is this the girl's first baby?' asked Anna tersely.

'Yes,' replied the midwife.

Anna shook her head slowly at the midwife and whispered that the head wouldn't engage, so the baby couldn't be delivered. She felt the girl's pulse; it was rapid and thready.

'She's not going to do, is she?' asked the midwife quietly.

'No. Where's the husband?'

'In the other room, shall I get him?'

'Yes, you'd better.' By this time, the girl was lying very still, not even reacting as the pains came, as her body continued to try to expel the baby, even though it couldn't.

'What's the matter, Mistress Physician?' asked the expectant father.

'I'm sorry; we can't deliver your wife's baby. The baby is too big to get through the birth canal. There is nothing we can do.'

'So what will happen? She looks poorly now. Look at her.'

'Yes, she is poorly and I don't think she can survive.'

'What about the baby, then?'

'No, it can't get out.'

'But can't you get it out for her?' pleaded the young father desperately.

'No, the only way I can do that would be to cut her open and get the baby out, but the operation would kill her.' At this, the husband reached for his wife and held her close, crying to her not to leave him, but she was fading fast, her body exhausted by the three days that she had been in labour: her breathing becoming shallow, her skin tinged with blue.

The girl wasn't conscious anymore and her life was slipping away, so Anna and the midwife went to the side of the room to give them some privacy. Suddenly the man cried out. His wife had breathed her last.

Anna debated whether to ask him a question, but decided to try.

'I could cut the baby out now for you, if you like? Your wife won't feel it. At least I could save the baby.'

The man nodded. Anna asked him to go next door, and asked the midwife to get the dead girl prepared, as there was no time to lose.

Anna cut into the woman's abdomen, through the layers of skin and muscle and opened the place where the baby was. She took the baby out of the womb and cut the cord. At first the baby remained quite blue, but then it suddenly took a gasp and started crying.

The midwife quickly wrapped the baby up in a blanket and took it to the father, whilst Anna sewed the abdomen together. She looked at the young face after she had finished and was making her look tidy and peaceful. She wasn't much above fifteen, thought Anna.

The father came in with the baby in his arms.

'Thank you for saving my daughter.'

'I'm sorry I couldn't save your wife.'

'These things happen, but at least I've got my daughter to aid my grief and always be a reminder of her.'

'That's true,' said Anna gently, thinking that it might be a greater burden to have saved the baby, as who would look after it whilst he had to work. As if he had read her mind, the father spoke.

'At least my mother lives nearby, so that she can look after her when I am at work.'

'That's good. You need your family at times like these. What are you going to call her?'

'We were going to call her Madeleine for a girl and Thomas for a boy, but I think I'll call her after my wife. She was called Esther. I'll call her Esther Madeleine.'

'That's lovely. Now let me check her over and make sure she's got everything she should have.' Anna took Esther into her arms and examined her. 'There you are, just perfect. Now, what are you going to do about feeding her? Do you know of a wet nurse near here? I've only just arrived in town, so I don't know anyone,' replied Anna. The father shook his head.

'The midwife will know of someone, I'm sure. I'll go and ask her.' A wet nurse was soon sorted out and Anna prepared to leave the house.

'Money,' said the new father, 'I must give you money.'

'No, better than money, will you make me some candles for my house? Not now, there's no hurry, I've got enough to be going on with. Just when you feel up to it.'

'Thanks. I'll do them soon, I promise, and thanks again for all you tried to do for my wife.

Anna smiled and left, finding Stephen outside, watching the world go by. Stephen was already aware of some of the drama of the day, so remained silent as they walked home. As they got home, Anna said, 'Not a good start to my career in Colne. I lost my first patient,' said Anna mournfully.

'Yes, but you got your first fee,' said Stephen trying to cheer her up. It worked; Anna laughed.

'I didn't even get that. I told him to make me some candles for the house later instead,' she said.

'Well,' said Stephen, 'if you carry on like that, I'll be having to find a new job.'

'I don't think so; I need you now for when my practice builds up. If it ever does.'

179

'I'm sure it will when word gets round.'

But word got round that Anna's first patient had died, and although those who cared to hear the whole story understood what had happened, others judged her on that first fact. Her first patient had died.

People were slow to attend, and Anna was worried that she would not be able to get a living in this village and would have to move again. But the children were so settled with the priest in their lessons, and she was loath to move them. The arrangement with the priest had worked well. He had a parishioner who was a widow and she kept asking him what good works she could do in the village, to wile away her time. He hadn't thought of anything until Anna asked about lessons.

The widow was a very well educated woman, so the priest asked her if she would like to teach the children their reading, writing and sums. She was delighted, and so they developed a small school within the church for all the children in the village. The widow taught the little ones like Isobelle and the priest taught the older ones, including Jack and Edwina.

Anna and Eloise amused themselves by sewing whilst the children were at school, and Eloise even took in sewing to raise a little money for them, although Anna wouldn't take anything off her. Stephen took on small jobs for local farmers, or offered to cart anything in return for small amounts of money or produce. They also sold eggs from their hens and their surplus cheese.

Anna had just returned from the market one day when Stephen called to her.

'Mistress, we've got a servant here from a local landowner. They want you to attend one of their servants.'

Anna's face lit up.

'Really? Where do they live?' said Anna as they hurried inside. But the servant answered instead of Stephen.

'Please Mistress, could you come and help us. We live at Alkincoates. Our dairymaid is very poorly with a fever.'

'Certainly, I'll just get my bag. Stephen, could you come with me for the return journey?'

'We would bring you home, Mistress,' replied the servant.

'That's kind of you, but Stephen and I need to get to know the area and our way around, so I'd like him to come.' The servant nodded and the three of them set out, after Anna had told Eloise and the children that she was going out. They climbed into the carriage and Stephen followed behind, with two horses.

'Where is Alkincoates, then?' asked Anna.

'It's on the outskirts of Colne, down the hill then up again. I'm afraid this area is all hills, Mistress.'

They soon arrived at Alkincoates Hall and were taken inside to the main hall. Mistress de Alkincoates was talking to the cook.

'Are you the new barber-surgeon?' she asked.

'No, I'm actually a physician, but I have done some training in surgery.'

'We were expecting a man. There are very few women physicians.'

'I know, but my aunt is one, down in Brun Lea.'

'And what is your name?'

'Mistress Anna de Ribbleside.'

'Is that where you came from?'

'No, originally I was from Rexar, but my parents moved to Ribbleside. Then I was married to the Lord. I trained as a physician when I was widowed.' Mistress de Alkincoates looked as though she had a few more questions to ask and Anna didn't want to go into any more details, so she interrupted her.

'Should I see your dairymaid now?'

'Yes, cook will show you to her bedchamber. I'll be in my solar afterwards.' Mistress de Alkincoates walked away, leaving Anna with the cook.

'This way, Mistress,' said the cook, taking Anna into a back room off a corridor, behind the main hall.

There was a fetid smell in the darkened room. Anna asked for some candles and a window to be opened, before she looked at the patient. The girl was about eighteen years of age and was tossing and turning in the bed, under lots of blankets. Her face was flushed, her eyes staring and her skin looked dry. Anna stripped the blankets off her and started to examine her, asking questions of the cook as she worked. 'How long has she been like this?'

'She's been under the weather for a few days, but got worse today.'

'Has anyone else been ill like this?' asked Anna, wondering if this was a case of plague.

'No, just her.'

Anna felt her skin, it was hot and sweaty and she could smell bad breath coming from her mouth. Carefully feeling all her limbs, the girl flinched when Anna touched her right arm.

'Is that sore?' Anna asked, but got no reply. She continued looking at the girl's arm, and then noticed a large swelling in the armpit. It was an enormous yellow-headed boil. Thank goodness, thought Anna as she checked the groin, no sign of black buboes, so it wasn't the plague.

'The girl has a boil, cook. Could you get me some hot water? I need to lance this boil. That is why she's so ill. The boil is poisoning her whole body. She'll be better after I've lanced it.'

Whilst Anna waited for the hot water, she stripped all the clothes off the girl, apart from her under things. Cleansing the armpit, Anna carefully sliced down the boil and released the pus, just as Robert had showed her. Then after cleaning it again, she fastened a piece of linen over it and sponged the girl down to cool the fever.

'Make sure she gets plenty of fluids to drink. That will help flush the badness away. Also, I'll just take a small amount of blood out, to purify the blood and get rid of the badness that has festered.' After completing her task, Anna was asked to go and see Mistress de Alkincoates in the solar.

'What was wrong with the girl?' she asked.

'She has a high fever due to a boil in her armpit. It's not the plague, thank goodness. I've lanced the boil and drawn some blood off her, so she should get better soon.'

'Thank you. You seem to know what you are doing. Please tell me how much I owe you.'

Anna stated a price and the lady went to her manuscript desk and took out some money.

'I'll come and see her again in a few days, if that's all right with you, Mistress de Alkincoates?'

'Certainly. Perhaps you will have a drink of ale with us?'

'Not this time, I have to get back to my children, but next time, I would enjoy that.' The women made their farewells and Anna and Stephen left. Her first paying customer. Today was a good day. They would celebrate at the evening meal. Also, thought Anna, as a high-bred lady, she might recommend Anna to all her friends. This could be very lucrative for her.

And it was. This visit heralded the start of a slow increase of patients to her door, until within the year, she was very busy.

Her parents managed to visit for the Christmas period again and were pleased to see Anna so settled in her new life. The children loved having their grandparents with them and being thoroughly spoilt.

The New Year dawned. What would 1348 bring for them all? thought Anna. But in her wildest dreams, she would never have imagined what did happen.

Chapter 16

At first, the rumours were just that. Mere rumours. But then more people came with tales of a fever that was sweeping the south of England, which was killing people in their droves. The fever had already affected large parts of Europe and they were calling it the Great Plague. The priests were saying that it was a plague visited on the people by God because of their wickedness and disbelief. It started a panic amongst many people.

People flocked to the churches and paid large sums of money to the priests, so that they would make intercession for them, so that they wouldn't be affected by the plague. Many others were asking for forgiveness of their sins, in the hope of appeasing God.

Colne was no less penitent. As they heard that the plague was moving up the country, the villagers became more fervent in their prayers, more generous with their gifts to the priest and the church, bought more indulgences, and became more self-searching in their confessions. Anna studied about the different types of plague, as she had had little experience in her training, praying that it wouldn't arrive in Colne.

There was an uneasy tension in the village, like waiting for something to happen. If a stranger appeared, he would be hounded out of the village, just in case he had been near a plague-ridden town. They didn't bother to ask questions first; strangers were just not allowed in.

But somehow, inevitably, the plague came to Lancashire. Ironically, it was the priest who was the first person to show signs of the disease. Anna was called to see him late one night. As she hurried there, she hoped that it would be the bulbar variety of plague, which mainly affected the lungs, from which the priest might survive.

It was not to be. Anna's heart sunk as she examined him. He had a high fever and was spitting blood, and then she found the black buboes in his armpit and groin, and realised that he was very ill and unlikely to survive. She did her best, trying to get him to take some fluid, but it was just gurgling in his throat. Within an hour of her getting there, the priest was dead.

Stephen and Anna looked at each other; the full impact of this death beginning to dawn on each other.

'It looks like we've got our first plague victim. Are you still happy working with me, Stephen?' Anna asked quietly.

'Yes Mistress. I enjoy my work. And I like being near Eloise. But this has frightened me. Would you let me marry Eloise? I don't want to think that I might lose her, when I've never held her in my arms.'

Anna was stunned that their romance had moved on so swiftly, but she knew that he was right; the plague took no prisoners. They could all be dead within a week or two. And what about her children? Would they get the plague? They spent all their days with the priest, learning their lessons. No, she closed her mind to that thought. She didn't want to even think about that. She concentrated instead on the question that Stephen had just asked.

'Of course you can. Will Eloise agree, do you think?'

'Oh yes, she would have mentioned it before, but she wanted to wait a little longer, till you were more settled.'

'Marry now,' Anna urged and then realised the ironic nature of what she has just said, standing over the dead body of the priest. 'But you'll have to affirm your vows, rather than marry in church.'

'That doesn't matter, as long as we can marry.'

'Come, we must arrange for the priest to be buried. And somehow, we have to tell people without them all becoming panic stricken.'

Anna and Stephen laid the priest out flat and called at the house of the old woman who laid bodies out, telling her what had happened. She agreed to lay the priest out and said she would get the grave men to bury him in the churchyard as soon as possible.

When they arrived home, Eloise was still up, waiting to see what had happened. She could tell by their faces that it wasn't good news. Eloise was sad to hear about the priest but then Stephen told Eloise that they were getting married the next day, which surprised her, but Anna could see that it was what she wanted, by the big smile on her face.

Without fine clothes or bridal attendants, or even a priest in the village, Stephen and Eloise made their vows in front of Anna and the children and then Anna sent Stephen to get some special foodstuffs from the market, so that they could have a celebratory meal. The news from the market was not good. Everybody already knew that the priest had died of the plague, even though Stephen and Anna hadn't told anyone.

Some people were already fleeing the village and streams of carts were going past the house throughout the day, as the villagers were desperate to get away from the plague. Anna reflected sadly that they wouldn't be received anywhere else, but their panic ridden minds hadn't thought of that.

Stephen quietly moved his belongings into Eloise's room but it wasn't the type of wedding day that Anna would have planned for them, or indeed that Eloise had dreamed of.

For the next week, there was a lull and no other cases of the plague presented. But the plague honeymoon period and Stephen and Eloise's honeymoon were both soon over. Case after case presented themselves in the village and Anna had her work cut out trying to keep up with all the patients. They were dying every day, sometimes before she could even see them. Most of the time, whatever she did for them, they still died.

Anna was becoming exhausted. Even during epidemics of fever that she had worked through, it had never been so relentless, or carrying on for so long: new cases presenting every day. The men who dug graves and arranged burials were amongst the first to go. After that, people had to be persuaded to dig graves and help bury the dead, but no one was very keen to do this job.

And then her worst nightmare happened. Edwina said that she felt ill. Anna examined her and found the tell-tale black buboes of the plague in her groin. Despite wanting to scream out loud, Anna controlled herself and asked Eloise to come into the bedchamber. She showed Eloise what she had seen and asked her if she was prepared to care for Edwina.

'Of course I will, how could you doubt me? She's like my own child. What can I do?' Anna gave her the simple instructions with a heavy heart, knowing that she would be unlikely to succeed, as she had failed with so many other patients in the last couple of weeks.

Although Edwina was so ill, Anna dragged herself round her other patients and hurried back home. There had been six more deaths that day. The small graveyard was filling rapidly and they were burying people in large graves altogether, not even marking the grave.

As soon as Anna saw Edwina, she knew that she had only just got back in time. Eloise was doing her best, but it wasn't good enough. Edwina was dying. Anna picked her up in her arms and cradled her and told her how much she loved her and that she always would, but when she looked down on Edwina, Anna noticed that she had already slipped away into eternity.

Anna hugged Edwina even more and wailed out loud, like a wolf. Eloise was crying too. Hearing the noise, Stephen entered and joined the wailing pair, holding Eloise and trying to comfort her. Unfortunately, Jack and Isobelle had followed Stephen into the room.

'Why are you crying, mother?' asked Jack, whilst Isobelle clung to his hand.

Anna turned to her son and little daughter and gently explained that their sister had died of the plague, and for them to kiss her goodbye. Stephen went out to get the old woman to tend to Edwina and arrange her burial.

Trying to organise things kept Anna going for the rest of the day, and fortunately, no one came to ask for a visit, but at night when she had gone to bed, she let herself go and broke into inconsolable sobs, rocking herself on the bed and banging her fists on the pillow. She couldn't bear it. Life would never be the same again, without her precious Edwina; her first-born child.

Eloise and Stephen heard her and Eloise wanted to go and comfort her, but Stephen stopped her and said that Anna would have to come to terms with it in her own time, and to let her grieve in peace.

But there was no healing respite for Anna. The next day brought a new outcrop of cases and Anna was in demand. The news had already got round the village about Edwina, and some of the villagers expressed their sympathy, but Anna kept tight-lipped about her feelings in public.

Only in the privacy of her own bedchamber, would she let go of her feelings. At other times, she tried to support her children who were bewildered by the loss of their sister.

Three days later, Eloise went in to get Jack up in the morning and found him still and lifeless in the bed, but still warm. She screamed for Stephen to go and get Anna who was out on visits, but it took him some time to find her.

'Just tell her Jack is ill, and get her home,' instructed Eloise.

Eventually Stephen found Anna and brought her home. She ran straight to Jack's bedchamber and collapsed in a heap on the bed next to him.

'Not my son, not my only son,' she kept crooning as she held him in her arms. 'See Eloise, he's still warm, perhaps I can save him?' Anna cried desperately.

'No Mistress, it's too late. His chest is still.'

'I can't bear it; I can't bear it to happen again. Two of my lovely children gone. How cruel is that?' Anna said to no one in particular. 'What have I done wrong in my life for this to happen to me? Holy Mother tell me?' she pleaded, and continued rocking Jack in her arms until Stephen gently took him away from her, and let the woman in to prepare him for burial.

Anna went to lie on her bed and when someone came asking for a visit, she made Eloise tell them that she couldn't visit anymore today. She lay on her bed keening, holding Jack's pillow and Edwina's blanket in her arms and rocking. She cried all day and all night, but next morning, got up with a resolute face and asked about her children's burial. Stephen had managed to arrange a separate burial plot for the children to share. It was under a small tree, against the farthest wall of the churchyard. Stephen had made a small wooden cross to mark the grave, unlike many of the other victims, who were in communal graves.

With a heavy heart, Anna resumed her visiting and realised that she wasn't the only one to lose children. By this time, many of the villagers who had fled the village had returned to Colne, as they had been refused entry at any other town or village. The news they brought back was grim. Brun Lea, Marsden and Exwhistle had all been devastated by the plague. No town or village seemed to have escaped.

Anna became neurotic about Isobelle's health, checking her for signs of plague every few minutes, when she was at home. Isobel had become very withdrawn since Jack's death as she was at a loss to understand what death was all about and missed her brother and sister deeply. She took to following Eloise about all day and hanging on to her kirtle.

By now, more than half the village had died; the children and old people being taken first, but healthy adults were taken as well. Anna was getting wearier and wearier as the days went past, as she dragged herself on her rounds. She had lost the will to live, but knew that she had to keep going, if only for the sake of her remaining child, Isobelle. Eventually she became ill herself and collapsed on the street outside the house.

Eloise was panic stricken and put Anna to bed, praying long and hard all the time. Remembering all the symptoms that she should look for, and treatments Anna had told her about, Eloise cared for Anna for three days, walking on tiptoes round the house for fear of disturbing her.

Suddenly, on the fourth morning, whilst Eloise was washing her, Anna sat up and asked for a drink. Eloise fell at the side of the bed in praise to Heaven that Anna had survived, making the sign of the cross. She was still far from strong, but by the end of the week, Anna felt strong enough to get out of bed for a while. She also managed to eat more normal food instead of the pobbies that Eloise had been feeding her.

Her first lucid words had been to ask how Isobelle was and was reassured to hear that she was all right. But as soon as she could walk, she was keen to get back to her patients. Although Stephen and Eloise were reluctant to let her go, they knew that she would go, whether they let her or not. Stephen insisted on being with her, even if she was only going across the street.

But whilst she was physically walking or riding round to her patients, in her mind she was far from well. Thoughts of her children played on her mind. Could she have seen the plague coming? Could she have prevented it? How could she be sure that Isobelle didn't get it? She relived both the children's deaths, wishing she could turn back time; her mind whirling round in circles.

And once she knew that Brun Lea was badly affected by the plague, she kept wondering about Judith. Had Judith been as badly hit by the plague? Had she survived? And had the plague got to Ribbleside? Were her parents all right? Anna had no peace. So concerned was she with her own thoughts that it was Eloise that made the statement.

'We've had no new plague victims for three days now.'

Anna thought for a moment. 'Have we not? The days just seem to run into each other.'

'Yes,' said Eloise, 'the last time you were called out to a new case was Sunday. It's Thursday now, so we've had three clear days. Four with today.'

'We've had a brief respite before. I wouldn't get excited yet,' replied Anna mournfully. But as the days went on with no new cases, Anna couldn't help but get hopeful herself. She went round the village talking to people, who all felt more positive that the plague was waning, and thankful that they had been spared. But only about fifty of the two hundred population had been spared and the village was trying to come to terms with their communal loss, so it was relief tinged with sadness.

Eventually a whole month passed without a new case. Anna cautiously declared to Eloise that it was over and they had a celebratory meal together that night. But Anna was still worried about her family and had had enough of death and dying. She needed a break.

'I've decided to go back to Brun Lea to see how Judith is. Do you two want to come?' she asked Eloise and Stephen one night.

They looked at each other and didn't speak for a while. Then Stephen spoke first.

'Would you mind if we don't come, Anna? We like it here and we have a chance of getting some land to farm, now that so many people have died.'

'Will you manage Isobelle without us?' asked Eloise, looking worried.

'Of course,' said Anna, 'you have your own life to lead now. Isobelle and I will be fine. After I've been to Brun Lea, I've a mind to go to Ribbleside. I'd like to see how my parents are.'

'Will you get a message back about my family too?' asked Eloise.

'And mine, in Brun Lea?' asked Stephen.

'Yes, and I hope it's good news for all of us. We've lost enough in this plague already,' replied Anna, thinking sadly about her own two children. Leaving them behind in the graveyard would be hard, but it was something she must do.

The following week, Anna got ready and set off to Brun Lea. She told Stephen not to come with her, as she needed to get used to being on her own now. Taking Isobelle by her hand, she lifted her on to the cart and waving at Eloise and Stephen, she clicked at the horse to set off. She needed to know about everybody or she would never rest.

Chapter 17

The journey to Brun Lea took most of the day and Anna thought that she would be glad to get some rest at Judith's and a good nights sleep. She tried to cheer Isobelle up as they went along, with little success. Only when she started singing some little songs to her did she get any response, and Isobelle started to join in.

Eventually she arrived at Judith's house, only to find it all in darkness. She went across to Robert's, but that too was in darkness. Dear God, thought Anna, surely they've not all died? She made her way to the Lamb Inn and found the landlord sat alone in his hostelry.

'Mistress Anna Physician,' he said with delight, 'how good to see you alive and well.'

'And you too,' replied Anna.

'Have you come to take over your aunt's practice?'

'No, just to see how she is.'

But Anna knew the answer by the look of sheer horror on the landlord's face. 'She's died, hasn't she?' she asked. The landlord nodded.

'Aye lass, I'm sorry, she has. I thought you knew. I'm sorry to have to break it to you like that.'

'What about the rest of the household? The servants?'

'All gone.'

'And Rupert too?'

'No,' smiled the landlord, 'Rupert's still alive. He's staying here with me, as he didn't like staying in your aunt's house on his own. He's just gone an errand for me. He'll be back shortly.'

'And what about Robert, the barber surgeon?'

'No, he's gone too. He tried to carry on with Judith's work after she died, but he got taken as well. Then Mr Elliott died too.'

'Mr Elliott?'

'Yes, he and your aunt got married at the start of the plague, and he lasted longer than most. Only took ill on the last week of the plague.'

'Married? How long were they married?' asked Anna.

'Only a month. But they seemed very happy.'

'I'm glad she was happy then, before she died,' reflected Anna sadly. The landlord nodded in agreement.

'I'm back, landlord,' cried a familiar voice and Anna was thrilled to see Rupert come through the door. The two of them threw their arms round each other and hugged for a long time, until Isobelle pushed her way forward and asked Rupert for a hug too.

'Hello, little Missie Isobelle. Where's your brother and sister?'

'They've gone to live with Jesus in heaven,' she lisped in reply. Rupert looked as if he was going to cry, until Anna changed the subject.

'Rupert, will you stay with me in my aunt's house tonight? Is that possible?'

'You can stay here tonight, if you'd prefer,' suggested the landlord.

'Yes, I suppose that's a better idea. But I'll need to go and sort things out tomorrow and decide what to do.'

'I'll come with you tomorrow then, Mistress Anna,' replied Rupert.

The landlord hurried round getting them a meal and getting rooms ready for them both to stay.

'Only prepare one room,' asked Anna. 'Isobelle and I need each others company at night at the moment.'

'Of course, I can take you up now, if you only want one room. I've always kept one room ready, but haven't needed it of late,' he said mournfully.

Anna and Isobelle went upstairs and cuddled together until Isobelle fell asleep. Anna found that it was better this way, as she had to contain her tears when sleeping with Isobelle. After the trials of the day, Anna soon fell asleep herself, her body wearied by months of extra work, even though her thoughts had been whirling round after Isobelle had gone to sleep.

Next morning, Anna sat with the landlord, whilst Rupert took Isobelle for a walk.

'What are you going to do now?' asked the landlord. 'Will you stay here?'

'I don't think so,' replied Anna, 'I need to find out about my family in Ribbleside. I'll probably go there once I've sorted things out here.'

'Did your aunt have any other relatives?'

'Yes, my father, and his family. I don't know about on Uncle Edward's side. I don't remember there being anyone else.'

'Well, you'll inherit all that is in her house then.'

'I suppose so,' replied Anna. 'What a sad way to inherit anything. I'd rather have my aunt back.'

'I'm sure you would, but so would many others. Do you want me to help you with her things?'

'No, I'll be fine. I'll take Rupert with me. And thank you for looking after me last night. It was so much easier staying here with you.'

'My pleasure. Are you going across now?'

'Yes, can you send Rupert across when he gets back please?' The landlord nodded and Anna made her way up the street to Judith's house. The door wasn't locked and Anna went straight inside. It felt so quiet and unusual, to have no servants scurrying around upstairs, no one caring for the animals, and no laughter and gaiety.

Anna went into the solar and looked round. The first thing she saw was Judith's bag that she used to take on her rounds. Anna burst into tears and held the bag gently to her chest. She would keep that always as a memento of Judith. On the manuscript box, there was a letter. It was from Mr Elliott.

Dear Anna or Richard or whoever comes here first.

My dear wife Judith died peacefully in my arms and now I have the same symptoms that she had, so I know I have not long to live.

I have no family left now, so please take everything as yours. I do hope that the rest of you have survived. Until we meet again in Heaven

Your obedient servant.

Micah Elliott

Anna sat down with the letter on her lap and that was where Rupert and Isobelle found her. Forcing a smile on her face, Anna asked Isobelle where she had been and what she had seen, and the child's bright chatter raised her spirits.

'Shall we sleep in Aunty Judith's house tonight?' she asked Isobelle. The child nodded in agreement.

'Could you arrange that, Rupert?'

'Yes, Mistress Anna. I'll light the fire now, so that we can eat later.'

'Yes, light it, so that we can be warm, but I've a mind to go to the Lamb Inn for our meals. It'll save cooking. What do you think?'

Rupert nodded. 'I like the food at the Lamb Inn,' he replied.

'Good, that's what we'll do. What have you been doing since everyone died, Rupert?'

'I've been helping the landlord.'

'Would you like to come to Ribbleside with me?'

'To live forever there?' he asked.

'Possibly forever.'

'Yes, I would, got no one now Mistress Judith gone,' he said sadly.

'I want to go and see the rest of my family. Do you remember Richard and Jane in Ribbleside? I may come back here afterwards, but I don't know what I'm going to find when I get there.'

'I'll come,' replied Rupert. 'I'll stay wherever you are. You'll look after me, like Mistress Judith.'

'Yes, I will Rupert, and I know that you'll look after me, as well.' Rupert nodded.

'We'll go in a few days, then. Now, let's go and get some food. Come on Isobelle, food.' Isobelle needed no further prompting and jumped up from playing with a doll and followed Anna and Rupert out of the door.

The next day, Anna looked all through her aunt's house, deciding what she would take with her and what she would leave. She found a hoard of money in the manuscript chest and put that into a bag, reflecting that her aunt's money would mean that she didn't have to work for quite some time, if she didn't want to.

Within three days, they were packed up ready to go. There was too much to go on one cart, so Anna hired a larger cart and a young man who offered to help them get back to Ribbleside. She took some of Judith's furniture with her, in case she needed it, not knowing what she would find when she returned to her parent's home. Then she asked the landlord to try and rent the house out and gave him her address in Ribbleside.

Taking a last look round Judith's house, Anna sadly said goodbye to all her memories of that house and its occupants, and climbing up beside Isobelle and Rupert, they set off on the journey; the young man, Arthur, driving the other cart.

Along the way, Anna noticed that many of the houses were empty and hardly any people seemed to be around in the villages they passed through. Eventually, they arrived at Tom the pedlar's sister's house. It was empty, Anna sadly noted.

After a while, they went over the Nick of Pendle and started descending to the other side, where Ribbleside lay. Pendle Hill was looking cheerful today, thought Anna, and hoped that it was a good omen for her return.

On arriving in the village, Anna first noticed the stillness. No noisy children; no animal's noises; no birds singing; no women chattering; no workers on the estate shouting to each other; no smoke coming from the huts or houses. Surely the whole village hadn't been wiped out?

Anna stopped outside her parent's house. The door was ajar. It felt cold and dank and unlived in. It looked as if all the occupants had gone away in a hurry; there were things still left on the table as if someone was coming back to them. Finding no one there, Anna grieved for her parents, although she had a fleeting idea that they may have hurried away at the onset of plague and that's why there were still signs of activity.

Reluctantly, she went out of the house and went next door to her old marital home, the Manor House. Again, there was no one around and no sign of life. Had the evil Max died? She certainly hoped so, and slowly. Then feeling shocked at what had come into her head, she asked the Holy Mother to forgive her sinful thoughts, and made the sign of the cross.

Anna and Rupert left Isobelle with Arthur, and then went slowly round the village, finding no one in any cottage or hut. Indeed, the huts looked dilapidated, with roofs falling in and shutters hanging off. Then suddenly she heard a faint sound. Was it a child? Or an animal? Anna wasn't sure. She walked towards the sound that seemed to be coming from a large cottage at the far end of the village.

Entering the cottage, it took a few seconds for Anna's eyes to adjust to the gloomy interior of the cottage. Then she saw about eight pairs of eyes staring back at her in sheer terror.

'Who are you? What are you doing here?' Anna asked but nobody answered; the smallest children cringing back against the older girls. 'Come on, I won't harm you,' Anna coaxed.

Eventually one of the oldest girls answered in a tiny voice.

'I'm Jessie, and I'm looking after the others 'til he gets back.'

'And how old are you Jessie?'

'I'm eight Mistress.'

'And do you all live here?'

'Yes, since our parents died.'

'And nobody looks after you?' asked Anna; completely appalled at the state the children were in.

'Yes, I look after them, and what business is it of yours?' growled a man's voice from the doorway of the cottage. Anna turned to look and saw a shock of bright red hair.

'Matthew Fox? How glad I am to see you.'

'Why Mistress de Ribbleside, I'm sorry for speaking to you like that,' said Matthew, bowing to her.

'Oh blow all that Mistress stuff. I'm just Anna to you. Now tell me what's going on. No better still, let's go up to my parent's house, and bring the children with you. Do you remember Rupert? My aunty Judith's man?'

The two men nodded to each other and gathering the children together, Matthew followed Anna to her parent's house.

'What were you doing whilst you were out?'

'Trying to catch some carp for the evening meal. The nuns all died with the plague and no one has returned to take their place, so I use their carp,' said Matthew.

'Why didn't you live in the convent with the children then?'

'I didn't like to. I was afraid I'd be in trouble with the church if they sent new sisters.'

'I'm sure that the sisters would have been glad that you'd cared for the children. Can the oldest girl make any food?'

'Yes, she's had to grow up quite a lot in the last few months.'

'What's her name?'

'Jennet.'

'Jennet,' called Anna gently, 'come and make some porridge on the fire that Rupert will light and then we can all eat. There seems to be plenty of grain around.' The child went over to the fire that was starting to burn in the grate and seemed to know what she was doing. Isobelle had started playing with the other children and seemed happy, so Anna sat with Matthew and tried to catch up with all that happened.

'Tell me about my parents, Matthew. I did hope they might have got away before the plague started. And anyway, how did the plague come to Ribbleside?'

'It was Tom the pedlar. He came to the Manor House and fell down sick. They did what they could but he was dead within the hour. It went right through the household. Master Max was first.'

Ha, thought Anna, he got his just desserts, but didn't let her face change at all. Matthew hadn't stopped anyway; he just carried on talking.

'They just died one after another. I tell you Mistress Anna, I was scared stiff, wondering when it was my turn.'

'Just call me Anna. And then what happened?'

'It spread right through the village. Your parents were next. Died on the same day as each other.'

'At least they weren't grieving for each other then,' said Anna, but grieving for them herself.

'No, I suppose not. But it was relentless. Nothing we did seemed to stop it. Nobody was immune. Even the priest and nuns.'

'I was living and working in Colne, a village near Brun Lea when the plague started. The priest was the first to die.'

'Did you train as a physician, like you wanted to?'

'I did. But it didn't do me any good. I couldn't save my own children,' she said bitterly. 'I lost Edwina and Jack. And my aunty Judith. And all my friends. Well, except for Eloise and Stephen.'

'Do you mean Eloise that was Ethel's sister?'

'Yes, she met and married a man called Stephen and they both survived, even though Eloise nursed my children and Stephen helped me in my work. What about Ghislane? Did she die?'

'No, but she wanted to. She was with child by Master Max, forced himself upon her he did, and so she went home to her mother. I don't know what happened to them. It's taken me all my time to look after these children; I haven't been out of the village since the plague started, never mind finished.'

'You've done an amazing job with the children. But now, I'll help you look after them. We'll all live here in my parent's house and you can go back to tilling the land and growing some food for us, if that's what you would like.'

'I'd like nothing better. There are still some animals alive. I've been milking the cows, so we have plenty of milk, but I need to do more work on the farmland to make sure there will be food for the winter.'

'Good, that's settled then. Now, introduce me to these children.'

'Jennet and Jessie you've already met. They're the daughters of two of the estate workers. Then this is Eleanor, she's six, and was Mattie's little sister, their father was the miller, you'll remember. Then we have Joshua, he's six as well. And little Jonathan, he's nearly six.'

'Is that Jonathan the bowman's child?'

'Yes, he never came back from the war, so when his mother and grandparents died, he had no one left. Now this is Madeleine who's four, and then the twins, John and Peter, they're three.'

'Goodness, what a family,' said Anna. 'And are they the only ones left?'

'Oh no, I forgot with you arriving, Mistress Cobb is still alive. She's in her own cottage, but finds the children too noisy all day. She's very weak.'

'Mistress Cobb? Oh go and get her. She helped me when I had the children, so I want to help her now. Bring her now, Matthew.'

'I will. She needs looking after, more than I could do.'

'I'll take great delight in looking after her,' said Anna. Matthew set off with Rupert to get her and Anna prepared a bedchamber for her, well away from the ones she'd decided to use for the children.

But when Mistress Cobb arrived, Anna knew that she would need a lot of care if she were to survive. Her chest was noisy and rattly and Anna knew that it didn't bode well for Mistress Cobb. Sometimes she winced as she took a breath in, at other times, she seemed to forget to breathe at all, then suddenly took a breath. Mistress Cobb lingered for two weeks, then slowly slipped away during the night. Matthew quickly arranged her burial in a new plot near to the church, as the original graveyard was too full.

Matthew commiserated with Anna, and said that it seemed hardly worthwhile having moved her, as she didn't survive, but Anna shook her head at that.

'It's always worth trying. Perhaps her last days were easier because she was here being tended to. Sometimes that is all I can do. I feel that I've done my best for her, in return for how she cared for me during childbirth. As a physician, you have to accept that you are not God and can't always cure your patients.'

'It wouldn't do for me,' replied Matthew, 'looking after these children has been enough for me, and they weren't sick.'

'But you've done an amazing job with them. You've kept them alive, against all the odds.'

'I'd rather be tending animals or growing crops.'

'I know that, and you will again. We need to go round all the farms and find out which tenants are still alive. I suppose I'm the lady of the manor again until somebody else turns up, now Max is dead. If only little Jack had survived. He would have been able to inherit all this, but never mind, too late now,' she said with a heavy sigh and a heavier heart. 'Yes, we'll go out again, just like old times when we used to go and visit the tenants,' said Anna trying to produce a smile.

'What about the children, though? We can't leave them alone.'

'True, but perhaps we can take them to the nearest farms, that will be fun for them and a change from sitting here all day. That's a good idea. Have we still got a cart?'

'Yes, or you could go and visit the farms with Rupert, whilst I stay with the children, so that they won't be scared with a stranger.'

Anna thought for a moment. 'We'll do both. We'll all go to the nearest farms and then Rupert and I will visit the outlying farms and cottages. I think we're going to need some new tenants. But then I suppose every village is the same, no men left to work the land.'

'It's a good opportunity for anyone who is available to farm, as they could have the pick of the land,' said Matthew.

'Where would you pick, if you could choose anywhere?'

'I'd pick the farm just outside the village, on the road to Chatburn,' said Matthew enthusiastically. 'It's got some good acreage, which isn't spoilt by lots of uneven ground. There's a good farmhouse and outbuildings, too. Also there are lots of streams to water the land when it's dry. I'd keep cows and sheep and pigs, and perhaps breed horses.'

'You have thought about this, haven't you?'

'Every day since I first looked after the farms for you. I planned what I would do. Then I thought about it even more whilst I've been looking after the children. It sort of kept me going. And I've got plenty of labourers to work my land with the children, haven't I?' he laughed.

'So that's why you're looking after them, just so they can be labourers in your fields?'

'Not really, I wouldn't force them if they didn't want to.'

'I know that, I was just teasing you, Matthew,' replied Anna.

The next day being fine, they all set out to go round the farms and cottages. Some of the children had never been outside the village in all their life so they were very excited and giggled and laughed together, teasing each other. Anna had made a picnic and they sat by the river and ate their fill. Then the children happily ran around for a while, until they were ready to drop. After finding only two farms and one cottage with tenants, Anna realised the full impact of the plague in Ribbleside and the difficulties she was going to have to keep the land in good order.

Slowly, the children got into a new routine. They all had little jobs to do around the house. The little ones had to feed the chickens and collect the eggs, a job which Isobelle adored. Jennet and Jessie learnt how to cook meals and keep the house tidy, whilst Jonathan followed Matthew round all day, trying to emulate him on the farm, doing simple tasks. Eleanor supervised the little children, but also was taught how to do some of the simple tasks in the kitchen. Life was settling down again.

Chapter 18

One day, as Eleanor was returning to the main hall, she looked up and saw people approaching. 'Mistress Anna,' she called. 'People coming. Oh look, they're sisters.'

Everyone came out to have a look at the group of people. It was indeed sisters. A line of sisters in the familiar habit of the Little Grey Sisters of Mary were walking slowly towards the village, leading carts that were pulled by small horses. Anna went out to meet them.

'Welcome sisters. Please come and take refreshment in my house. Are you travelling far.'

'No my child,' replied the oldest nun, 'we have reached our destination but we will be glad of some refreshment. But can you cope with twenty of us?'

'Indeed. We are a large family here so a few more won't be a problem. Come inside and sit yourselves down in the main hall. I don't think you would fit in the solar.' Anna ushered them inside, asking Jennet and Jessie to get some bread and ale for the nuns.

After they had all been fed, Anna asked them to explain what had been meant by the remark about arriving at their destination.

'We have arrived at Ribbleside. We are the replacement nuns for the convent across the river.'

'Oh good. We have missed having the sisters here since we returned. I was so sorry to hear that the others all died. I was taught by Sister Bernadette myself. Will you be resuming lessons for the children?'

'Yes, as soon as we have got ourselves organised. Are there any children left to have lessons?'

'Oh yes, I've got nine here.'

'Nine? The Lord has seen fit to bless you graciously my child.'

'Oh, they're not all mine. Only Isobelle is mine. I acquired the rest on my return here.'

Your return? Where have you come from, if you were taught by Sister Bernadette?'

'I was brought up here in this house. Then I married the Lord of the Manor and moved next door to the Manor House, and had three children. Then he died, so I went to train to be a physician in Brun Lea, then I moved to Colne, then after the plague, I came home,' said Anna breathlessly.

'Goodness, you have had an eventful life. A physician? That's interesting. You know of course that we are a nursing order as well as a teaching order.'

'I do indeed. Your predecessor tried to encourage me to become a novice so that I could undertake duties in the hospital. But I preferred the life of a physician.'

'That is a blessed calling. Now, we mustn't take up anymore of your time. We will make our way over to the convent. I'll let you know when we are ready to resume lessons again. Thank you for your kindness.'

'It's a pleasure,' said Anna, 'and if there is anything else we can do for you, you have only to ask.' The sisters set off, leaving Anna pleased that they had returned; it would be more adult company to enjoy. It would also be good for the children to have some lessons.

Anna decided that it was time to go in to Clitheroe and see if she could find anybody who would be prepared to come and work for her as cook and housemaid. It was good that the children were learning the chores, but she preferred them to have lessons as well, and with such a large family, help would be appreciated by all of them.

Next day, Anna went into Clitheroe with Rupert. They needed some provisions that they couldn't make or grow anyway. They set off with the cart, leaving the children looking unhappy because they weren't going too. When they got to Clitheroe, Anna was surprised at how many people there were around the town. Calling at the hostelry for a meal, she asked how the village had been affected by the plague.

The landlord said that they had been very lucky and that only about fifty of the villagers had died, which was far less than all the other villages locally.

'Why do you think that is?' asked Anna.

'We don't know. The priest says it's because we all confessed our sins, but so did all the other villages. There was a real panic to have confession and people were making allsorts of bargains with God.'

'Yes, it was like that in Colne, where I was,' replied Anna.

'You're not from these parts then?'

'Yes, I'm from Ribbleside, but I moved to Colne after my husband died.'

'You're young to be a widow, perhaps you'll marry again.'

'Never, I would never have a husband again,' Anna said with feeling. 'Now,' she continued, trying to change the subject, 'I've come today to try and find a cook and housemaid. Ribbleside has been very badly affected by the plague. There are virtually no adults left.'

'Aye, I believe all the nuns died too,' replied the landlord.

'Yes, but a new lot have just arrived, so things should get better.'

'I don't know of anyone who wants a post, but I'll ask around and send word to you.'

'Thank you. I'm Anna de Ribbleside but I'm currently living next door to the Manor House in my parent's old house. I'm also looking for tenants for my farms as well, should you hear of anyone who wants one.'

'I'll get a message to you, for either job.'

Anna left the hostelry and went to the market. She got all her purchases, plus three large home made game pies for the evening meal. Deciding to go home via Chatburn, Anna called in at the home of Martha's sister.

A thin, weary looking girl opened the door, with a toddler at her knee. Anna stared in amazement. It was Ghislane.

'Ghislane,' she said with joy.

'Mistress Anna, what are you doing here?'

'I've just been to Clitheroe and I'm going back home.'

'Back to Brun Lea? That is kind of you to call.'

'No, Ribbleside. I've moved back to my parent's house. What are you doing now? Is Martha in?' The girl's face clouded over.

'Martha died during the plague, and my mother with her. I was ill too, but for some reason I survived. I needed to, to look after my little boy.'

'He's a good sturdy lad, what is his name?'

'Jacob.'

'A strong name. I heard that you had had a baby and how it was conceived. I'm so sorry that I left you there at Max's mercy, but I was already turning up at my aunt's house with four others, and I didn't feel I could impose on her anymore than I was already.'

'It doesn't matter now. I was upset at the time, but I wouldn't be without Jacob now. What made you come back to Ribbleside then?'

'I wanted to see how my parents were. I'd lost all but my youngest child, Isobelle, and I needed to have my family around me.'

'You lost your children? I'm so sorry. And are your parents all right?'

'No, they are gone too, and my aunt Judith. No, Isobelle is the only relative I have left now as far as I know, although I haven't been over to York to see if anyone survived there.'

'I've no one left either. I'm quite struggling at times.'

'You are? I don't suppose you'd come and live with me then and be my housekeeper and cook? We could get another girl to help you and the children are training up nicely now in the kitchen.'

'Children? I don't understand. I thought you'd lost your children?'

'I did, well I lost Edwina and Jack, but when I arrived back in Ribbleside, I found Matthew Fox looking after eight children. Only Mistress Cobb had survived as well as them. They were quite destitute.'

'I'd love to come and work for you again. I can bring Jacob, can't I?'

'Of course, and he'll have lots of playmates and will go to the sisters when he is old enough to learn his lessons.'

Ghislane beamed at Anna. 'When do you want me to start?'

'As soon as possible. Do you happen to know of a young girl who could help you?'

'Not really, but I could ask around. I'll come later in the week if that's all right? I'll need to get a tenant for this cottage. I own it now that my mother and aunt Martha are dead,' she said sadly.

'That's true. Just come when you can. I'll look forward to seeing you. It'll be lovely to have another woman to chat to. I'm fair starved of talking women's talk,' Anna grinned, and Ghislane nodded in agreement.

Anna and Rupert set off back to Ribbleside, and were greeted with a loud cheer by the children when they arrived home. And then another loud cheer when they saw the game pies. They were also delighted when Anna told them that a lady was coming to help in the house.

The children weren't as delighted that a sister had been across to tell them that they were starting lessons the next day. The children had lost the discipline of lessons and quite enjoyed their freedom, but Anna insisted that they return next day.

Although some of them were a little nervous, Anna escorted them all across the river bridge to the convent on the following day. The new sister who was designated to teach them was called Sister Margaret Rose and she welcomed the children. She said for the first day, they would just get to know each other and play some spelling games and sums, so that it eased them back into lessons. Anna was pleased at this approach, as she knew how apprehensive some of the children were. Even though the little children were too young for lessons really, Sister Margaret Rose said that she would take them all, to make up the class.

'There will be another young boy coming to live here soon as well, my former cook's child. I've persuaded her to come back to work for me again.'

'The more the merrier,' beamed Sister Margaret Rose. Anna decided that she was going to like her.

'Thank you, I'll leave you to it, then,' replied Anna. 'They've all got something to eat at midday,' she said as she left the room.

Returning to the house, Anna sat in the chair in the solar and relaxed. It was the first time she had been on her own for a long time. It will be good to have Ghislane living here again, she mused, and I do miss adult company, even though I've got Matthew. Her eyes started to droop, and she dozed for a little while, until there was a loud knock at the door.

Hurrying down to the door, Anna wondered who it might be and was surprised to find Mother Veronica at the door, the new Mother Superior of the convent.

'I'd like a word with you, Mistress de Ribbleside,' she said in a stern voice.

'Certainly, do come in,' replied Anna politely. 'Can I get you something to eat or drink?'

'No thank you. I'll come straight to the point. Sister Margaret Rose was talking to the children today and what they told her concerns me greatly.'

'Oh? What have they been saying?' asked Anna, also a little concerned.

'They tell me that you live here with two men, and you are not married to either of them. What do you have to say about that?'

'But I just took all these children in, and Matthew was looking after them, so he stayed with me. And Rupert served my aunt for many years, and since her death, he now serves me. As it happens, Rupert has chosen to stay in the stable bedchamber, not under my roof.'

'And do you think that this is a good example to children, to see unmarried people living together?'

'But we don't live together. We merely share a house. We have separate bedchambers; why they're even at the opposite ends of the house. These children have all been through a lot in their young lives. Most of them have lost everything, and would probably have died if it wasn't for Matthew rescuing them and feeding them, until I arrived.'

'That's as may be, but it is not a good example to them.'

'So what are you suggesting?' asked Anna, getting a little annoyed.

'You should look to the example you are setting the children. Perhaps the men can move out?'

'Why should they?'

'Because it is a breach of decent behaviour. We are due to get a new priest here soon, and he would be most upset to see this state of affairs in his village. Besides, I could take them all from you, until the situation changes. As the Mother Superior, I have those powers. We are well equipped to take charge of children at the convent and will do so if there is no improvement in the situation.'

Anna was shocked into silence by the threats that Mother Veronica was making, and let her walk out, without even passing a comment on her last statement.

After a while, Anna went to find Matthew, but he was out in the fields somewhere, Rupert said, and wasn't sure just where he was, or how long he would be. Anna fretted and fumed about what to do. She wasn't sure if the threat to take her children away was true or not. She certainly wouldn't let them take Isobelle. In fact, she would fight for all her children.

By the time Matthew got home, Anna was really angry.

'You'll never guess what that interfering busybody from the convent has just said?' Anna ranted.

'Yes, I would,' Matthew replied grimly, 'She's just caught me as I was going past. Waiting on the bridge for me. Looked like a stone statue she did.'

'What are we going to do?' asked Anna in desperation. 'What if she takes the children?'

'I don't think she can.'

'But she says she can. These children have had enough. They don't need any more disruption in their lives.'

'I don't know what to do. We'll have to think about it.' They were both silent for a while.

'I suppose we could always get married,' said Matthew in a quiet voice.

'Married?' asked Anna in disbelief.

'Well, they couldn't complain any more then.'

'But I don't want to get married, ever again,' replied Anna.

'I don't mean properly married. I mean we'd just get married to keep them quiet, but go on living like we are now' suggested Matthew.

'You mean separate bedchambers?'

'Definitely.'

Anna thought about this for a while. 'But what if you met someone and wanted to marry them in the future?'

'I'd run away with them and pretend we were married,' Matthew laughed.

'Oh yes, and leave me with all the children to bring up on my own?' answered Anna.

'Sounds like we're bickering like an old married couple already,' teased Matthew.

'We'll both have to think about it. Mull it over for a day or two and then we'll think again.'

'Right. I'll go and chop some wood now. I feel like swinging the axe around, it'll get rid of my temper,' said Matthew.

'I might join you,' replied Anna. They both went their separate ways, but carried on thinking about the proposal of sorts that Matthew had made. It was a good answer to the dilemma, but Anna was worried about the future for Matthew. She wasn't worried about herself, because she was never going to marry, but if Matthew met someone, she would hate it if he couldn't follow his heart's desire.

After a sleepless night, during which Anna changed her mind many times, she sought out Matthew after the children had gone to the sisters for their lessons.

'Matthew, it was a very kind offer to make, but I don't think we should marry. It's not fair to you in the long run. But what you could do is sleep in the Manor House at night. Nobody owns it now. That should shut them up. For the rest of the time, you can be here, but just go over there at night time. What do you think to that idea?'

'Sounds good to me. Why didn't we think of that straight away? Yes, we'll do that, starting from tonight. I'll move my things now. And Anna, why don't I take the boys to sleep with me over there? That way there can be no question of indecent behaviour or whatever they said.'

'Excellent. That's a brilliant solution.' Anna breathed a sigh of relief. She hadn't wanted to get married, even if it was in name only

210

and as a marriage of convenience. She just didn't want to have to tell anyone that she was married. Being a widow was the best situation, she decided. She had the status and the freedom without having to put up with a man.

When the children got home from the sisters, they told them about the new arrangements. They all thought it was a good laugh and cheerfully collected their belongings and trooped after Matthew as he led the boys to their new home. Anna fretted over them a little but was reassured when the boys told her that it was better in the Manor House because they could have a room each.

Next day, Anna made a point of telling the sisters about the new arrangements and could tell that they weren't too pleased about it, but couldn't really say anything. Within the week, Ghislane arrived with Jacob and another thin young girl in tow.

'Hello, who's this?' asked Anna when she opened the door.

'Oh Anna, I hope you don't mind, I found this young girl in Chatburn. She was living off the land and her parents are dead. She has no one. Can she be my kitchen help?'

'With pleasure, we seem to be making a speciality of adopting orphans in this house nowadays. What's your name young lady?'

'I'm Katie, Mistress,' she replied, giving a little bob to Anna.

'There's no need to curtsy to me, Katie. You're very welcome and you can have a home here for as long as you want. Ghislane will be your teacher and show you what is needed in the kitchen. How old are you?'

'I'm ten, Mistress.'

'Good, that's a suitable age to start work. Have you had any lessons before?'

'No Mistress. I haven't had any lessons,' replied Katie a little bewildered, not sure what a lesson was, but knew she hadn't had one.

'Then we'll have to get the other girls to teach you after they've helped you in the kitchen.'

'Other girls?' Katie asked.

'Yes, there are quite a few live here and when there is nothing for you to do in the kitchen, and you've learned your lessons, you can go and play with the others.'

'Play?' asked a puzzled Katie.

'Yes, run around and act silly and go exploring in the countryside.' But Katie merely nodded, not quite sure what play meant either. She was just glad to get a roof over her head again and plenty of food to eat, so she gave Anna a beautiful smile.

'Can you find her some clothes and get rid of those, Ghislane? She needs a whole new outfit but she'll have to do with cast-offs from the other girls for now. Give her a bath too. I'll go up and sort the bedchambers out. We've just got rid of the boys, you'll never believe it but the sisters complained that I was living with two men without being married!' Anna laughed.

'I'll put you and Jacob in together in a bedchamber, but all the other boys live next door now at night, since the complaint from the sisters. But if he wants to go and join them he can, but he's a little young to be away from you yet, isn't he?'

'Yes, he'll need to be with me for a while yet,' agreed Ghislane.

'That's fine. I'll show you to your bedchamber when you've sorted Katie out. Now Katie, would you like a room of your own or would you like to share with the other girls?'

'Share with other girls, please,' said Katie in a quiet voice, not wanting to admit that she was terrified of sleeping in a room on her own.

'Right, I'll put you in with the bigger girls,' said Anna as she set off up the stairs to the bedchambers.

The new routine soon became the normal pattern. The children all worked, learnt, ate and played well together, and then separated at night to go to their own bedchambers, in their own house. It seemed to work even better than when they were all in together; perhaps thought Anna because they all had more space now that they were in two houses. Katie soon settled in to her new home as well, becoming much more lively and outgoing than when she had arrived. Ghislane also thrived in her new routine, and the house was well organised and happy.

212

In the evenings, Anna sat by herself sometimes and reflected on the needs of her village and her adopted children. There was no candle maker in the village and that had been a real pressing need. She had already talked to the candle maker in Clitheroe, and he had two sons who were learning the trade. He promised that in a years time, the younger boy would be ready to set up in business on his own, but the father worried that he was too young to live alone yet. Anna told him about the set up at the Manor House with the children and said that young Jake could have a cottage to make his candles in, but sleep at the Manor House at night, near Matthew and the other boys.

When he heard about these arrangements, the candle maker agreed to let his oldest boy, Thomas, come and live in the village straightaway, as long as he lived at the Manor House at night. Soon twelve-year-old Thomas joined them, and Anna and Matthew had another mouth to feed.

Some day, they would also need a bow maker, but as there was only Matthew, Rupert and Thomas who were old enough for bow practice, she could leave that for another few months. They had enough bows to be going on with, but would need more some day in the future. And hopefully she could get Jonathan to train as a bow maker in a few years time, like his father before him.

Perhaps Tom could train Joshua as a candle maker. That would be good, she reflected. But then he might want to follow whatever his father's trade had been. She wanted all her children to get a trade so that they could be self-sufficient. The girls could train in cooking and sewing and housework, and perhaps Isobelle would be a physician, like me, thought Anna.

She wasn't sure what young John and Peter could train as. They were both such scallywags, that she couldn't imagine them being anything serious at all. Still, compared to the silent, pale frightened boys they were when Anna first arrived, she was glad to see their naughtiness sometimes. She just wasn't keen when they involved all the other children in their pranks. And then she laughed at herself. She was making all these plans without even enquiring what the children would like to do with their lives. That was one thing she had learned from her own life: she would not force any of her children to do what she wanted them to do.

But we still need a miller and a carpenter, and the forge was still idle, Anna carried on worrying to herself. Where would she get all these tradesmen from? She'd love her village to be complete again, but it would take time to get people back in for some of the jobs. So she kept her eyes and ears open when she went into Clitheroe, or anyone called round at the house.

But a small part of her resented the worries that she had about these children's futures, as she remembered that her own two children had no future. Never would she get over the loss of her two children. She thought about them daily, remembering how old they would be now, or recalling some part of their life together. No, she would never forget them, but her present life was so busy that she had to get on with her life, and it grieved her that Isobelle seemed to have forgotten them, with having so many new little friends to play with. Whilst there were good things in her life, there were also many hard things, too, she reflected sadly when she was alone.

One night, when all the children had gone to bed, Anna and Ghislane were sitting by the fire talking, when young Joshua came flying through the door.

'Mistress Anna, Master Matthew says to come quick,' then he ran away again, without saying anything else.

Thinking it might be a medical emergency, Anna grasped her bag and ran next door, but it was no medical scenario that she was met with. It was an irate woman who was berating Matthew for stealing her things.

'Just a minute,' said Anna, 'what is going on here? And why are you shouting at my friend?' The woman turned round and the two women stared at each other in silence. Anna was first to catch her breath.

'Christine, what are you doing here?'

'Anna, I don't believe it! I've found this man living in my house. What's going on?'

'Actually Christine, by rights it's my house, but we won't argue about it. This is Matthew Fox, don't you remember him? He was at the sisters with us.'

'Matthew Fox? No, I didn't recognise him. Still I suppose you didn't have a beard when you were at the sisters,' quipped Christine, calming down a little. 'But what are you doing here?'

Anna answered for him. 'Matthew became my bookkeeper after your grandfather died. Then when I came back from Colne, I found him here in a small cottage, looking after all the children who had survived the plague. So we joined forces, I opened my parent's house and we all lived here together, but the sisters objected because we weren't married, so now we live together all day, and the boys and Matthew come here at night to sleep. But Christine, we must get you something to eat and drink and then we'll sort out a bed for you for the night.'

'Your parents survived then?' asked Christine.

'No,' said Anna sadly. 'Come to my house and then we can catch up on all our news. But you'll have to stay in the girl's house,' quipped Anna, trying to raise her spirits again. It would be so good to have Christine here; she couldn't wait to hear her story.

Over a meal, Christine told her story to Anna.

'After you said you were marrying my grandfather, I went to stay with my aunty in Ripon. There I met a young man from a neighbouring family and we fell in love and married. We had two children, a boy and a girl, and then like everyone else, I lost them to the plague. So I thought I would come home and see what was happening here. I sort of felt that I wanted to be back here, for I was happy here as a child.'

'Me too. I wanted to come back and see if my parents were alive,' replied Anna, and continued to tell Christine all that had befallen her since she had last seen her.

Christine was unhappy when she heard about Max and what he had done.

'He was always mean to me, I never liked him,' Christine

commented, 'but at least it meant you could follow your dream and become a physician. Do you still do that work?'

'I haven't really had time since I came home, what with looking after all the children and organising the house, but I mean to let people know that I'm available soon. Now that Ghislane is here as cook, and young Katie as helper, I'm going to be able to spread my wings a little more. In fact, I'll go to Clitheroe tomorrow and put the word around. I don't think they have a physician in Clitheroe. Perhaps you can come with me and we can catch up some more?'

'I'd rather not, if you don't mind. I'm weary. I couldn't think of anything worse than going on a cart to Clitheroe. No, I'll just stay here and rest.'

'I don't mind. We've a lifetime to catch up. Now I'll show you to your bedchamber and you can get some sleep.'

'Thank you for taking me in, Anna. I'm sorry I shouted at Matthew. I was just so tired and fed up after the journey.'

Anna laughed. 'You can apologise to him yourself tomorrow. He's been a tremendous help to me and the children. They'd all have died without him.'

'I will, I'll apologise tomorrow. You enjoy your time in Clitheroe.'

It was very late when the two women parted, both amazed by the other's story of what had happened to them. It was as if they had never been apart, as their old friendship resurfaced easily, and they picked up where they had left off all those years ago. How strange reflected Christine, that both she and Anna had lost a boy and a girl, but sadly, Christine had no others left to her. Being back with Anna wouldn't make up for what she had lost, but it might aid in the healing process. There appeared to be no shortage of children in these two households to keep her occupied. Not surprisingly, after all the talking, both women went to sleep as soon as their heads touched the pillows.

Chapter 19

Next morning, Anna got the cart ready to go to Clitheroe. Ghislane wanted some saffron and other spices and herbs to make her favourite dish of casserole of pigeon, amongst other items that she needed to stock up the kitchen. For once, it was a lovely crisp November day, and wrapped up in her old black velvet cloak, she didn't feel too cold. Rupert kept asking her if she was warm enough, and she assured him she was. As they passed Pendle Hill, it looked to be in a warm and welcoming mood and it lifted Anna's spirits. For some reason she felt glad to be alive today. Perhaps it was in contrast to the death and dying she had talked about with Christine last night.

They made their way to the market and stopped to do their purchases. Rupert wanted to have a look round on his own, so Anna arranged to meet him at the hostelry for a meal, later in the day. She bought some material to make some dresses for Katie and wished that she still had Eloise who was so handy with a needle. Would they still be farming in Colne? Would they have any children yet? Perhaps she could send for them now that she had many farms available here. That would mean she could have Eloise and Stephen around her, but they would continue farming. If only they still had a pedlar; it was so hard to get a message to anybody now. Perhaps she would send Rupert to invite them, when she got home.

Wondering how Eloise and Stephen were, made her think about something that Christine had said about her husband the night before. She said how much she had loved him and how she loved being married, especially the physical side. That was certainly not Anna's experience, but she knew it had been her parents. As she walked around Clitheroe, Anna pondered on what Christine had said about marriage, even though she knew that it would not be right for her.

Arriving at the hostelry, Anna met Rupert and they had some food together. Anna spoke to the landlord and told him that she was now prepared to have patients again, after she had ascertained that there was no physician left in Clitheroe.

'I'm glad about that,' said the landlord, 'I happen to have someone who needs a physician staying here at the moment. Will you see him?'

'Yes, of course,' said Anna getting the familiar excitement she used to get when meeting a new patient, with a different set of symptoms. 'But I haven't any instruments with me.'

'Well, have a look anyway. It's this way.' The landlord led Anna up the stairs and into a bedchamber at the back of the hostelry. A large man was lying in the bed, partly under the clothes, obviously in a fever. He was muttering to himself and throwing the bedclothes around. Anna felt his forehead. It was very hot. His pulse was weak and rapid.

'How long has he been here?' she asked the landlord.

'Two days, but he seems to be worse today. I'm glad you came.'

Anna continued the examination, at the same time noting that he was a very handsome man, with dark curly hair and strong arms. It was whilst she was examining his legs that he started stirring and saying a woman's name. 'Rosa, Rosa,' he crooned, with real love.

And then during her examination, Anna found a large wound on his thigh. It was festering and looked as though he had had something sharp in his thigh, like a knife or axe head.

'This is what is causing his fever. I'll need to clean and treat it, then take some blood. I'll send my man home for my instruments. In the meantime, I'll wash him down to break his fever. Have you anything suitable that I can use?'

The landlord scurried away, both to get her some spring water and some clean cloths, and to tell Rupert to go back home and get her bag. The landlord returned with the water and cloths and Anna asked what the man's name was.

'It's Owain, he's a Welshman but been living in these parts for some years.' replied the landlord. 'He was working for a farmer and got an axe in his leg. The farmer finished him and sent him off the farm. He came here to stay until he was better. He's not from Clitheroe. That's all I know about him.'

'Thank you. I'll deal with his fever now. I'll need some lemon balm to bring his fever down. Also, I'll need some weak ale. It's important that he gets some fluid down him, especially if I'm going to take blood later. It'll dilute the fever too.'

Anna started to undress Owain and wash him down, and cleanse the wound itself, getting rid of some of the nastiness that was within the wound. He again started stirring and saying Rosa. Anna wondered about him, and about Rosa. Was it his wife? Or his sweetheart? Or even his daughter? Only time would tell. She watched him carefully as she waited for her instruments. He had obviously had a hard working life as his hands were calloused, but she admired the line of his jaw, and his neatly trimmed beard, and the way his hair curled over his forehead.

Stop it, thought Anna. What are you doing thinking these thoughts about a man who is a patient? And for all you know, he belongs to Rosa too. Anna blushed at the way her thoughts had been going. Fancy, admiring a man she didn't even know. She had never felt like that since the first stirrings of feeling that she had had for Donald as a young girl.

Donald! She'd never asked about Donald in all this time. How could she have been so awful and uncaring? It was strange that Christine didn't ask about him either; the three of them had been so close. She must find out about him first thing tomorrow. Perhaps he never returned from the war, or perhaps he too, was lost in the plague. It was surprising that neither of them had mentioned him, even though they had talked about a lot of people that they had both known.

Just then, Rupert arrived with the bag. She took a lancet and carefully scraped the edges of the wound. Owain cried out at times, but Rupert held him down, so that he didn't knock Anna's hand away whilst she was doing the cleansing of the wound. She put a poultice of marjoram on his wound, sprinkling it with periwinkle first, in case it bled where she had been scraping it. Afterwards she took some blood from him, then asked for clean sheets for his bed and settled him down.

He was much calmer now, and Anna gazed down on him, strangely loath to leave him. Eventually she tore herself away, and told the landlord that she would be back tomorrow to see how he was doing.

'I don't know how much money he has, Mistress Anna, he might not be able to pay you.'

'That doesn't matter. He could always come and help me on my farms to pay for his care, I need some good strong men,' she laughed lightly, wondering why her heart was beating faster at the thought of Owain working on her land.

Rupert and Anna went back home and Anna couldn't keep her thoughts off the young man that she had treated. She wanted to know more about him. And wanted to know who Rosa was. She didn't really need to go and see him again tomorrow if she was honest, as she had done all she could and it was up to God whether he survived or not. But she felt as though she wanted to know how he was and willed him to get better, so that she could get to know more about him.

But all thoughts of strange young men were driven from her mind when she got home. There was a dispute between the little ones about whose turn it was to feed the chickens. In the end, she told Katie that she could be in charge of looking after them and that the little ones had to help her.

'In fact,' said Anna to Katie, 'you can go to market and sell the surplus eggs and keep the money,' knowing that it would keep Katie happy and show the children that they had lost an opportunity through being selfish.

The atmosphere soon calmed down and eventually everybody went to bed, but not before Anna had asked Matthew, what had happened to Donald.

'He never came back from the war, but his widow did,' said Matthew.

'Widow? He was married?'

'Yes, it was the daughter of one of his officers. Apparently he was very well thought of amongst the soldiers.'

'So how did his widow find her way back here?'

'Her parents died, so she couldn't stay with the soldiers anymore.

So she decided to come back to live with Donald's parents, with her little boy.'

'He had a boy?'

Mathew looked bewildered. 'I thought you knew that? It's young Joshua. That's Donald's boy.'

'No, I didn't realise that. Now you mention it though, I can see the family likeness. He's very like Donald's father.'

'Yes, it would be good if he could set the old forge up in the future, but I suppose there is no one to teach him.'

'What happened to the widow?'

'Died in the plague, like everyone else. She still lived in the forge whilst she was here.'

'We've been lucky to survive, haven't we?' asked Anna.

'Yes, we have. And Christine too.'

'Yes, all of us. Well, are you going to your house, or the sisters might come across to check up on us,' teased Anna.

'Yes, Mistress, better go back to the boys barracks,' he said laughingly back, as he left the room. Anna made her way slowly to bed remembering Donald fondly, but also remembering the man she had met today with much stronger feelings.

Next day, Anna set off early, telling Rupert she would be all right travelling on her own. After all, the plague seemed to have killed off some of the robbers and thieves that used to abound in the area.

She smiled at Pendle Hill as she drove past; it was tipped with mist, drifting down over the side of the hill. It would probably rain later, but for now the weather was fine. She felt lucky to be alive again. Her heart lifted as she approached the hostelry, but also she felt apprehensive as to what she would find. Her man might even have died in the night. Oh no, please God, Holy Mother and all the saints, she intoned, not died.

Anna hurried into the hostelry and asked about her patient.

'Much the same,' said the landlord, 'still thrashing around the bed. But he doesn't seem just as hot today, and I did get some fluid down him last night and this morning.'

Anna went up to the bedchamber and thought that he was quieter,

221

so she made the sign of the cross, whilst thanking God. She checked the wound and it looked better than it had the day before. So far so good, she thought, but he was still unresponsive and not aware of anything at all. But he did feel cooler. The landlord had cared for him well, thought Anna.

After sponging him down again, checking his wound and carefully giving him a drink, Anna just sat and waited by his side. She gazed down at him, wondering what he was dreaming about, and if he was thinking about Rosa. When she could think of nothing else she could be doing, she reluctantly tore herself away from his side.

'You seem to have made a good job of caring for him,' she said to the landlord. 'I'll call again tomorrow, goodbye.'

'Goodbye Mistress,' he replied as she left the hostelry. On the way home, Anna exulted that her patient was still alive. Well, I'm always grateful when my patients survive, thought Anna, but knew that this patient meant more to her already than her other patients. She really must take control of herself, she reflected. For all she knew, he could have a wife, Rosa, and several children. No, she must put all thoughts of him out of her mind.

Sighing heavily, she pulled on the reigns to get the horse to set off, and tried to think of other things, but her mind wouldn't behave and kept returning to Owain. Owain, she said his name softly. Even his name was wondrous. Oh stop it Anna, you're wasting your time, she chastised herself, but laughing out loud at the same time. So she deliberately sang a long and difficult song for the remainder of the journey to keep her thoughts from straying.

The following day found Anna back at Owain's side, and she continued to visit him for a further three days, but still with no response. By the seventh day, his fever was almost gone, but he was still not speaking or responding. After her treatment of him, she sat gazing down at him again and hadn't realised that she was stroking his forearm, but was aware of the tingling feelings going up her own arm as she touched him. Suddenly, he opened his eyes and looked straight at her, with a confused expression on his face. He tried to reach out to her but missed so Anna took hold of his hand.

'Where am I? Who are you?' he said with a croaky voice, that had a Welshman's lilt to it.

'You are in Clitheroe in a hostelry and I'm your physician,' Anna replied with rapidly beating heart, noticing that his eyes were a rich brown colour, his lashes heavy, and his lips were . . .

'How did I get here?' Owain interrupted Anna's wayward thoughts.

'The landlord says you were in a farming accident and you came here to recover.'

'So how did you come to look after me?'

'I came to the hostelry for a meal and to say that I was starting up my practice as a physician again, and the landlord told me about you,' Anna replied breathlessly.

'How long have I been ill?'

'This is my seventh day visiting you.'

'So long? I don't remember anything after getting here.' Suddenly he tried to sit up. Anna held him back, realising that she was still holding his arm anyway. 'I lost my job, I remember that now. What will I do? How will I pay you?'

'Don't worry about that now. Just get better, and then come to see me. I have plenty of farms going spare. I'm sure I can find you one.'

'Where do you live,' he asked.

'Ribbleside, about three miles from here.'

'I know it, on the way to Yorkshire,' he nodded.

'That's right. I'm glad you are so much better. I had to cleanse your wound and take some blood to get rid of the poisons. But I think it's done you well.'

'You've done all that for me? How can I thank you? It doesn't seem right that a woman has to do such jobs.'

'Nonsense, we're doing it all the time for our children,' laughed Anna, and then wished she hadn't said it, when she saw a look of pain shoot over Owain's face.

'Oh, I'm sorry, I shouldn't have said that,' said Anna mortified.

'No, you weren't to know. I lost my children in the plague. I originally came from Wales, but we've been living in Lancashire. We were trying to escape the plague in our village.'

'I lost two children as well,' replied Anna softly, 'it hurts doesn't it? Even more so when you are a physician and you can't save your own children.'

Owain stared at her then, and said, 'Yes, I suppose it must. And your husband, did he survive?'

'No, he died long before the plague, thank goodness.'

'Thank goodness?' said Owain, rather shocked at this admission.

'Yes, I was married to an old man when I was thirteen, and he was awful. Unbearable.' Anna shuddered, even after all this time at the remembrance of Jack. 'But at least I got three beautiful children out if it.'

'Three? Then has one survived?'

'Yes, my youngest, Isobelle, she's seven now.'

'Thank God for that then,' he replied.

'I do, daily.' replied Anna.

'And do you have a farm that I could manage for you? That would be my life's dream. Rosa and I always talked about buying a farm one day.'

'Rosa?' asked Anna, her heart trembling.

'She was my wife,' Owain replied sadly.

'I'm so sorry,' said Anna, trying to look sad, when she really wanted to shout Hallelujah in a very loud voice because he was free. What was the matter with her? She managed to calm her thoughts.

'Did you lose Rosa in the plague?'

'No, in childbirth. Just before the plague started. The baby survived, only to die of the plague, with the other children. It's been a terrible time, hasn't it? But it's time to move on now and face the future. I've only myself to bother about, so if you would let me have a farm, I would work hard every day to make it a success. I can't give you a bond though, will you still let me farm?'

'Of course, there is no one left to work most of the farms, so I'd be grateful if you'd have one, and I'm not bothered about bonds.'

'But you don't know me, and yet you'll trust me?'

'I don't have much option nowadays, if I want my farms to be worked. I'm sure you'll be a good farmer. I have no qualms,' replied Anna.

'Well I thank you from the bottom of my heart, Mistress. I'm sorry, I don't know your name.'

'Anna, my name's Anna de Ribbleside.'

'And I'm Owain of Gwynned' He shook her hand formally. 'My word is my bond. I'll work hard for you, Mistress de Ribbleside,' he promised.

'Oh please call me Anna.'

'I can't, that's too impolite when you will be my landlord. I know my place.'

'But life has changed now. I need you to work the farm as much as you need a place to live in. Times are changing; the old orders are breaking down. Call me by my first name.' She suddenly realised that she was still holding his hand, but didn't want to leave go of it. The feel of his hand in hers was making delicious little tickly feelings in her tummy.

'Right Anna,' Owain said, releasing her hand, 'I'll be over to see you as soon as I'm fit.'

'Good, I'll get my manager, Matthew, to sort out the farm for you. I'm living in the house next door to the Manor House at present, and Matthew lives in the Manor House.'

'That seems a strange arrangement?'

'Yes, it just happened that way. It's a long story. Come for an evening meal when you are better and we can talk.'

'Thanks, I will look forward to that,' he smiled. Not half as much as I will, thought Anna, trying to stop her face from breaking out in a silly grin.

Gathering herself together, Anna held out her hand again, 'Until you come to my house, then.'

'Yes, soon,' Owain said. Did he give a light pressure to my hand then? thought Anna, or is it wishful thinking? Giving a small sigh, Anna left the room.

Leaving the hostelry, Anna almost skipped back to the horse and, completely forgetting her other errands, set off back home again. All the way home, her mind was in a daydream. Pulling herself together, she reflected that it was a long time since she had had a daydream. Whilst she was married to Jack, it had been her way of escape from what was happening to her body. But since then, her life had been too stressful to daydream. And during her training to be a physician, she had been too busy. And she was certainly too busy to daydream with all her current children to look after. Until now.

As soon as she got in, Anna searched for Matthew. She found him laughing and talking to Christine. They both jumped apart when Anna said hello. So was there something developing between her friends, she wondered? Or was she just imagining that everyone was having feelings for others? How interesting, but time would tell.

'Matthew, I've got a tenant for Mearley Farm. He's called Owain and he's from Wales via Lancashire.'

'Where have you found him?' asked Matthew.

'It's a patient I've been treating in Clitheroe. He got turned away from his last job because he had an injury with an axe.'

'But do you know anything about him?' asked Christine. 'He could be a murderer for all we know.'

'I don't think so; I've got to know him whilst I've been treating him.'

'Oh you have, have you?' teased Christine. 'That's all right then, if you know him,' she winked at Matthew much to Anna's embarrassment.

'His wife and children have died, and he's a hard-working farmer. He just wants to have his own farm,' said Anna trying to defend her actions.

'You seem to know a lot about him already,' commented Christine.

'We've only really talked today. He's been pretty much unconscious until now.'

'And yet you've offered him a farm on the strength of one days conversation?' asked Matthew, rather shocked.

'The landlord said that he was a hardworking man, who paid his bills. That's good enough for me. I haven't seen too many applicants streaming down the valley looking for places to farm, have you?' Anna answered rather tartly.

'No, I suppose not,' admitted Matthew. 'We'll see how it goes, then,' and Christine nodded her agreement.

'As soon as he is fit, he's coming over to discuss the tenancy,' said Anna, 'so you'll both get to meet him. He wants to start working as soon as he can. Now, let's get some work done.'

Anna hurried away from the two of them, who smiled at each other knowingly after she'd gone. She busied herself with jobs to keep her mind from going over her conversation with Owain, because each time she thought about him, her tummy flipped over.

Although it felt like months to Anna, Owain turned up for an evening meal four days later. He was still limping slightly, but looked much healthier than he had done previously. Anna knew that he would make a full recovery. Matthew and Owain were soon talking as if they had known each other all their lives, and comparing farming methods and stock rearing practices.

Owain planned to start work the following day and Anna suggested that he stay with them overnight. Laughing, she told him that he'd have to sleep at the boy's house, and told him the saga of the sister's complaints. He happily agreed to go to the Manor House with Matthew and the boys.

Anna watched him as he played with all the children, even though she knew that it must be painful after losing his own children. Isobelle seemed especially taken to this strong gentle giant.

Anna found it hard to sleep that night, knowing that he was only next door, and wished he could have stayed in her house. Never mind her house, she wished he could have been in her bed. The thought shocked her, and she blushed, even though she was alone in her bedchamber. After all her bad experiences with Jack, she couldn't believe that she wanted to go through with all that business again. But somehow she knew that with Owain, it would be different. She knew that with him, she would have what her parents had had in their relationship; what Christine had experienced in hers.

Next morning, Anna escorted Owain to his farm cottage and showed him the extent of his land. He was ecstatic. He was so overjoyed that he took hold of Anna and hugged her and whirled her round. And Anna hugged him back. Before they knew what they were doing, Owain was kissing her and Anna was kissing him back. She couldn't believe what was happening to her body, it was totally betraying her. She was feeling sensations that she'd never felt before and it was very pleasant and she didn't want it to stop.

Suddenly, Owain pulled away from her, speaking hoarsely. 'Anna, we must stop this. We hardly know each other, it isn't right.'

'It felt very right to me, Owain. And why is it not right? We're both widowed?'

'That's true. But let me prove myself with the farm, and let me come and visit you. It's all happened too quickly. I want us both to be sure before we commit ourselves.'

'As you wish,' said Anna, 'we'll take our time. But don't take too long,' she quipped, 'I don't think I can wait.' Owain grinned at her and Anna knew that he would come to her. Knew that they would be together. Knew that their joint loss of children would be a basis for their future life together, as they helped each other with their grief. Knew that this was going to be the happiest time of her life. Knew that she and Isobelle would be all right.

Anna walked away home towards Pendle Hill. There was no mist, no mysterious brooding. It was smiling at her and she smiled back. Life was good.